THE EYES OF ATHENE

TAPESTRY OF FATE
BOOK 9

MATT LARKIN

INCANDESCENT PHOENIX BOOKS

The Eyes of Athene
Tapestry of Fate Book 9
MATT LARKIN
Editors: Sarah Chorn, Regina Dowling
Cover: Felix Ortiz, Shawn T. King
Map: Francesca Baerald

Incandescent Phoenix Books
mattlarkinbooks.com

A QUICK NOTE

I had always planned Pandora's myth to be a big part of the Eschaton Cycle. In 2016, I took a research trip to Greece to see firsthand the locations inspiring the story. When we went there, my baby was in a carrier strapped to mine or my wife's chest. Now, with the final book coming out, she's eight. It took a full-time year of research, reading, and planning to hammer out the plot for *Tapestry of Fate* before writing the first word, and years more to finish it. I can no longer imagine carrying my daughter on my chest up to the Acropolis.

For full colour, higher-res maps, character lists, location overviews, and glossaries, check out the bonus resources here:
https://tinyurl.com/hw52dzss

And if you liked this book, be sure to check out my offer for a free books at the end.

TITAN ERA
OKEANUS
THULE
HYPERBOREA
KELTIA
ILLYRIS
SALON
RASSENIA
MNEMOSYNIA
THRINAKIA
OLMECATL
TARTESSOS
KARKHEDON
KARTH
KEMET
MEMPHIS
TIWANAKU
TIWANAKU
INUMIDEN
OSIRION
THE GREAT VELDT
KUSH
KONGO JUNGLE
HY-BRASIL
KGAUAGADI DESERT
AZANIA

KER-YS

XIRONG

ISSEDONIA

NYXLANDS

ARIMASPIA

FLAMING MOUNTAINS

FIRE MOUNTAINS

YAN

JINYANG

WAKOKU

PHYLEAN WOODS

KIMMERIA

YINDAI

XIANYANG

YING

YAMATO

PHLEGRA

THEMISKYRA

GEBI DESERT

XIAO

OLYMPIAN MOUNTAINS

KOLCHIS

XIANG

BO

WANGGEON

ELLADOS

AXEINOS SEA

KOLCHIS

DANGUN

PHAEAKIA

DELPHI

THEBES

IOLKOS

PHRYGIA

KUNLUN MOUNTAINS

ITHAKA

ARGOS

KORINTH

ILIUM

ARAD MOUNTAINS

BYBLOS

YUESHANG

KROKYLEA

NERITUM

SKYROS

LESVOS

PHOEBA

PHOENIKIA

VYADHAPURA

AEOLIA

NAXOS

CHIOS

LYDIA

TYROS

NUSANTARA ISLES

ATLANTIS

KNOSSOS

HELION

AIAIA

HAWAIKI

OGYGIA

ATLANTIS

THALASSA

NUSANTARA

UGART

NESHIA

MUGEDANG

BADIAN STEPPES

NINEVEH

ASUR

DREAMING DESERT

BABILIM

BABILIM

KISSATU

DREAMING LANDS

BULU

EMPTY DESERT

DURANKI MOUNTAINS

RAPAI

NYSA

MU

SUMERU MOUNTAINS

SHALMALI

TAKHKHASILA

HUANG MOUNTAINS

BARBARIKON

PATALIPUTRA

HINDUSH

DHANYAKATAKA

KUMARI KANDAM

THE WHISPER

It starts with a whisper, a haunting intimation of a World askew. That we are, in the end, caught in a death spiral, time nearly played out, whilst entropy tugs ever harder upon the Wheel of Fate.

Looking now into the dying embers, we at last apprehend Truth, and in it the revelation that the vaunted tales of old were not what we thought ... And neither, in fact, were we.

For if we have lived before, might not all we've dreamt be but our souls' memories of Worlds become dust ...

PROLOGUE

Asura Era, Dark Age

In the wake of the Pandavas' war, the world had grown more violent still, and Matarśivan wandered the breadth of Kumari Kandam, watching as Men denied all bonds of kinship and precepts of compassion. As mothers sold children for gaudy jewels and brothers murdered one another for petty jealousies. As cities burnt to ash, families starved, and civilisation collapsed.

Ever he concealed himself from his erstwhile brethren, for they could not understand what he had become: a vagrant striving against the inevitable end that lurched ever closer with each passing year. As now, when he crouched in twilight in a battlefield south of Ayodhya, watching the ravens gather for their feast. Blood and faeces had turned the rolling hills to foetid mud that sucked at the feet of those who searched for survivors or plunder.

The Danavas—Asuras, now—had risen again and struck out against the Adityas, who thought to deny them Amrita. From the shadows, Matarśivan watched their war and the petty, fool part the remnants of the Dodecadic Circle took in it. The Rishi walked among both sides, wilfully ignorant to the true threat.

He watched, wondering if aught he might do would avert the visions he saw now with damning clarity in flame. The rise of the Archon Lord impended, and it would devour the sum of all Prakasa. So many times, he fought the temptation to seek out another Rishi alone, to try to win *someone* to his side.

But he had sworn to face this alone, to never trust them again, and sworn it with good reason. Still, he watched Arundhati slink amid the war-torn wasteland that had become Kosala. The need to call out to her —perhaps the wisest and most primed to truly hear his words—it whirled about him, almost as ever-present as Surtr's struggles to claim his body.

The Rishi moved now through the gloaming as if part of it, mostly unnoticed by those Men and Adityas still dying. Matarśivan saw her kneel among them, siphoning off bits of her Prana to save those who might live. For those beyond saving, she would end their suffering with mercy. And could she abate *his* suffering? Could she offer him any ally in his struggle against the end he had foreseen? Perhaps, but Matarśivan could not afford to trust. She might just as easily summon others of the Rishi to try to apprehend him. Some must still blame him for the sundering of the Circle. He had brought them only the truth, but they condemned him for the ramifications of that revelation.

Without warning, a tremor seized the ground and Arundhati stumbled, dropping to the mud some distance away from him. Dread apprehension filled him, and Matarśivan rose, turning to survey the convulsing landscape. Hills bucked and flowed toward one another as if they had become part of a turbulent sea, heaving and perverse.

The tremors redoubled and Matarśivan flailed, unable to keep his balance. His knee sloshed down in the muck and he landed on his hands. His fingers squelched down into the mud, but even as he touched it, it began to lose its viscosity, as though some force had desiccated the whole of the battlefield. Mud become dried-out dirt caked his fingers.

Struggling to regain his feet, he beheld the woods beyond the field, just visible in the growing darkness. But ... it looked like the whole of the forest had begun to crack and flow like motes of dust half seen in the twilight. Boughs snapped like dried tinder, and the wood collapsed inward.

Now Arundhati looked to him, hand to her mouth. He had no time to wonder what she made of the torment that wracked Ayodhya. The land a hundred feet away exploded upward in a rain of dehydrated turf and withered corpses, as if a volcano had burst from the field. Rather than magma, the geyser spewed out a sinuous black form that stretched on and on, its saurian maw rushing up toward the moon as though intent on swallowing it whole. Great spines ran along the back of the creature, and a forest of horns sprouted from its head, any one of which must be larger than Matarśivan.

Where the serpent thrashed, the desiccation increased. Its squamous bulk slammed into the field, creating fresh tremors and hurling dust and cadavers skyward. The impact nigh sent him to his knees once more.

The serpent seemed endless, for even as it darted about the field—swallowing corpses!—it continued to pour from its subterranean nest. The scope defied comprehension as if it was but a tendril of something greater. Because, of course, it was. The corpse-gnawing abomination was but a sliver of the writhing nest of serpents that composed the greater scope of the dread god at the heart of the World.

Balking, Matarśivan could do naught save stare in rapt terror.

Yaldabaoth, the Lord of Archons, had come, had breached the scope of the Mortal Realm and now, at long last, begun to feast upon the living and dead. The World convulsed and withered at its passage.

Shaking himself free of his stupor, Matarśivan cast about himself, looking for a source of flame, knowing that naught he could muster would impede this horror. Whether the Asuras had intentionally unleashed this draconic abomination or it had been drawn out simply by the unrivalled slaughter that now seized the World, still, the end he had foreseen had arrived.

His worst fear, the prescient nightmare that ravaged his sanity and threatened ever to drag him into despondency, had arrived.

He had seen ... in the flame ... He had seen himself seeking out the greatest warrior among the Adityas. Had seen himself finding Kali, imploring her to go into battle. For this moment, no doubt, given that he could not have defeated this eldritch god—his visions made that clear enough.

Arundhati had taken to the air and flew over the lurching serpent, perhaps searching for some weakness. She would not find one.

Matarśivan dared to hope she would not try to engage the dark dragon.

Either way, he did the only thing he could. He ran.

A mad dash away from the field—if ever there was a time he missed the freedom of wings!—and dried mud cracked under his sandals with each fall of his feet. He ran, knowing he abandoned the fallen here to be consumed by the devouring darkness that would feast upon their souls.

Utter desperation had him now, and no option lay before him save to trust that, if his vision showed him calling upon Kali, perhaps she could do the unthinkable and overcome this aspect of the dark god.

It was the only play left before the ending of the World.

PART I

From the apples of the Tree of Life, using a formula known only to Hebe, daughter of Zeus, we ferment the Ambrosia, the golden lifeblood of the Titans. This liquor alone sustains immortality, enhances Pneuma, and—as has been observed—acts as a rather potent aphrodisiac. Titans who have drunk even have their blood take on its golden tint, turning to ichor. And the first, greatest law of the Olympians is that no Man shall ever taste its splendour.

— Polyhymnia, Analects of the Muses

1

PANDORA

1550 Silver Age

*P*andora's heart was broken, its pieces scattered across the sea of time, the sum of it beyond the chance of ever becoming whole once more. Such were her thoughts as she stumbled back to the manse she shared with Prometheus, outside Tyros. History had played out as it had always did, and she remained trapped within the coils of the ouroboros. She had, given the chance, chosen not to prevent her child self's worst torments and abuses. She had chosen to stand by and allow Europa, her adoptive mother, to be abducted and raped, all in the name of the preservation of a timeline loathsome beyond endurance.

Thus, dolorous, drained of Pneuma, and filled with choking bouts of self-loathing, did she collapse on the beach before her house, unable to bring herself to even open the door. Instead, she beat the sands as if she might pulverise them and, along with them, tame the currents of history that so abused her and her kin.

History was merciless.

As she stared up the firmament, the stars seemed to swirl, the heavens caught in a maelstrom overhead, as powerless to escape the currents of Fate as she was. If Hekate was right and, given what Prometheus had said of the Elder Gods, Pandora believed it, then, somewhere out there, beyond mortal perception, lurked cosmic predators. In the dark between the stars, in the fathomless depths of the Okeanus, they waited. Hungry.

Tiamat, the Leviathan, was but one such abomination, and it alone fit to consume the whole of Gaia if she failed. And, if Pandora sought to avert the future, she had failed at every step along the way. Not once, so far as she could tell, had she changed the course of history. There had to be some other way, some route past this obscenity, toward a destination she could stomach for herself, for her loved ones, for all of Mankind. Her fingers dug rivets in the sand. For a moment, she relished the grit, the sheer, unadulterated *realness* of it. Faced with invisible, unknowable horrors, forced to look again and again upon the all-encircling coils of the ouroboros, this grime alone became the thing she could touch and thus ground herself upon.

She could surrender now, could she not? She could say, *this much is enough*. Let Fate attend to itself, for were it so inviolable, it could well enough endure without further input. She could stay here, in this house, beside her husband, and just live. That, and wait for him to be imprisoned in Tartarus. Wait for her past self to grow to adulthood, start her journey, and begin this cycle all over again.

A sigh tore from her, and into it she poured her doubts and her despair, for there was no solution in hiding, and one could not outrun the pace of time itself. So, at last, she pushed herself up off the beach, rose, and brushed the sand from her peplos as best she could.

There was ... such darkness, out there in the World.

But Pandora refused to believe darkness was all there was. Time and again, as oft as it took, she would carry the flame to push back the shadows. Always, always one more attempt to find a way free of these coils.

She found Prometheus upon their portico, legs folded, staring out at the waves. Mostlike, he sat here awaiting her return. Perhaps he'd known she was on the beach and had left her there to sort through the moil of her thoughts, to face the battle of her despair, trusting her to emerge victorious in the end. He did not speak or even look to her as she came to sit beside him, but she felt the warmth of his regard brushing across her, nonetheless. Their passions forever blazed like the Flames within their breasts, and she knew he would not turn from her, in this, or any, life.

"I think ..." Pandora swallowed, for though an incipient plan had wormed its way into her mind, it seemed blasphemous to give voice to it. And still, it was her last, most desperate ploy to find a way free of the maze in which she remained lost. Prometheus had his gambit with the Destroyer, and maybe, when time played out, his would prove the path of Man's last hope. Still, she knew he saw but fragments of the future and thence extrapolated everything else and, thus, might fail. Pandora too had to be willing to bet all she had, her soul, upon the ends she sought. Succeed or fail, she had to be able to say to herself she had taken every chance, even those others would not dare.

So she cleared her throat and began again. "I will see the Moirai themselves."

Now, slowly, her husband turned to look at her, his expression unreadable save for the hint of dread in his starlit, sapphire eyes. Fear for her, perhaps, and behind it, something else. A realisation they had always been heading here, and he must now deliver her to his mistresses or else refuse Pandora. That, she suspected, he could not do. "An audience with them will not avail you. They shall not be swayed from the course set at the dawn of time, least of all by the will of a mortal already accounted for within their weaving."

"Nevertheless," she said, firming both her jaw and her nerve. "I will look them in the eyes and I will hold them answerable for the obscenities they have made of our lives." She was proud that only the slightest tremor had slipped into her voice, considering what she proposed. She would confront, with ire in her breast, beings beyond gods, beyond time itself, and demand they explain themselves to *her*. The audacity of it surpassed even what Men would term hubris until it became something else, something without name or precedent.

Some private war raged behind his crystalline eyes and, after a moment, he shut them, steadying himself. "Long ago, when the World was yet young, I too made that choice. I came before them to demand answers, and answers they gave, though at the cost of the pact I made with them. For me, they revealed the Ontos, confirming my greatest fears. Superseding those terrors, even, for the Truth I learnt then was worse than I imagined. You cannot begin to imagine the price of that knowledge, borne through the uncounted millennia of my life since that day. It has left me to devote nigh every moment since toward a solution, no matter how desperate." He paused, clasping her hand, squeezing her fingers. "I would not wish such a burden upon you, and I shudder to imagine what price they might ask, only to give you answers you, in your heart, already apprehend well enough. You cannot stop the Eschaton. You cannot forestall a future already in motion."

Pandora stared at him a time before pulling free her fingers. She believed every word he spoke, and yet, she could not live with herself if she did not press forward, all the way to the end, however bitter it proved. "Where do I find them?"

He sighed and rubbed the bridge of his nose with two fingers. "It was a riddle, of a sort, one I had to solve. The answer, it led me to the place where life began, in the shelter of mighty boughs." He dropped his hand from his face and fitted her with that piercing look of his.

"The Tree of Life."

He nodded and blew out a breath. "I found a hollow, inside the tree, and trod down amid the roots until I came to a well. There, I found the three weave women, those loathsome creatures who bound me to an oath I did not, at that time, yet understand. Only later, when I found time would bend back to prevent my death, did apprehension of the true depths of my pact dawn upon me. Only when I looked upon the eldritch, unfathomable true form of an Archon did I believe. Only when I had stolen the First Flame and saw my fate."

A realisation came upon her then and, with it, a chill that sent shudders down her spine, though the night was warm enough. "You went to them because I—Aditi died."

He didn't answer, instead taking her hand once more. "I know there is some time for us, in years to come. Go back to that time, beloved, and make a life for us, such as we may. Do not go to Atlantis. If they see you at all, they will not deign to appear save at the final moments, when it will be too late, regardless."

Her mouth was dry. He spoke of their days on Mu, as Maui and Hina, the best days of her life. Her heart ached at the thought of disappointing him by refusing his counsel, and yet ... "I cannot go to that life with you and watch millions of people die without knowing I took *every* chance to avert it."

He shut his eyes once more, pain creasing his face. "Such fancies strike those who cannot conceive of ends worse than death for the ones they strive to save."

To see him so distraught twisted her chest into a knot. All she could do was lean forward and plant a kiss on his brow. "Long back, on Atlantis, we played draughts, you and I. That game, you planned farther ahead than I could imagine, and I played right into your gambit, do you recall?" He nodded, opening his eyes. "I have somewhat refined my strategies in the days that followed." She paused. "I'll see you again, my love. When the last chances are played out, then we shall see which of our gambits might save our world."

He did not deny her, only pulling her into an embrace. Yes, she could use the warmth and the sleep and one more night of comfort. For in the morn, she would go to Atlantis, and at long last, she would seize her answers from the Fates.

PANDORA FOUND it easiest to use the Box to transport herself to a place with which she was familiar, so she chose the city of Atlantis, in an alley outside the *Bay of Dreams*. Time had weathered the guesthouse, and it was no longer the posh establishment in which she had once found Prometheus. Rather, it seemed an office for some harbour official, and a rundown office at that. History was merciless.

Given that Prometheus had made plain the Moirai, if they deigned to show themselves, would mostlike appear in the times of transition, she chose a moment not far from the impending Eschaton. Parts of the city remained familiar, but so many of the buildings seemed foreign, changed by the ravages of time. The edifices of her past were torn down to the foundations, with new constructions built upon their rubble, until she scarce recognised the streets in which she'd grown to adulthood.

The city was abustle, not with the usual charged passions of commerce, but with a frisson she soon learnt hinged upon the citizens' fear of Kumari Kandam. Some spoke of an impending sorcerous war between the Queens of Mu and the Kandamian Magi, wondering what spillover from such a conflict would impend. Others carried on about disastrous battles in Elládos. She heard one man claim all the poleis there had surrendered to Babilim, whilst another swore a handful of Spartans had held back an army of Babilimian warriors and thus broken the spirit of their foes. No two tales agreed on quite what had transpired on the continent, but all admitted Zeus was driven to a rage, his wrath would prove dire.

That, at least, Pandora had no doubt about as she wended through the crowded breezeway, looking to make for the mountains. Once, with Perseus, she had travelled to the Garden of the Hesperides, there to dig up adamant arms to use against Medusa. Maybe she should have tried to send herself to the owl rock, but if her aim went awry, she could wind up lost in the woods. Here, she could plot a course from the city to the Evenor Mountain, and from there find the Tree of Life.

Would Ladon prevent her from reaching the Tree to confront the Moirai? The Old One drakon had created a constant niggling in her mind, reminding her ever of the dread it had stirred in her back then, with Perseus at her side. She had not beheld the horror at that time, only felt the mammoth weight of its fell intellect pressing against her consciousness.

She passed the bridges spanning the concentric canals that divided Atlantis and, beyond them, into the sprawling fields of golden wheat. She amused herself—distracted herself, perhaps—with idle fancies, imagining if, in those days with Perseus, she had known the Moirai laired so close and she had then confronted them. She mulled over what she might have said to them back then, or if she could have ever formed a coherent argument before having experienced all she had in the days that followed. She knew so much more now than she had before, but as Prometheus had warned, with each glimpse of the Ontos she gained, more of her comfort in the World atrophied, falling away like detritus from a crumbling ruin she had once mistaken for a palace. She was like a child who, having grown up, could never go back to the innocence of childhood, could not return to days before she had known it as a blessing.

Beyond the golden fields lay foothills, and among them, as Hyperion vanished beneath the horizon, she made camp, such as she could. In truth, she picked a flattened patch on a hillside, shadowed by a plane tree, and lay in the dirt. Through gaps in its canopy, she watched the stars, trying not to imagine squamous enormities hidden in the empty spaces of the black betwixt them. But as with other aspects of the Ontos, what Pyrrha had shown her could not be unlearnt, and the fear of what lay beyond might well haunt her the rest of her days and, even more, her nights.

With a sigh, Pandora rolled onto her side, forcing herself to look away from the firmament. From what she had gathered, the darkness above Gaia was more metaphor for the Khaos lurking out of sight than a physical abode of the predators hungering for a way in. Prometheus had been right when he'd claimed she would have been happier not knowing all the truths. And, oh! What a strange, bitter thought, to admit such a thing. That Pandora, who had always sought the answer to every riddle, who had prized knowledge above all things, considering it the only good of true merit, should now lie here, wishing there were things she did not know. No ... down that road lay condemnable self-pity, and she would never indulge in such. Better that she knew what forces arrayed themselves against Man, for only in such knowledge could she hope to confront those foes. She could never have been content to remain amid the ignorant masses, passing through life clinging to comforting illusions. Not for her, such an existence. Not for her.

SHE HAD to skirt the lower slopes of Evenor Mountain before she could reach the forbidden valley beyond, where grew the Tree of Life. The land was rocky, covered with scree, though she recalled it seeming steeper and harder last time she'd come here. That was before the Phoenix fortified her Pneuma and thus her stamina, and before training with Artemis, the Amazons, and Prometheus had toughened her to what she had now become. It was a day before she espied the burgeoning forest on the far side of the mountain, and there, beneath the shelter of its trees, she camped once more. She caught herself, along the way, wondering where she once made camp on her earlier journey here. Even the land was changed by the centuries.

The next dawn seemed to light the canopy ablaze, and Pandora pulled away from the wood just enough to get a fair look at the towering Tree of Life. It rose above all other trees, visible even from a distance, for it must rise thousands of feet into the air. The morning glare turned its leaves into a viridian shimmer, like the sunlight glinting upon water in a sea of green. The Tree's boughs stretched like arms welcoming the valley into its embrace. For a time, she gazed at its majesty, letting the moment draw out. She wanted to tell herself she lingered only to drink in the awe such a place inspired, yet dread anticipation had her gut fluttering; that she could not deny.

The moment might have called for audacity, but that did not mean it wise to cast aside all fear of the powers before her. Yet she had not come here to gawk at the great Tree or to turn aside from the path she had chosen. So, with a last steadying breath, she headed back into the forest. The lesser canopies obscured her view of the higher, great canopy above, and she had to trust to the woodcraft she'd learnt from the Amazons to keep her course true.

Soon enough, she came to the river that threaded through the valley's heart. She did not spy the owl carving. Perhaps time had eroded the rock beyond recognition, or perhaps she had come to the river along a different path this time. Either way, she expected to feel the weight of Ladon's alien intellect pressing in upon her mind, and yet it never came. Not as she skirted the riverbank, looking for a crossing. Not as she, on finding a place where rocks protruded, leapt from one to the next, arms out for balance. Slick stone threatened to send her spilling into the water, but years of training had improved her balance beyond what it had been.

On touching down on the opposite bank, her sandals sinking in the silt, Pandora breathed a sigh a relief.

"You there!" A Kroniad woman exclaimed, brandishing a xiphos as she stepped from around a tree. It took Pandora a moment to recognise her as Zeus's daughter, Hebe, whom she had seen in Athyras, during the Titanomachy. The woman's face screwed up as she drew nigh, the point of her sword dipping. Perhaps she recognised Pandora's face but could not place it; it had all been so long ago for her, had it not? "Eh, you are not supposed to cross that river, dammit. Every time some annoying cretin comes tromping over the water, I have to go and kill them. Bleh." She gestured randomly with the xiphos as if not even Hebe knew what she meant to say here. "I mean, *really*. Do I not have better things to do than this? Like, what say you return whence you came, and we dispense with the thrusting and dying and shit, eh?"

Pandora frowned. She didn't think she'd ever had the displeasure of needing to speak to Zeus's daughter afore now, and, based on this conversation, she could happily have gone the rest of her life without that bothering her. "You do not recall my face, I take it."

"Well, yeah, no. Am I supposed to remember every face I encounter? Do you have any idea how many *faces* there are on Gaia? I bet you don't know. Because it's a lot. There's lots of faces, yeah. Shit, even I have a face, and we're not talking about that one, right? So you have a face, and maybe I've seen it before. Who knows. Fuuuck, already."

Pandora didn't know whether to roll her eyes or laugh at the fool Zeus trusted to manage the production of Ambrosia. Was that it? The girl was, in the end, too simpleminded to dream of subverting her father's will and thus made the perfect servant? Pandora's hand drifted to the hilt of her xiphos. "I've not come to interfere with your duties, though I am going to the Tree. You may not recall me, but I know you, Hebe. I do not think you much care to fight me, and I've no wish to harm you, either. I will, though, if you try to bar my passage."

The Kroniad's eyes widened and she hefted the sword. By her pose, she knew how to use it with some proficiency, though Pandora had little doubt she could overcome the woman if need be.

"I am Nike," she said, after a moment, hoping her name might avert a fight. "You know of me. You know, too, that if we cross blades, it might go ill for you."

Now the woman moaned, her head lolling to either side. "Fuuuck. Goddess of Victory, now? And I'm supposed to stop her? Yeah, that's not happening, is it? Shit. That was the whole damn reason I was supposed to have Ladon. Stupid oaf going and slaying monsters that didn't even belong to him. Pshaw!" She sheathed her blade, then threw up her hands. "Fine! Do as you will. I mean, don't take the apples or Ambrosia or such. But besides that, yeah, whatever."

Pandora eased her grip off her sword hilt and, with a nod, edged around Hebe, continuing on her route toward the Tree. Nevertheless, she cast frequent glances behind herself to make certain the Kroniad did not follow. Hebe might not have wished a martial conflict with Nike, but that did not mean she would not change her mind and sick whatever guards served her on Pandora. It was best if Pandora was done with her business here before such could happen.

2

HEL

750 Bronze Age

From across the Veil, Hel watched the chaotic moil unfolding within the caverns of Katpatuka. She watched as Artemis and Phaethusa and Apollon sent the souls of Maenads screaming across the Veil, to be seized up by Hel's waiting ghosts. Hel had sent Hermes to Artemis, had forced her will upon him through the ring which had lent him his powers, and now he too served to send a feast into the Spectral Realm. So she bided her time, watching the slaughter, with growing hunger.

Time in the Mortal Realm dilated compared to the Spectral Realm, so despite the Titan speeds many of the combatants moved at, from Hel's perspective the battle seemed relaxed, almost lethargic. She might have taken the time to feast upon a soul, but she would not turn away from the fight, would not risk any distraction that might allow her prey to escape.

Dionysus, preoccupied with the Titan assault, did not notice Hel nor her gathered forces across the Veil. Whilst the Maenads seemed but muted smudges viewed through a gossamer shroud, the Titans gleamed with pulsing Pneuma, and Dionysus—oh, that blighted fragment of Pan blazed bright as a corrupted star. Hel drifted close, daring him to perceive her. She passed so nigh she could taste the vestiges of his eldritch power seeping into her Realm, like the aroma of fresh baked bread filling the air, setting her gut roiling with anticipation.

Apollon planted arrows in Dionysus, yet the abomination did not fall, and for a moment, Hel hesitated. Was it possible the twins would fail this day? That, through Hermes, Hel had sent them to their deaths? She hoped otherwise, for she bore Artemis no ill will, even recalled once caring deeply for her, though such sentiments were now but memories. Regardless, she needed the living to weaken Dionysus. She needed to be rid of this thing before she could move to secure her throne in the Underworld.

Hermes crossed the Veil, appearing in the Spectral Realm. He'd used the technique oft enough he did not bother to gawp at the gathered shades and wraiths or so much as glance Hel's way before racing toward the gleam that was Dionysus. Given the relative speed of time across the Veil, Hermes would have seemed to almost instantly vanish from one spot and appear in another. He stepped back into the Mortal Realm and plunged his sword into Dionysus's gut. Hel allowed herself a vicious grin at that, for well had the dark god earned his suffering. But still the avatar of Pan did not fall; rather, he grabbed Hermes's skull and, with a single motion, ripped off his lower jaw.

When next Hermes appeared in the Spectral Realm, it was as a shade, dazed and agonised and unable to speak for his missing face. Hel grunted in annoyance and made no move to save Zeus's son from the wraiths that descended upon his soul. Instead, she turned her attention back to Dionysus and his battle against the Titans. They were tearing into him, might soon fell his vessel. Last time Artemis had slain him, he had managed to shift his soul into a newborn and thus prevent his death.

Hel would not allow such a thing to repeat. A sudden thought came unbidden to her: Artemis deserved to know this was over. Too long had Dionysus's perversion of her will haunted Hel's former friend. She, a wraith queen, ought to care little what some living soul feared or suffered ... and yet ...

Grim faced, Hel pushed her soul into the corpse of a Maenad. Her senses blurred, shifting to the Mortal Realm. Colours sharpened, replacing the ultramarine haze of shadows with the crisp tones of life. The thrumming of Pneumic auras vanished even as the pains of the Maenad's dead body mingled with the omnipresent agonies of Hel's death. She lurched to her feet, disoriented. This was how revenants took corpses, though more oft dwelling inside their own bodies; it was harder to hold someone else's carcass.

Apollon planted arrows in both of Dionysus's eyes, and the creature fell to its knees.

"... the living and dying ... god ..." the horror croaked, in threat.

Hel almost chuckled. "Just dying this time ..." she rasped, striding closer. Already, the skin on the left side of the Maenad's face had begun to slough off, becoming like unto Hel's. "He won't be coming back this time ..."

"H-hekate?" Artemis gaped at her.

Hel cast a last glance at one she had once held dear, one she should not have cared for now. "Farewell ... old friend ..." It was all she had come to say, all she would spare for such sentiments now, from beyond death. She released her hold on the corpse and the Spectral Realm formed around her once more. In her disorientation, she did not see the blow that felled Dionysus.

She did see, however, when his soul seeped into the Penumbra and began to cast about for a new host. Hel launched herself at the weakened soul, latching onto Dionysus's shoulders with skeletal claws that bored into his etheric flesh. The thing shrieked in pain and—Hel delighted to think—terror at the realisation that his time had come. Hel bit down quick to glut herself on the feast of so rich and perverse a soul.

This day would be the end of two of Zeus's brood.

THE APTLY NAMED Eternal Glacier exuded a sense of timelessness that made it easy to lose oneself in its meandering tunnels. Even flush with the power she had consumed through Dionysus, Hel felt minuscule beneath the cyclopean weight of ten thousand feet of ice over her head. She was but a speck, but still, it seemed she brushed against something so vast that, if she could understand it, she would be one step closer to comprehending the breadth of the Ontos.

She shifted her satchel upon her shoulder, treading ever deeper into halls that seemed bored out of eternity. A fell, sourceless iridescence flickered within the ice walls, the boreal plays that lit the night sky in places within the Rimefells or the northernmost reaches of the Mortal Realm. It offered pale illumination for the maze of tunnels and occasional vast cavern of ice as she explored.

In one such cavern, beneath the ice below her feet, she perceived a mammoth shadow. Curious, Hel knelt and pressed a palm against the ice. Between darkness and the distortion of the ice, she couldn't be certain what the shape was. Something serpentine? A drakon, perhaps. Did that mean some Old One, spawned by Primordials in the early days of the World, had once swum here, before an underground sea froze?

Despite all she had learnt over her long life and death, she still had many questions. The cosmos might well open before her, if she could but grasp the secrets buried in these layers of ice. The Elder Gods and their Old One progeny predated Mankind by orders of magnitude. Indeed, before Man arose, the Elder Races had warred for control of the Mortal Realm, or so she suspected. It was possible—likely, even—that Titans were the descendants of one of those races.

Still, she needed more knowledge. More answers, if she was to succeed where the Gnostic Cabal had failed and break the hold of the Wheel of Fate.

The Mist that saturated the Rimefells barely penetrated this deep into the caverns, yet still it coiled about her feet as if alive, as if objecting to her presence here. The World, or at least this Realm, begrudged its hidden lore to any mind, but Hel would brook no denial.

For so long she had wandered down here, until she began to suspect she had passed beyond the reaches of the glacier and under the Fimbulvinter Mountains. Once, she had journeyed beyond those mountains to gaze upon the glorious Hvergelmir, a spring whence flowed the freezing Elivagar rivers that carved the Rimefells between them. Shards of ice the size of fortresses framed the depression in which the spring rested, and above it dangled the roots of the World Tree. Immense power radiated from beneath the Hvergelmir; even from a great distance Hel had felt it, rippling along psychic currents. It was, she suspected, one of the foundational blocks upon which the World had been constructed. If so, more clues to the nature of the cosmos might lurk in that spring, or beneath it. Hel had but to find her way there.

Further she wandered, days beyond where she'd seen the frozen drakon. Forward, ever deeper into the frozen core of the Rimefells, the chill seeping even into her dead flesh. At last she came to another cavern, if cavern was even the right word for the misshapen, mind-wracking sight she now beheld.

Reality had turned nebulous, and the space bent back upon itself in violation of all rules of mortal geometry she had ever learnt. Spherical recessions broke into blocks whose shapes seemed to shift and flow before her gaze. A maze of spine-like protrusions crisscrossed the space in sinusoidal waves, bursting with pulsating spurs.

And carved among all of the fathomless horror were endless whorls, parabolic arcs, and geometric designs. Hel huffed. These were no architectural flourishes. The longer she stared, the more certain she became of that. Slowly, reverently, she withdrew the grimoire from her satchel and paged through the tome until she found what she sought.

In frightful mirror of the space before her, Raziel had transcribed these designs as some of the foundations of the sorcery he had encoded into the book. Here the arcs and lines were absent spirit glyphs, but the underlying principles remained. Either Raziel had visited this place—or something akin to it—or whoever had trained the ancient sorcerer had done so.

And here, in the place beneath Hvergelmir, she could fill in the missing pieces to understand the foundations, not only of the Art but of the cosmos.

Amid the spines were what she took for steps. They bent back at perverse angles that ought not to have allowed one to walk along them, yet when she chanced them, she found she could follow the path, even as it inverted itself and she was hung suspended upside down. Pace by pace, she plodded on, noting the eldritch markings in as much detail as possible, given the mercurial nature of this place. Glancing below, she saw—to her chagrin—*herself*, staring back at her.

Her mind reeled at seeing herself bilocated, and Hel stumbled, tripped upon a step and pitched over, falling up the stairs. Dazed a moment, she did not, at first, recognise the looming of a mammoth intellect.

YOUR MIND IS GUARDED, YET THERE IS NO CONCEALING THE MALICE LURKING WITHIN.

Hel pressed a palm against her brow in an attempt to block out the booming voice in her head. The sense of awful puissance, of something that was ancient even before the Eternal Glacier ever formed, closed in upon her. It threatened to gnaw the fringes of her sanity.

Groaning, Hel scurried forward, desperate to escape the maze of spines. Yet retracing her steps seemed to take her farther from the entrance, as if in denial of all sense.

NO MORTAL MIND OUGHT TO GLIMPSE THE MESH OF GEARS UPON WHICH THE WORLD HINGES.

Another groan escaped her, and she looked to an opposite spine closer to the entrance. "Get out of my head ..."

YOU WOULD SPOOL OUT YOUR ENTRAILS IN VAIN PURSUIT OF UNDERSTANDING OF HOW THEY WORK.

Flooding Pneuma to her legs, Hel leapt across the gap. With unexpected force she collided with another spine, landed on stairs, and tumbled back to the ground.

GIVEN ANSWER, ALL THAT WOULD REMAIN IS UNRELENTING TORMENT.

She had seen enough. Grimoire tucked under her arm, Hel scrambled from the chamber, intent on scribbling down all she had beheld. If she had inadvertently drawn the attention of an Elder God—if the Archon had penetrated her thoughts—she risked losing everything.

The Shrouded One could reveal her plans before they were underway, and Hel needed time to study what she had learnt here, not to mention enact it. She had to hope whatever had touched her mind here had been able only to brush the surface of her thoughts. Else, she imagined *something* would be coming for her, and soon.

3

KIRKE

17 Golden Age

*I*t had taken time to begin recruiting members to the Circle of Goetic Mysteries. Most people feared the Art, with common folklore claiming it hailed from the Time of Nyx. Damkina saw no reason to educate the public, for cultivating a certain air of mystique did behove sorcerers. They found Isis and Nephthys in Kemet, which remained a burgeoning kingdom along the Iteru River in Hy-Brasil. Strange to think one of the oldest lands on the face of Gaia now lay in its nascence, and she could have, had she been so inclined, helped its shaping.

Of course, they were soon joined by Enki's daughter Ningal and her daughter Inanna, both of whom regarded Damkina with suspicion. They were of the Anunnaki genos of Kumari Kandam and mistrusted those from other continents, or so it seemed to Damkina. From what she gathered, the Anunnaki were descended from Enki and his friend Enlil, with Inanna representing the joining of their two bloodlines. Ningal insisted on bringing vipers into the sanctum, refusing to cast them out even after Heka had almost died from a bite suffered in his sleep.

Heka was Hy-Brasilian from somewhere beyond Kemet. The Jungles of Kush, perhaps, though the man said little of his past. No, but his talent was undeniable. He had been a jungle shaman before Enki found him, and he had taken to sorcery as though born with Supernal incantations buzzing upon his tongue.

"I shan't be told what to do by my father's whore," Ningal snapped when Damkina called her into her private chambers to demand she keep the serpents contained.

For a time, Damkina stared at the Anunnak. Yeah, mostlike Enki would take it amiss if she turned the woman into a snake herself, or even something more useful, like a coconut or whatever. Something had vexed Ningal from the moment she'd arrived, but Damkina could rarely suss out the depths of others' hearts—rarely her own, were she honest— and she'd little patience for the woman's vitriol. "You know ... our noviciate lies in fevered dreams, his soul wandering sidereal spaces, perhaps prey to the eidolons haunting those Realms." That Damkina had brewed an antidote after slaying the viper and Heka would mostlike survive accounted little in the current conversation. "But sure, yeah, my sexual proclivities are clearly the matter at hand, right? Whether or not I've lain with your father—" And, sure, she had, once, "—that excuses your callous disregard for the safety of others, doesn't it? Hmm, but if your blood qualified you to lead this Circle, why then did Enki recruit me, I wonder?"

"You are naught but a whelp, saved from consumption in the Dark by my father! My elder daughter would have smote you, left your entrails strewn across a mile of cobbles for your temerity." Ningal had lost a child during the Time of Nyx, one Ereshkigal, if Damkina recalled correctly. Well did Damkina know the pain of being torn from a daughter and might have pitied Ningal if Ningal did not insist on incinerating every kind thought directed at her with that boundless hubris of hers.

"Yeah," Damkina said, quirking a malicious grin. "Can't imagine what she'd have done if she learnt I took her younger sister to my bed, as well, hmm. Thoth's hidden arse, I bet she'd be vexed at such." Ningal's haughty facade cracked, her eyes widening as she caught Damkina's meaning about Inanna. "I mean," Damkina continued, knowing well she ought not to, but unable to help herself, "if her mother was not such a colossal jackass, I might try for her too, and call that family my conquest. Still, hard to justify the risk of such venomous lips upon my flesh."

The Anunnak's eyes widened further, and she sputtered in incoherent rage. Thus did Ningal leave the Circle of Goetic Mysteries, though her daughter remained. Inanna insisted on delving the arcana, and there was nowhere else upon Gaia for her to learn such things so deeply as she might in this necropolis.

Damkina had assumed Enki would prove wroth with her, but he took it in stride. "In truth," he said, "I have suspicions that she may have collaborated with the Gnostics, long back. I thought to have her here, beneath our watchful eyes, but perhaps such was ill advised."

"You think she betrays us, and yet you let her roam free?" Damkina demanded.

Enki frowned. "I would not turn against my child unless forced to it." Forced by Ananke, he meant. For if the future demanded he sacrifice Ningal, Damkina could see it writ upon his stern visage he would do so without question. *History must unfold.*

WHEN ENKI RECRUITED the Titans Phoebe and Helios, Damkina took to concealing her face beneath a hood. Of course, her father would not know her, two centuries before her birth—and less now that a few streaks of silver had appeared in her auburn hair—but best she not give him the chance to associate Damkina with Kirke.

Then, some years after the founding of the Circle, they received another recruit, and none of the other practitioners of the Art held a candle to the sorcerous inferno that was Mormo. More Gígas than Titan, the woman had clearly tasted Man-flesh, and it warped her, body and mind, leaving her with canine fangs and saurian-like eyes. Rumour followed her like a trail of poison, giving tale she had slaughtered children in Elládos and been chased from the land by Kreios for her crimes.

Ninurta, the son of Enlil and uncle to Inanna—a man dedicated to driving every last monster out of Kumari Kandam—had captured Mormo and, instead of destroying her, brought her before Enki for trial. Given the choice, Damkina would have barred the disquieting wretch from their midst, but Enki insisted they ought to have among their number more with experience in the greater arcana. And experience Mormo had, with talents more developed than Damkina's, though Damkina would never let Mormo realise that. If she had to guess, sorcerers of her day would have rated Mormo in the third echelon, perhaps even the fourth, behind rumours of Morpheus's power.

Mormo shared her experience with the others—primarily through what she termed the Sea of Oneness, which, as it turned out, was an orgy designed to evoke frightful gods from the Otherworld. All of this had happened before, Damkina oft reminded herself and thus that she bore no culpability for any perversity resulting from it. If she contributed to the damnation of these people, then they had *always* been damned. History must play out as it always had; that refrain Enki had hammered into her with the tenacity of a grizzled smith slaving over his forge.

Indeed, Enki had demanded, night after night, that she tell him everything she knew of the years and Ages to come. Every detail, no matter how trivial, he explored, though never did he bother recording any of it. He said he stored such things in the palace of his memories, whatever that meant. He asked, in particular, for tales of Kirke's mother and her daughter, for news of what Prometheus had done and would do, for all the wretched details of Zeus's benighted reign and the Titans who would rise. Everything he cared for, and Kirke was uncertain why ... save for the simplest of answers: that Enki wanted to hold the future to its course.

Thus, though Damkina liked some few among the Circle, and Isis in particular, she dare not let herself grow too attached. Their damnation was part of the Wheel of Fate, and through their suffering, they bought reprieve for the rest of the World's souls.

Of the Sea of Oneness ... Well, Damkina, had, in fact, helped induct a few members herself through shared intimacies that allowed the transmission of knowledge. But like Enki, she steadfastly refused to take part in the Sea of Oneness. She could guess at Enki's reasons. As for her, Damkina would not risk any situation in which Helios might try to come to her ... The thought brought a shudder out of her. Some lines, one did not cross, not even in the name of history.

Their sanctuary was called the Lodge of Whispers, for in touching the Realms beyond, they began to hear the hint of voices from beyond the Mortal Realm. Susurrations and lamentations, like warnings that none of these sorcerers would ever heed.

And through whispers did the shadowed halls of Kirke's earliest memories begin to take shape.

SO IT WAS, during one of the all-too frequent orgies, that Heka came to Damkina in her private chambers, sweaty and naked. Damkina had been poring over old Kandamian scrolls, trying to translate them from a forgotten language. Her eyes burnt from too long working by the dim light of an oil lamp and her neck ached from sitting in an awkward position on the floor.

Neither of which much endeared her to anyone deigning to interrupt her here. Perhaps the man thought that, as she had brought him to her bed once or twice—eh, perhaps thrice?—he was entitled to call upon her as he pleased.

"What is it?" she snapped, determined to disabuse of him of the notion he could intrude upon her privacy. "Not enough orifices in the main hall to suit your liking? I already told you, I've no intention to join."

The Hy-Brasilian shifted and groaned. "In the Sea ... I saw visions."

Damkina shrugged. That was, in the end, the point of the thing, loosing the tethers that ordinarily held consciousness fixed in time and place. A brief fusing of minds—perhaps of souls?—that allowed transfusions of unconscious knowledge. Of course, the right drugs helped the process along, and whilst Damkina did not partake of the activity, she did instruct Isis in alchemy to facilitate it.

"I saw ... dark intent in Mormo, I think."

Damkina frowned, straightening and stretching her back. She had known inducting a Man-eating wretch like Mormo would invite woe among them. They ought to have let Ninurta slay her when first he found her. The Anunnak warrior bore a mace that crackled with lightning, and, so far as Damkina knew, he had never met his match. Drakons and chimeras, perhaps even Old One demons, all had fallen before his thundering wrath. Yet Enki had commanded Mormo brought in alive ... *History must play out.* Enki would have had his reasons. "What intent?"

"I think ... she intends to spirit away the book."

The Sefer Raziel. Enki had taken to keeping it in the main library so that the others could peruse it at liberty, trying to suss out its secrets. It was a test, she assumed, such that only the worthiest of sorcerers might begin to fathom the lost lore of the Time of Nyx. Damkina scarce bothered with it, knowing how dangerous the damn thing was and knowing, too, Enki would have told her aught he needed her to know.

"You are certain?"

Heka hesitated. "The visions are a rush, a blur of sensations. I can never be—"

Damkina waved him to silence. She knew how it worked. "You did right to bring this to me."

Intoxicated and sated, participants of the Sea of Oneness tended to sleep deeply, drifting through turbulent dreams that may have held import even to non-oneiromancers. Such states made it easy to slip into Mormo's slumbering mind and confirm her treachery. It did not, however, tell Damkina what she ought to do about the traitor. Mormo had bound a wraith inside herself, and Damkina rather misliked her odds of overcoming the woman in a physical struggle.

Enki was away with Ninurta, pursuing some new oneiromancer he'd sensed in Kumari Kandam, leaving Damkina to deal with the situation herself. Thus, she unlocked Enki's private chamber and riffled his trunk until she found the treasure he had told her to use only in times of greatest need.

An orichalcum chain.

So, whilst Mormo yet slept, Damkina wrapt the fetters around her wrists. The Man-eating sorceress started awake, but it was too late. With a Potency-infused blow, Damkina smacked her fist into the woman's temple, sending her sprawling.

"What in Nyx!" Isis blurted.

But Damkina flung the semi-conscious woman over her shoulder. "I have seen perfidy in this one's mind. Now she must await the judgment of Enki."

So they had bound Mormo, still naked and caked in various fluids, to a ring they hammered into the wall. Some of the others, Damkina knew, delighted in seeing the mightiest among them brought low. There was a sick satisfaction in witnessing the proud fall.

When Enki returned, he brought a young boy, raven haired and dark of eye. "This is Morpheus," their leader explained. "Like jewels sieved from filth, I pulled him out of the slums of Nineveh." Damkina wondered if Enki had already given the boy oneiroi dust, for surely this was the one they had gone to find. Dosing potential oneiromancers with the dust tended to bring out the gift—at least if they survived the harrowing maelstrom of the nightmares such things induced.

"Something has happened," Damkina cut in, though she might have preferred the chance to inquire more about this Morpheus.

After she had told him of Mormo's intent, Enki nodded, little surprised. Maybe he had known all along. Maybe it was just another revolution of his Wheel of Fate. Either way, he soon stood before Mormo, having painted a summoning circle around her. The woman hissed defiance at him, but Damkina had little doubt that behind her veneer of bravado, terror had settled in the sorceress. Damkina knew she would be pissing herself in Mormo's place, even if she did not know what Enki intended.

Clearly, it was to be a public execution, though, for he had summoned the whole of the Circle, even young Morpheus, despite Damkina claiming the boy ought not to witness death at such an age.

"If he is to walk into the dark places where a sorcerer must tread," Enki had answered her, "he must do so with his eyes open. There is no shelter from the truth of what we do or what we are."

Beside Damkina, Isis clutched her sister Nephthys's hand. Damkina wore her cloak and concealed her face, and yet she allowed Morpheus to cling to her side. If Enki demanded he watch the spectacle, watch he would; yet Damkina would offer the child what comfort she could. Well did she know the dread such things worked on an impressionable young mind. They left bruise-like shadows upon the soul, wounds that would never heal.

The cants began, vile sounds in the Mortal Realm, thrumming reverberations across the Penumbra. With vicious intent, words flooded the ether, calling to wretched creatures of the Dark: the keres. Damkina blinked away the Sight, not wanting to see more of this than she must.

Mormo must have felt them approach, for the serpent-eyed, fang-mawed sorceress whimpered, "You need not do this!"

"Truth lies within dreams," Damkina whispered to Morpheus. "Cultivated oneiromancy allows one to suss out a person's heart and perceive the movements of their soul." She paused. "Sometimes, the lesser arcana are more powerful than the greater."

The boy pressed his cheek against her belly, fingers knotting the folds of her peplos. What she'd told him was truth. But then, the greater arcana had their power, which, as Raziel, Enki had once named harnessing the currents of Hell.

Mormo shrieked as strips of her flesh were flayed. Pieces of the sorceress vanished into the ether as if something swallowed what was carved from her.

Sobbing, Morpheus buried his face in Damkina's dress. The reek of urine now underlay the iron scent of blood, and she felt something splash over her sandals but did not bother moving them. She could scarce blame the boy for such a reaction.

Sanguine cataracts poured down Mormo's convulsing body, pooling in the seams of the floor, running toward gutters along the walls. The woman tried to keel over, but something held her on her knees. Sinew shredded and was ripped away just as flesh had been, gnawed on by invisible maws. On and on the macabre horror went until all that remained was a skeleton that, mercilessly, did not collapse. Rather, it raised a fleshless hand before its face and its jaw distended as if to scream.

No sound came, save for the grinding of bone upon bone.

Enki placed his palm upon the skeleton's brow. "As you have feasted upon the flesh of children, so too have they consumed yours." He looked to the gathered throng, several of which had retched. Isis was hiding her face behind her hands. "We do not consume Man-flesh." He turned his gaze back to wretched Mormo. "Lesson adjourned. You may now die and embrace damnation." He squeezed and the skull cracked before the skeleton collapsed in a heap.

But as a sorceress, death was only the beginning of Mormo's suffering, Damkina knew. They all knew. Just another part of the lesson, she supposed.

❧

"They say, in whispers when they think me not listening," Damkina said, sitting on a mat in Enki's chamber, "that to visit such horror upon one of our own, for a crime she had but dreamt of undertaking ... They name it a step too far. We risk breaking the Circle if we do not address this."

Enki had sat on his divan, staring at his wine bowl, but at her words he jerked his head up to meet her gaze. "Breaking ... the Circle ..."

Not for the first time, Damkina wished she understood more of this man she had dedicated her life to. Oh, she believed him when he spoke, believed in the Ontos he had shown to her. But there were depths to him that made her certain she did not and could never understand the sum of his motivations or the breadth of his personal history. As Raziel, he was something altogether different in kind to her, and who knew if he had been other men besides.

After a moment of intense staring, Enki shook himself. "Well, it matters little. If it appeases them, I shall go and leave things in your capable hands. You need but cultivate their Art and hone their minds until we can be certain of the worthy among them."

Huh? "Worthy for what? You said you did not want the greater arcana lost to the Ages. That the Circle needed to exist because I had been born of it, and, yeah, I get that. But uh ... why does it matter how much they cultivate their arcana?"

Enki huffed as he rose from the divan to come kneel before her. "You place a great deal of trust in me, so I will offer what answer I can. The Circle serves as a secondary purpose, namely as a proving ground for those who might be of use to a greater, more crucial Order, though one which, as yet, must remain unseen."

Damkina could only guess his meaning, and besides, his other words left her disquieted. "I mislike the thought of you leaving." Enki had, after all, become more or less the purpose of her life. What on Gaia's arse was she meant to do without him around? Who even was she? Who was this Damkina, if not his creation? He was the tether keeping her bound, stopping her from falling back into the wretched melancholies of Kirke.

But Enki shook his head. "Worry not over that. We shall see each other oft enough, even if I do not reveal myself to the rest of the Circle. I will, after all, still bring potentials as I find them and will spread word of this place to those who ought to know." He cupped her cheek, then spooled one of her hairs around his finger. "Besides, you have other things to which you must attend."

It took her a moment to realise he had singled out one of her silver hairs. "Yeah, what, of getting older?" They lived in a world without Ambrosia, and though Titan blood meant she aged slower than Men, still, she had resigned herself to mortality, as she had resigned herself to all aspects of Fate. "I'm fairly certain I can accomplish this whether you are here or elsewhere."

"Quite the contrary. For the order of the world you have known must be built up by Titans, and for them to truly rise, they must have Ambrosia. And yet, none of this Era have the alchemical experience to craft such a draught." A chill rose along her arms at his words and the incipient thought they evoked. "It would take, after all, an alchemist with centuries, perhaps millennia, of experience in making such a decoction. Long ago, when the world was young, the Elder Races discovered such secrets, called it Amrita, but their knowledge was lost after a terrible war. Can you think of anyone who has worked with something akin to Ambrosia?"

Damkina could scarce swallow over the dryness in her throat. "You mean in crafting ... Nectar."

"All you lacked was the apples of the Tree of Life."

"I created Nectar in imitation of the Ambrosia." It was a half-felt protest, considering the other perverse circles Ananke had wrought in her life.

"And now you shall invent Ambrosia based on what you learned in so doing. I will bring you the apples to work with, and you will grant Ambrosia first to the members of the Circle, reaffirming their loyalty to you."

She nodded, licking her lips. *This has always happened*, she told herself. "History must unfold."

"History *must* unfold," Enki agreed. He offered her his arm and she clasped it. "We walk in the shadows that fill the spaces between moments. We are Unseen."

Damkina swallowed. "We are Unseen."

4

ATHENE

399 Dark Age

Athene found herself in a darkened cavern overhung by fibrous roots. She had no memory of how she had gotten here, but her feet carried her forward of their accord. As she trudged through the cavern, she spotted stone plinths set in sporadic intervals. When she noticed them, flames sprung up from them, fires held within sconces, though they smelt neither of woodsmoke nor the reek of burning oil. Indeed, as she passed closer, she saw the fires seemed to appear among the iron frames without any obvious source of fuel.

Ahead, water dripped from a frayed root, splashing into shallow pools gathered in the uneven ground. Mithra ... She had agreed when he told her to speak with the Fates. Was this their place? She turned about, gazing into the hidden recesses, but able to make out naught save the leaping shadows cast by the torches.

Her sandals squelched upon damp loam, sinking in a hair, as she pressed onward until, at last, she came to a well so wide that the torchlight failed to more than hint at the far side. The fire sent amber streaks playing along the surface, their perfect pattern disrupted every so oft by a pair of swans—one black, one white—gliding across the water in concentric circles. The walls of the well seemed comprised of knotted wood, as if the roots had grown around it, formed it, beholden to some strange master.

"Moirai?" Athene asked, turning about for any sign of those she had come to meet. "I weary of games, Moirai!"

"This game ..." a voice said, and Athene spun to see a woman, her face concealed beneath her cowl, her features hidden within the voluminous folds of a dark robe.

"... is played across the ambit ..." another woman continued, appearing beside the first, an almost mirror image to her.

"... of all history," said a third. Though clad like the others, this one had a stoop to her. From beneath her robes, a wrinkled hand grasped a cane for support.

Athene folded her arms across her chest, glowering from one woman to the next. "It will take more than well-rehearsed stage plays to impress me, Moirai, if such you are." Once, Athene might have thought the Fates more metaphor than physical beings. Assuming, of course, this dream space, whatever it was, even counted as real.

"She comes for an answer."

"... As did the precursor ..."

"... As will the one to come."

Athene held her peace on that, though she continued to glare. These beings either could not form thoughts that seemed coherent to those who experienced time in the way of mortals, or else they chose not to, amusing themselves at the expense of hapless supplicants. If the latter, she found it even more vexing than the former.

"Ire sparks."

"No matter how oft she tries."

"To extinguish."

"Its burning flames."

"A heat that scours."

"She is of his blood."

"She is of her blood."

"We gave him all our strength."

"But his."

"Will."

"It seeks, ever."

"*To subvert.*"

Athene threw up her hands. "*I've no idea of whom you speak, nor at the moment, do I care. Mithra swore you could prove the truth of his words, that he had shown me the Ontos.*"

"*He thinks he sees all.*"

"*Though close he holds.*"

"*His secrets.*"

"*So another was needed.*"

"*Direr purpose, writ across the Ages.*"

"*She will die.*"

"*The mantle must pass.*"

Athene closed the distance between herself and the first of the women, seized her robe, and yanked her close. "*Speak plainly! What is the Ontos? Tell me the Truth! Is Typhon real, is it out there, waiting to consume the World?*"

"*Yes ...*" all three women hissed in unison, their words sibilant and echoing through the cavern. "*The damnation ... of all the cosmos.*"

Athene dropped the woman and backed away. She had not wanted to believe it, the horror that Mithra presented to her.

"*It feeds.*"

"*Upon the Wheel of Fate.*"

"*But should the Wheel ever cease to spin ...*"

Athene could not swallow. The words rose to her lips unbidden. "*It wakes.*" They must feed the sleeping abomination with feast after feast of souls, for the alternative would prove worse. And Hera was a member of this Gnostic Cabal, desperate to drive Zeus to war against Mithra in the hopes they might all escape Fate. But Fate, in all of its vicious cruelties, remained the only shield they had against utter Khaos. Against Typhon and the fathomless Dark it carried alongside it.

"*Make the pact.*"

"*Become the assassin of Fate.*"

"*Take the place.*"

"*Of the one who will die.*"

All three women exposed their hands, indicating the water. "*Become the Nemesis.*"

Nemesis. The foe Hera had begged—demanded—that she destroy. There were so many things Athene yet did not understand. But in the face of the Ontos laid bare before her, how could she make any other choice? She had *wanted, had so long dreamt of finding a way to aid Mankind. She had wanted to help them stand. Now, she must take the steps needful to ensure there could even be a Mankind to save. Swallowing, Athene strode to the well and bent until she could see her reflection thrown back at her by the still water. There was fear in the depths of her grey eyes, that she could not deny. She could never know just what this pact entailed, but the sense came upon her that whatever bargain she made this day, it would live with her for the rest of her days. However many or few those might prove.*

"Those who would unravel the Tapestry of Fate ..." the women said, "must be brought back into line with Ananke."

With Necessity.

Athene understood. She leant over the edge until she could cup the water in her hand. It was cool, like a mountain spring. The tiny pool she had claimed ought to have flowed out through her fingers already, but it lingered in her hand, demanding she sip. Athene brought the draught to her lips. If Fate was all, if the Tapestry must remain absolute, then every moment of her life, every mistake, every deed for good or ill, all had served to bring her to this moment.

She let the water brush over her lips, chilling. Something flashed before her eyes. A lucent cloud bloomed in her vision, and all around it, a sea of prurient Darkness ever lashing at the Light with assaulting tendrils. A Wheel took shape, colossal, spinning in time with the revolutions of the cosmos themselves.

Pain exploded across her eyes as though sight was burnt from her with scalding pokers. But when she blinked, she could see once more. And the eyes looking back at her were no longer grey but luminous blue, irises faceted like crystals.

And at last, though he had never become Nemesis, Athene understood who the Moirai's first avatar had been.

"The next Nemesis arises ..." The Moirai no longer spoke aloud in overlapping cadences but rather in a singular chorus that echoed through her mind. Athene looked down and realised that an aureate panoply had appeared across her body, vambraces and greaves, a cuirass, and at her side, a Korinthian-style helm that would conceal her face. "Enforce Ananke ..."

And she would.

ATHENE AWAKENED within the chamber of the god-king, her legs folded beneath her. As awareness dawned, she realised she must have fallen into a trance and that her experience had been a mental one. Save that the golden armour remained, and, she assumed, so too did the lucent blue eyes, so like her grandfather's.

Mithra, who sat across from her in much the same position, opened his eyes and stared at her with the piercing daggers of his gaze. After holding her like that a moment, he climbed to his feet and made his way to a table on which sat a small locker. While the god-king stared at the chest, Athene too gained her feet and stretched out a stiffness that had settled upon her neck and back.

The Unseen One too serves, in overlapping threads, the needs of Ananke. The voices of the Moirai remained a blended chorus in her mind, disconcerting and all-consuming in their insistence. She wondered at their choice of words. Mithra, as the head of the Unseen Order, seemed one of the most direct agents of the Fates upon Gaia; but he was not the only one.

Still, when Mithra turned, Athene fell to a knee before him. The emperor of Babilim had kept his word; he had shown her a Truth she could no longer deny. The future of Man, the existence of the cosmos, all hinged upon obedience to the will of Ananke. Having seen the absolute horror that lurked just beyond the World, having witnessed the Ontos, Athene would do whatever was needful to avert the rise of Typhon.

"You have become the Nemesis, now."

"Yes, Unseen One," Athene said.

Mithra strode forward, a strange metal puzzle box in his hands. "Then receive the gift of time, that you might trace its ambit and perceive the streams that flow about us. Fulfil your destiny."

We shall instruct in the setting of the Box. Once activated, it will carry you to the times and places where you may reinforce the threads of the Tapestry and thus maintain Ananke.

As she accepted the Box, a bombardment of knowledge burst into her mind. The use of the Box, and with it the understanding of why she, and she alone, could use it, as no other Nemesis could. Because she carried the blood of the one Prometheus had created this tool for, the blood of Pandora, her grandmother.

"No!" a voice screamed from the window even as Athene turned the

Box in her hand and, pressing the indentation the Moirai led her to press, activated the device. The top popped open and Mithra stepped away from her. The air rippled in an engulfing bubble, light collapsing inward around Athene.

And she was gone.

ATHENE APPEARED kneeling upon a bough of a tree so massive it could only be the Tree of Life on Atlantis. The sudden shift through time and space left her momentarily disoriented. A flash of lightning in the distance drew her gaze. Mighty thunderclouds ringed distant Evenor Mountain, lit by fulgurations of growing intensity.

The sounds of battle below her cut through Athene's daze. She crawled to the edge of the branch to look down. Some fifty feet beneath her perch, on a lower bough, a stranger engaged in battle with ... Athene? For the figure below was Nemesis, clad in aureate panoply, striving to hold off a foe whose Pneumatikoi seemed so strong his blows blurred before her vision and rang like gongs upon Nemesis's breast-plate. Was that Athene's future self?

Behold, sounded the Moirai's chorus in her head, *witness the last stand of the Nemesis who was. In her ending comes your true acceptance of the mantle.* A pause, and the battle continued, the old Nemesis badly over-matched by the stranger. *Keep this man away from your grandmother. The Eschaton must arise and unfold,* the Moirai commanded in her mind. *Thus must you and the veiled assassins forestall her attempts to avert the end.*

Only now did Athene realise Pandora, too, was below, though lying on the ground, bloody and struggling to rise. She had no idea what was going on, but she had sworn herself in service to Ananke, and if the Moirai said this man was a threat to Pandora, Athene would take them at their word. She rose. Wings burst from her back, and with a start, she realised she knew how to use them. She kicked off the bough and took flight, circling the mountainous Tree of Life.

Flashes of lightning tore through the firmament, distant still, followed by cacophonies of thunder. Athene circled higher, to give momentum to her dive. She saw as the stranger crushed the skull of the prior Nemesis against a tree. Saw it, winced. For the Moirai had left their servant to her fate. Of course they had; Fate was all that mattered. When the time came, Athene knew, she too would be discarded in whatever way proved needful. And still, the alternative was to allow Mankind to be swallowed by Typhon and damned to eternal torment within the Khaos.

Like a diving falcon, she shrieked upon Nemesis's slayer. She had not thought he would detect her, and yet he moved, twisted aside. Almost fast enough. Athene caught him in the chest with both feet. The impact sent the man hurtling off the branch on which he'd fought. He flailed his arms as he fell, then vanished into a vast gulf beneath the Tree, lost in darkness. As so befit one who would stand against Ananke and thus risk damning all the cosmos to Khaos.

Athene had landed where he stood and realised it was a platform leading into a hollow within the Tree. What lay inside?

Ananke ... came the answer in her mind. *You cannot answer your grandmother's questions.* Athene turned, looked to Pandora. Wanted so badly to speak to her. Instead, she withdrew the Box from her belt pouch and set it as Ananke-born instinct demanded.

"Wait!" Pandora shouted, even as the Box's light bubble rose to swallow Athene.

But Fate waited for no one. And Athene would follow any path that saved Mankind from Typhon, even unto the unceasing of an Eschaton.

5

ARTEMIS

399 Dark Age

"Indeed," the god-king Mithra had said when Artemis and Marduk had asked him if, after all the centuries of planning, the time had come to move upon Elládos at last. So they had sailed for the lands of Artemis's erstwhile home, every plunge of the waves sending her gut reeling with anticipation. Her nerves were frayed, her mind awhirl with a thousand incipient thoughts she could not have articulated to save her life. For so long she had dreamt of this day, clinging to visions of revenge even as Men worshipped idols of their deities, daring to believe in the fulfilment of retribution she might make right all that had gone wrong.

But to have the day arriving at last, now, it seemed to her more as though she remained trapped in one of those dreams, stuck inhabiting the surreal landscape of her fancies.

"Is it regret?" Marduk asked by her side as the fleet passed the first of the Aegean islands, heading for the greater poleis of Elládos and Phlegra. They had sailed out of Ilium and everyone would know they were coming. The empire would demand tribute of earth and water, symbolic submission to the might and will of the god-king. Some of the poleis would offer it up, fearing the annihilation they would face to challenge the greatest empire on Gaia. The city-states were fractious, used to forever warring against one another for land or bounty, and the Olympians had made no effort to unify their worshippers, save by common allegiance to their false gods. So, many of them would cave, join the Empire, and avoid the carnage.

Others would refuse, of course, sick with pride that ran thicker in their veins than blood. They would tell themselves, perhaps, that their city could challenge the might of hundreds of thousands of soldiers converging upon them. Only when they saw the horizon blanketed by an endless procession of foes would they, far too late, begin to glean the depths of their hubris.

Artemis would not savour killing these folk now. The more poleis who submitted, the better for all. She had come not to slay Men but to destroy the gods of those Men. Of course, some who might have otherwise offered tribute would balk and revert upon learning Babilim intended to wipe out their entire religion. They would kill the King of the Gods of Elládos, bringing an end to worship that spanned more generations than most mortals could conceive of.

"It's not regret," she finally answered her betrothed. Not exactly. "Rather, I struggle to grip the impending reality. But I have no doubts, love, have no fear of that."

"There is no turning back ..."

No, there never had been. As Mithra had instructed, the Wheel of Fate necessitated everything she had endured must transpire to bring her to each successive moment of her life. This one included. "Zeus must die."

MARDUK HAD GONE to Iolkos with Phaethusa, while Artemis travelled for the island of Athenai. To the other great poleis of Elládos—to Korinth and Argos and Thebes and Delphi and Mykenai—she sent emissaries. Too, other captains had sailed for ports along the Aegean Islands, for many would have seen the fleets and grown nervous, primed for absorption into the Empire. The lesser poleis of mainland Elládos, and of the Ionian Islands, they would attend to later.

A palpable frisson held the port of Athenai taut when Artemis climbed from the small boat she had taken off her trireme and paused, letting her gaze sweep over the gathered throng. Soldiers and fishermen all stared at her, caught in the throes of an anticipation that seemed almost to match her own. The tension held so thick, she knew, that a single misspoken word, an innocent gesture thought to conceal aggression, could lead to an eruption of violence. Warriors and civilians alike would sweep over her delegations like pyroclastic flows cascading downhill, heedless of the devastation left in their wake. Or in this case, the carnage that would ensue in the aftermath.

Then Athene came striding through the throng, a head taller than most Men, and the crowd parted around her like children ushered into the wings. In truth, Artemis had hoped to treat with the Athenian Senate. She had heard they had, some years back, deposed Theseus. A chain of ill-loved successors had eventually led the Athenians to oust the kings and found a democracy some years following the Ilian War. The last person she wished to see was her former friend, with the judging grey eyes, and that unwavering loyalty to her despotic father.

"Artemis …" Athene said.

Artemis fought not to sneer at the woman. "Some memories have a taste so bitter they cut through the haze of our unending lives, remaining forever acrid, churning our guts."

"Apollon fell in war, the same as my brother." The Olympian had the grace not to feign ignorance about what Artemis spoke.

"Yes, but it was your side who slew the both of them, so you can hardly call us even."

Athene bristled, then stilled her rising temper. "Ares fought for Ilium because you enticed him into your wretched war."

"He fought for Ilium because your deranged father threw him off a mountain for imagined disloyalty!" Artemis knew she was shouting but found it so hard to hold her tongue. This woman had once named her "sister." But her familial loyalty extended, in truth, only to a sybaritic father who used her as he used everyone else in his life. "Nyx's dark bosom, Athene! What would it take for you to open your eyes and behold Zeus as the blight on this world he truly is? How can you, for centuries, live alongside a festering cancer and not smell the rot? Are you inured to the stench, having known it all your life?"

Artemis wanted to draw her blade and slit the woman's throat for what she'd done to Apollon. She wanted to attack her here, even knowing it would mean her death. But she had come on behalf of a higher purpose than revenge against Athene. This city must have the chance to submit to the Empire.

"You speak as though a self-proclaimed god-king who would rule all the Earth, by the sword if need be, is somehow more worthy. Somehow less a tyrant than the kings of your homeland."

"I am Lydian," Artemis spat. After so long living in Elládos, thinking herself one of them, there was a certain freedom in the recognition that this land had not birthed her. "And I do not come to treat with you, but rather with the Senate."

"They appointed me to speak on their behalf and deliver the simplest of messages, Artemis. Athenians will never bow before the Babilimian Empire. Elládos will not cave. If you would have peace, turn your ships back to Kumari Kandam. Flee across the Thalassa Sea and never think to encroach a single pace further than you have in claiming Kolchis. Fail to heed this warning, and you will face foes more dire than those you have fought thus far on behalf of Mithra."

If the Senate had sent her with such words, there would be no swaying her, Artemis knew. Still, she would make one last attempt. One last jab she could tell herself was a chance to spare Athene from the bloody fate before her. "You think your cause righteous, but your vaunted father is but a puppet to one who pulls his strings from the shadows."

At last, Athene seemed stricken by her words, eyes wide. "What nonsense do you spout?"

"The Gnostic Cabal has *infected* the Olympian Order, and you do not even realise you are no longer masters of your actions." And maybe, it was enough. Maybe Artemis had tried for long enough to get Athene to break with her father. Now, let her pay the price for her loyalty to the madman, even as Apollon and Ares had paid the price for their convictions. "In the end," Artemis taunted, "your father will cast your life aside as a mere token and never once grieve for your death. At best, it will serve as a pretence for venting his petty rage."

"Return to your ship," Athene snapped. "You have no welcome here, or on any shore of Elládos. And if I see you again—"

"The next you see me, it shall be with my blade at your throat." Artemis spun on her heel. She was through talking to the Olympian. She was through with all of them.

It turned out that, while Thebes abstained—surreptitiously offering tribute not of the demanded earth and water, but of silver—and most of Phlegra had submitted to the Empire, none other major Elládosi poleis had sent the demanded tribute of earth and water. Sparta had, to Artemis's shock and chagrin, even murdered the emissary sent to them. With such knowledge in hand, she had regrouped with Marduk in Phlegra, where the armies of the Empire stood marshalled and readied.

War impended, awaiting but her command.

Her ship sat at anchor, swaying in the waves that battered the Phlegran shore. Artemis, in her quarters, looked at a map sprawled across her table, depicting the mass of the Elládosi forces. Some significant group of them had gathered at the coastal passage of Thermopylae which divided Phlegra from Elládos. To march the army against them, Marduk would need fight in narrow confines that would render his vast numbers, if not useless, then severely hindered.

Though Artemis had an impressive navy, she could not ferry the entire Babilimian army by sea. Between the Babilimians themselves and the numerous subject kingdoms, they had more than three hundred thousand warriors to account for.

Part of her wished to stay, to fight beside her betrothed. Her skills in narrow confines could well make the Elládosi alliance—now led by Sparta—regret their choice of location for a stand. But as Marduk had pointed out, they had other apt generals and talented warriors, including his Immortals and Phaethusa. Artemis was now admiral of the largest of the fleets. The best way they could aid the efforts at Thermopylae was not by throwing more bodies at the breach—for Babilim had numbers aplenty over the Elládosi—but rather by sailing around their foes and cutting off further reinforcements. Sparta and Athenai led the alliance, and should either of those fall, the morale of their citizens would crumble.

It did not make letting Marduk or her sister wade head-first into an ambush more appealing. "Are you certain there is no other way?" she asked, knowing the question inane. Who knew the geography of these lands better than her? The Olympian Mountains made marching an army along any other land route a mission of suicide. The narrow passes, buffeting winds, and steep declivities would chew up their forces like a herd of cattle devouring a field. It was Thermopylae, or else march for months out of the way, giving their enemies too much time to prepare whilst watching their supplies dwindle to the dregs.

"This will not be the place I die," he promised.

"I'll hold you to that." Artemis kissed him.

INTERLUDE: MARDUK

400 Dark Age

The verdant mountains of Mu seemed, to Marduk's eyes, emerald waves frozen mid-undulation. Palm trees swayed in a gentle breeze and birds cawed. Beneath the cerulean sky, beside the lapping azure sea, he might have called it paradise upon Earth. Might have, were it not for the fields of corpses, their spilled blood imbruing the sands crimson. Too many were his soldiers, infantry and Immortals alike, slain by the ferocious tattooed Muian warriors who moved with speed and strength like unto Titans.

Marduk unfastened his lamellar cuirass but had to peel its linen backing away from his sweat-drenched tunic. Despite the heat, a chill wracked him at the shedding of the layer. He let his armour fall, knowing one of his aides would gather it and return it to his flagship.

At first, when Marduk's forces had landed upon these shores, they had seen their foes and thought their lack of armour—their lack of clothing, in fact, save grass skirts or sarongs—meant their opposition ill equipped to oppose them. Here though, beneath the punishing sun, the Kandamians had learnt otherwise.

With a groan, he hefted Sharur—his blood-spattered mace—over his shoulder and trudged amid the carnage. He'd made it but a handful of paces before Tishpak came tromping toward him, dented helm tucked under one arm and bleeding scar along the line of his jaw. Even he, even an Anunnak, he'd taken wounds aplenty here. Tishpak's bloody club trailed behind him, cutting a rivet into the sand.

The Queens of Mu would not fade quietly into the oblivion of history. Did they know the end approached? Did they see the noose that settled around their necks, even now? Would that they had made the offer of earth and water and ceded their lands to the Babilimian Empire. Would that they did not, through their foul sorcery and affiliation with dark forces, threaten the whole of the Earth and make such conquest needful.

"The path to the walls of Mugedang seems clear," Tishpak said, unbothered by the blood dripping from his chin. Unlike Elládosi Titans, who indulged so deeply in Ambrosia as to turn their blood to golden ichor, the Anunnaki of Kumari Kandam bled crimson as Men.

"Seems?" Marduk peered into the distance, where the mountain-like temples of the city peeked over the horizon. The Muians had too much control over the sea for Marduk's forces to land their navy at the city. Besides a fleet of dhows and war canoes, it was said Queen Pokoharau could command the waves. If such proved truth, Marduk would not risk her casting his triremes into one another, not knowing how disastrous that could turn out. Salamis had gone poorly enough, and he was not the naval commander Artemis was. If only she were here beside him now.

"Sirsir says Lady Hubur—his kin name Pokoharau thus—has made a pact with rival Deep Ones from an undersea kingdom. He believes they will intervene on behalf of their Muian allies."

"In daylight?" Sirsir was sworn to Marduk's father from days long back and thus trusted as much as one from beyond this Realm might ever be. For all that, the spirit was a Deep One, and his ways were unknown and unknowable. Whatever politics and machinations unfolded beneath the waves lay beyond Marduk's ken. Still, he knew Deep Ones shunned daylight when able, and Sirsir avoided showing himself save at night.

Tishpak shrugged. "Mostlike they will strike us after dusk."

Marduk glanced at the waning sun. "About when we hit those walls."

The other Anunnak nodded, at last bothering to wipe away the dribble of blood from his chin. Already, it had seeped into the grooves of his lamellar. The scales would need tending when this was over, if the armour was to be saved from rust and ruin. "Sirsir says they are led by Kingu and by Kulullu."

"Should the Deep One names mean something to me?"

Tishpak grunted, looked to the sea. "He called them demon gods born of Tiamat, said the Queens bargained for eleven such abominations to destroy Kumari Kandam and all its gathered armies." Something in the way the Anunnak spoke had a fresh chill hitting Marduk. He had his doubts about whether such fabled abominations as Tiamat— supposedly an Elder God from some unfathomable deepness beyond the Earth—could exist. Still, if such tale spread among the army, it would do little for morale.

"Sirsir will come to our aid?"

"So claims the Deep One. He says Poseidon is overthrown, though the Sea King's children squabble over his domain."

"Did you take Sirsir's oath?" Marduk asked, and Tishpak nodded. The gesture relieved some of the tension, for what little he knew of Deep Ones, they could not break an oath, though they might otherwise lie at will. "So be it. We press on, come what may. But have a runner sent to my father in Hursag. If the Queens think to unleash demon gods, he must call for the Magi to bind them with their prayers." That, or at least to buoy the nerves of the men called to face the Otherworldly in combat. "As for us, we make for Mugedang. Pokoharau's dark bargain only serves to reinforce how needful our victory is."

THE MARCH toward Mugedang gave Marduk rather too much time to think. Heading to a battle was always like that. Better, when Artemis was by his side. Her mere presence calmed his nerves, stilled the racing of his mind. Where was she now? On what mission had his father sent her?

Once, years ago, Marduk had begun calling her Sarpanit in jest. It was a name given to her by the people of Sarpan, after she'd saved them from marauders out of Kissatu. Those marauders had been funded by separatists trying to break away from Babilim's authority, which was bad enough in and of itself. Far worse, when they armed bandits with imperial lamellar and sent them to prey upon imperial towns, trying to stir up support for their sedition.

According to the tale Marduk had heard, Artemis had snuck into the midst of the raiders' camp, killed their sentries, and challenged their leader to a duel. When the man had lost, others had tried to kill her, and she had single-handedly driven out the handful of survivors of that error. Men fared ill when they sought to engage a Titan in melee. For a Titan as fortified with Pneuma as Artemis, her speed and strength made her an unstoppable force. Yes, well could he see how the Elládosi had worshipped her as a goddess.

So the people named her Sarpanit and, on hearing of it, Marduk had started to call her the same, at least until he'd realised it made her uncomfortable. She wouldn't admit her disquiet over it, would have thought such an emotion another weakness. Artemis could not abide men thinking her a hero. Somewhere, inside her breast, she felt herself a wretched soul, no matter how oft he tried to show her otherwise. He'd spent centuries trying to get her to see herself with the eyes with which he beheld her. But then, Artemis was thousands of years old, and that life brought, along with pleasures, burdens aplenty. The peril of memory, she once named it.

He did not know all the things she had done in service to the Ouranid League, or later, as an Olympian. He knew only what Father had said: Olympus sat above a gate to Khaos, and thus, any who dwelt there would have had their minds and souls poisoned by its influence. Artemis once said that the only reason she had any sanity left was because she never bided longer upon the mountain than Zeus insisted.

Ah, well. Whatever she had done, whatever she had been, she was a good person in his eyes—the best person. The one he wanted by his side now. Not least because he knew he went to face others whom Men would name gods.

When this was over, when the war was at last ended, then they could be wed. Then, maybe, they could afford to both be the people they wished they were.

§.

THE MILKY SEA of stars overhead glinted off the waves, would have lent them a blessed appeal, save for the terror emerging from the depths. At a glance, Marduk might have taken the water-bedraggled forms striding onto the shore for naked men and women. Only when they drew nigh could one make out the disquieting differences betwixt their forms and those of Man. Some had webbed fingers or feet, some tiny fins upon their ankles. All had gills flapping along their necks, almost concealed by their sodden hair. Their eyes—shielded by nictitating membranes— were oft solid pools of black, like onyxes, or in some cases opalescent as the finest pearls.

Such came the Deep Ones, slow at first, then lurching into motion with horrifying speed, curtains of sand and water streaming behind them as they launched themselves amid Marduk's men. He saw, from too far back, one leap, its jaw monstrously wide, baring shark-teeth the instant before it collided with a hapless soldier and bore him down. Life was rent from the warrior in the space of a heartbeat.

Gripping his mace—mighty Sharur—Marduk surged his Pneuma and raced forward leaving a wake of sand and wind. Too late, too late for the first victims. His Pneuma-fuelled leap hurled him twenty feet through the air, to land among the Deep Ones. A creature rose, turned to meet him, too slow. Sharur slammed into the chest of his foe, with a gong-like clang, the force of it impacting the fiend's Pneuma-hardened skin sending out a shockwave. The Deep One was sent hurtling away, flying like a missile dozens of feet through the air. Marduk did not see where the creature landed; already, he was leaping once more, flying toward another foe.

The Deep Ones had speed and strength beyond mortals, beyond even the main of Marduk's Immortal elite. Not beyond Titans, though. Not beyond a prince of the Anunnaki. Shrieking, he raced among them, dodging claw-like nails, deflecting tridents, and smashing the shark-things with sweeps of his mace. Sharur, a gift from his father, had once belonged to the ancient hero Ninurta, and Father claimed within the weapon lay quiescent power Marduk must live up to. This, he aimed for, always.

Tishpak, too, charged into the fray, and Sirsir, Marduk saw, the Deep

One rending his ilk without the least thought of kinship. Blood splattered Marduk, some of it his. Deep One claws gouged his unarmoured flesh, tore into arms and legs, scraped his back, for he focused his Pneuma into strength and speed rather than hardening his skin. Only thus could he hope to move fast enough to save his men, to save his people.

In the distance, he saw as the gates of Mugedang swung open, as more of her warriors sallied forth to meet his. Yes, now their Deep One allies brought death and carnage amid the Babilimian army, now the Muians would come, and the slaughter ensue. Faster—he had to move faster. He surged more Pneuma, knowing he must eventually pay the price for so draining his life energy, yet unable to see another way. A torrent of wind chased him as he surged at another Deep One. Scales punched through its flesh in places, lending it an ill aspect, profane in its alienness.

Its eyes, like gleaming pearls, nictitated, and it grinned, leaping aside from a colossal swipe of Sharur that would have shattered bones even of an Elder being such as this. "Prince of Kandam," the thing gurgled. It had a long, thick beard, beaded with shells and jewels. Even from paces away, the reek of brine reached Marduk. The Deep One brandished a spear, its reach keeping Marduk back.

"Do you know me, spirit?" Marduk answered, pacing around the creature. With his off hand, he drew his akinakes, working through a flourish to loosen his limb.

"Do not you recognise your opposite number amongst your foes? I am Kulullu, child of the Elder Deep. 'Tis her ineffable power that courses through my veins, little prince. 'Tis her timeless memories I was granted to recall the bygone days when yours and my race long warred to hold the Earth. Time came when Giants cast us down, aye, but tides that once ebbed now flow, and vengeance comes upon your ilk. Your world shall soon be claimed by the waves, and you Titans shall find the doom you earned yourselves in those forgotten days. Tiamat, who birthed all, shall consume all."

The Elder Deep? Sirsir had said that was what his kin named Tiamat. So then, if Kulullu was her spawn, here came before Marduk one of the eleven demon generals Pokoharau had called forth. Here, face to face with him, stood one of his greatest foes, surpassed, according to Sirsir, by Kingu alone.

"So then, when I break your mortal shell," Marduk said, circling, "and send your soul screaming back to the watery abyss whence it came, you may tell your *mother* that Marduk sent you, Deep One."

He lunged, tried to sweep the spear aside with his akinakes, but Kulullu was faster than his brethren and leapt aside. A swipe of that spear—its tip the wicked barb of some sea creature—forced Marduk to jump, wheeling his legs to flip away. The dance began, Kulullu whirling his spear about him with frightful speed, Marduk dodging and parrying, seeking an opening that would not come. Again and again, he feinted, lunged, then fell back, unable to penetrate Kulullu's flawless defence. Belatedly, Marduk realised the creature sought more to occupy him than fell him. In so doing, he had stalled Marduk's rampage among his kin and allowed the Deep Ones to rain slaughter among Marduk's army.

Only Sirsir and his few Deep One allies, and the Anunnaki, could hope to stand against such power as an Elder Race brought forth. Then, watching, he saw it was not only them but one of the Queens of Mu who waded into the melee. Pokoharau wielded a great club, about which swirled eddies of water that, when she struck, coalesced into swells of force that sent men flying with all the power of Marduk's blows with Sharur. Pokoharau was a scything tide of death, her hydromantic abilities beyond any he'd ever seen.

In his distraction, Kulullu lunged, tried to impale him with his barbed spear. Marduk bent backward, the blade passing within a hair of his face. His counter-swipe of his mace lacked strength but still, clipping Kulullu's knee, sent the Deep One stumbling, scrambling backward to get away. For a single heartbeat, Marduk considered closing, trying once more to subdue this supposed child of Tiamat.

The deafening roar of thunder, close at hand, stole the decision from him, and he turned, saw another of the Queens of Mu. Searing white lightning coruscated along the saw-toothed blade of her poleaxe, and he knew this must be Whaitiri, the Storm Queen. With each blow she struck, lightning leapt and burst to nearby foes, her power almost as horrific as Zeus's—as Ninurta's was in legend. Her axe-blade cleft into a skull and Marduk saw the victim's eyes turn to jelly. His head exploded and galvanic arcs shot among his allies, leaving them in convulsions that made them easy prey for Whaitiri's next attacks.

"Sirsir!" Marduk called, uncertain if his Deep One ally was nigh enough to hear him, or would try to stand against Kulullu in his place. Either way, Marduk leapt again, his Pneuma-filled bound sending him crashing down before Whaitiri. Though he landed in a crouch—having covered perhaps forty feet—he surged forward at once, sweeping at her with Sharur. The queen parried on her poleaxe. Marduk's blow sent her skidding across the sand, flailing to abate her momentum. But the lightning crackling along her blade sent shocks leaping into his limbs, had him gasping, though he might have expected to lose muscular control and fall into convulsions from such energies.

Whaitiri recovered first, kicked off the ground and spun end over end whilst swiping with her lightning-charged poleaxe. Marduk rolled sideways, narrowly avoiding a blow that exploded into the sand. The queen spun, whipping her weapon in a wide arc. Marduk rolled under it, surged Pneuma to his legs, and hurled himself at her, swiping Sharur. The queen backflipped ten feet in the air to land a dozen paces away, bringing her weapon to rest on her shoulder, panting with exertion.

Marduk rose, glaring. He had no idea whether the queens had Titan blood, but they certainly moved with the speed and strength of an Elder Race. Even he mostlike had not the amount of Pneuma in his body as they seemed to channel. For all that—and whilst they were well trained in arms—he didn't think they matched his skills. Keeping his gaze upon Whaitiri, he slung Sharur behind his back and switched his akinakes to his dominant hand. This was a foe to face with speed and precision, not the brute force of his mace. He pointed the blade at the queen. "Your obstinance in refusing to submit to the god-king only increases the death toll your people shall pay before they break."

The queen sneered. "Spoken like one so drunk on self-importance they cannot conceive that others might rather die than surrender to the authority of a foreign tyrant. We do not ask for your land—yet you think yourselves entitled to claim the whole of the World."

Marduk paced, shifting his footing as he took her measure. "Such is the mandate of Oromasdes; my father is the voice of the God of Light on Earth. All who stand against him unwittingly serve Khaos." He pointed to the Deep Ones surging over the shore, laying waste to his army. "Are not your allies the spawn of a demon god?"

Once more, Whaitiri brandished her poleaxe. "All gods are demons ... Names for primeval forces from beyond our Realm."

Her blasphemy stole any further argument he might have mustered, left him gawping for a heartbeat. Words were wasted on those who looked upon light and named it but another flavour of darkness. How was one to treat with an opponent who refused to acknowledge any semantic consistency? With a growl, he launched himself at her. She swiped again with that mighty poleaxe; Marduk leapt over it, thrust with his akinakes. Whaitiri twisted aside, kept herself from being impaled, though his sword gouged her shoulder, bloodied her neck.

He saw it, when panic took her, and she struggled to bring the poleaxe to bear, despite him standing too close for such a weapon. He caught the haft as she brought it up. The queen shrieked, and lightning coruscated along the weapon's shaft, surged into his arm. Such should have killed him, perhaps. Agonies shot through him, his nerves aflame with the energies coursing through him, but he did not fall into convulsions like her other victims.

Rather, he strained, bending the weapon downward, opening the way for his sword. Her eyes widened. Lightning raced through him, became him. He could almost hold it in his hands. He raised his blade to strike.

From the side, something shot toward him like a missile. Pokoharau crashed down on him, swinging her club-staff. Water undulated around the end of it. Marduk could not move, could not get out of the way. Could only surge Pneuma to his flesh to harden it. A tremendous crack—as of thunder—sounded and he was sent flying, the World rushing past in a swirl of colour and pain. A surface struck him, and he was beneath the sea, flailing weakened limbs, struggling to determine which way was up, how to claim a breath, even as saltwater raced into his lungs.

A whirl, a rush in the water. Iron-strong limbs seized him, dragged him down.

They called it Apsu, the aquifer that ran beneath Etemenanki, which breached the surface in vast pools of unknown depths. They said he'd been born here, a water birth. Marduk's sandals skidded upon the slick rock ledge that ran between the pools, his torch scarcely adumbrating the cavernous space. Which of these basins had it been, where his mother had died?

Was this memory? He was a boy now, though he had no boyhood memories, not from before he was about ten.

In the welling darkness, the water seemed tar-black, as if he looked into bottomless wells of ink. Into ... lidless eyes. So many eyes, staring at the shadowed recesses, unseeing, dead things. Motionless, still they peered, seeking for something. For a trespassing soul that dared wander into this lightless, breathless, timeless place. Of a sudden, he knew he had intruded upon a primeval deepness. Those wells—eyes—delved into the aquifer, a watery abyss that called to him.

One of the eyes nictitated.

Marduk froze, unable to move, unable to draw breath. His limbs were stone, his chest a solid lump of petrified organs, useless, fossilising beneath the enormity of such alien intellect. The eyes, the Apsu, it saw him. Not just the man, a hollow shell, but the paltry soul within, every depth of his being plumbed in an instant of the abomination's regard. His self was violated, his sins and doubts and failings unfurled as some papyrus scroll, read at once and found wanting.

It held him in its cosmic mind. He had sunk into a fathomless sea, engulfed until neither up nor down still existed, until direction became a fading memory. All around, infinite murky water.

Within that benthic eternity, something immeasurable stirred. Though the entity remained unseen, Marduk could feel he was but a mote of dust before the colossus. Yet he had drawn its ire.

A Deep One held him, pressed against the seabed, almost invisible in the darkened water, even beneath the shallows. Another form crashed into the one slaying Marduk, and he was free, sloshing, lungs exploding. He got a foot under himself, kicked off the ground, and shot skyward with all the Pneuma he could surge. The force carried him above the sea, launched him into the air where he could suck down a precious breath.

Just one, then gravity seized him and sent him smacking onto the beach. Marduk landed on his face, in a half foot of water.

Waves lapped over him, beat him, strove to drag him back into their embrace. His strength was failing, he could not endure. But if he let the sea reclaim him ... Marduk forced Pneuma back into his arms, dragging himself further inland until the receding waves no longer threatened to pull him under. Then he collapsed, gasping, groaning.

Sharur was still strapped to his back. Belatedly, the thought occurred that, had he fallen the other way, the mace might have broken his spine. For once, perhaps landing face-first in the dirt was a blessing.

The sounds of battle—diminished now—came to him. Much though he needed to rest, to regain his strength, he pushed himself up. In truth, his Pneuma was less drained than he might have suspected. Almost as though ... as though some part of the galvanic energies Whaitiri turned on him had seeped into his core, feeding it rather than ravaging his flesh. Was that Sharur's power? Something quiescent in himself?

He drew his mace from his back, then tromped toward the battle once more. So long as breath remained in his body, he would not allow his men to fight alone. Once more, he pulverised Deep Ones and their tattooed Muian allies. Once more, he slaughtered, turning the land into a reeking mess of bloody viscera and splattered gore. Such was the price of war.

Then Morpheus arrived from the south, bringing fresh Immortals and infantry, and Marduk knew the night was won. The Muians with drew behind the city walls once more, and Marduk allowed himself to slump, arms upon his bent knees. To let his mind wander and escape all this.

UNSHOULDERING HIS BOW, *he looked across the bank of the river. In the shadows there, behind the trunks of thick trees, he saw something massive and squamous slithering. The crunch of underbrush came to him even over the burble of the river.*

He doubted he would do any sneaking past such a creature. Well, it would not grow easier if he lost the daylight. With cautious steps, he plodded into the river, slowly wading across. It must have poured down from a mountain, for despite the heat of Atlantis, the waters had an icy bite. At its greatest depth, the river reached almost to his shoulders but soon receded as he drew nigh to the opposite bank.

Rustling filtered through the treetops when he reached the shore, and he peered up, gazing into the incandescent eyes of a saurian head as large as his torso. Its sinuous neck arced down above the leaves, watching him with malevolence unlike aught Man saw upon the face of Gaia. Its horn reminded him of tales of Hy-Brasilian rhinoceroses. Its fangs dripped acidic venom. Its scales glistened with black virescence.

Such dire intellect as now pressed upon him he had felt only once before, in the very pits of Tartarus. The serpent whose gaze bombarded his soul had the aspect of foulness beyond reckoning, and its assault upon his senses turned now from probing intrusions to a full attack.

Under the weight of its regard, he could scarce move. Every step forward required a battle of will. Every motion became an uphill charge. Teeth gritted, he nocked a black-fletched arrow to his bow. The Old One watched him with disdain as if daring him to keep his feet. Cyclopean will pressed upon his shoulders and demanded he take his knees before the calamitous enormity whose ire he had drawn. A thousand pleas for mercy would not prove enough to sway this demonic abomination, and yet it demanded he plead, nonetheless.

Arms trembling, he raised his bow instead. Confronted with absolute malice, the only viable answer came through responding in kind. Incredulous, as if unable to believe any mortal could have such temerity as to raise arms against it, the dragon head peered at him, unmoving and unblinking.

"Uhh … little brother …" a woman whined from across the river. "Stealth has failed you …"

He loosed, his poison-laced arrow streaking through the late-afternoon air. Such force had he instilled in his bow, the missile punched even through draconic scales and landed with a crunching sound. The demon recoiled, shaking its head one way or the next. Would the hydra venom fell even another drakon?

All at once, the Old One convulsed, its head cutting a collapsing arc through the wood. It pitched through the treetops, shattering branches as it plummeted sideways, the sound of its fall a series of crashes. The corpse slapped down on the shore not far from where he stood. An earthy reek of snakes and decay wafted off the carcass.

Strange. He had heard tales this Old One had many heads, like the hydra, and he had thought ...

More rustling in the trees drew his gaze skyward. Another head peered at him now. Another, and another. Dozens upon dozens of serpents, all glaring at him from different angles. They enclosed him, some watching from left or right or behind, some from above. He could not see where flesh joined or if the demon was, in fact, a nest of serpents rather than any singular entity.

Either way, a hundred scathing, colossal minds now scraped across his mind. They glared at him with terrible wrath for what he had done. Any time in which he might have begged for mercy had now passed.

IN PREDAWN GREY, Sirsir came to him, face ravaged by claws, one eye torn away. The Deep One, a lesser god as it were, seemed scarce able to stand. Marduk caught the creature's arms as Sirsir stumbled.

"Do I have you to thank for my rescue?" he asked.

Sirsir grunted. "Kingu had you. It was unwise for me to challenge such an ancient one, but sometimes the bloodlust drives out sense, I fear." Was that his way of making light of the risk he took? Or perhaps Sirsir meant his kin flew into blood frenzies, explaining their ferocity.

Tishpak, Marduk had learnt, was slain by Pokoharau, as had been hundreds of Immortals and more infantrymen than anyone had managed to take stock of. Babilim may have driven the Muians into retreat, but the cost had come high, and the walls of Mugedang remained unbreached.

"I shan't forget what I owe you, Sirsir," he said, to which the spirit nodded, face creased in his agony.

"Kingu did not retreat within the city. He will be nearby, ready to prey upon your forces once more come nightfall."

"I can scarce hunt a foe beneath the sea."

"He did not retreat into the deep but rather followed a river inland."

Marduk looked in that direction, then winced. The demon general seemed inclined to ensure Marduk's father could send no further reinforcements from their holds in the Hursag Mountains. "We cannot allow him to wait in ambush for our forces or supply train."

"No. You cannot. But neither can I aid you further at present, Prince.

If I push this host beyond its limits, I could wind up driven from your Realm entirely." Sirsir did not say what such an event might cost him, but Marduk got the impression a hint of fear lurked beyond the god's statement. Whatever lay outside the Mortal Realm, Sirsir had no wish to be thrust back into it.

"Go then," Marduk said, releasing the Deep One's arms, "and regain your strength. I would have you by my side before the end of all this."

Sirsir nodded and slumped to the water.

Marduk must rest a little, then he would need to set off after Kulullu. When next he faced the Queens of Mu, he would do so without Deep One foes at his back.

PART II

What then, exactly, is the Spirit Realm? We must look to define other Realms—that is, states of existence—in contrast to that which we know, namely the Mortal Realm. While the Mortal Realm is definitionally a physical space, the other Realms are etheric in nature. Here we live and die, and in death, our souls pass from this Realm into the Spectral Realm, commonly called the Underworld, or sometimes the Penumbra by sorcerers. Beyond this Underworld, however, lies yet another Realm, where the Primordials and the elemental spirits dwell. If it is possible to travel to this Otherworld, none have done so and returned.

— First Chronicle of the Circle of Goetic Mysteries

6

———————

PANDORA

400 Dark Age

*A*mid the roots of the mighty Tree, sections of the ground fell away into an abyss, over which dangled fibrous tendrils of the behemoth, thick with clinging dirt. Pandora could not spot any hint of a bottom there, nor did she wish to find out just how deep into Gaia the hole bored down. Rather, the roots themselves formed a misshapen bridge up to a hollow within the trunk. It was overshadowed by gnarled protrusions large as boulders, and thus concealed well enough, but not so much she thought Hebe would not have discovered it in centuries of dwelling here. Had the Kroniad ventured within?

Or perhaps, if this was the abode of the Moirai, the opening now appeared before her because they deigned to speak with her, and Hebe would have seen but a solid trunk here.

Amid the roots, she saw colossal stones twisted into strange shapes. Only when she had drawn close, looking down on them from the protruding root, did she recognise them for fossilised bones. There, vertebrae bigger than her whole body, and there, half covered in loam and moss, a saurian skull, one empty socket burgeoning with weeds. Was this what became of Ladon?

Arms out for balance, she trod along the first section of root, willing herself not to look down into the endless void that spread out to either side. Step by plodding step she edged toward the aperture within the Tree, but this root would not reach the bore, for, once she came to the root's middle, the path onward lay some twenty feet overhead. It was another root, crossing this one, but she could see no means of reaching it, save to jump.

Phoenix wings could have borne her up there, but she would have immolated her clothing, and besides, a wild flight could have her over-shooting the mark. Instead, she flooded Pneuma to her legs and made a Potency-fuelled leap, hurtling upward. Her fingers snared in the rough fibre of the root, leaving her dangling there, sandals kicking for purchase against the uneven surface and finding little to support her weight. Potency in her arms allowed her to heave herself up again and fling herself atop the root.

On hands and knees, she peered around. Ahead was a massive knot that acted as a landing, beyond which lay the bore into the trunk's hollow and, she assumed, the place where she could find the weavers of Ananke. All her answers, her last, most desperate hope, lay within this Tree, and somehow, she dreaded to cross the threshold. How could she not fear, for before her lay the risk of losing worse than her life. Here, she risked at last being forced to surrender the hope that had driven her so far these past years. So long as she lingered upon the threshold, that flame of hope lay crackling within her, and she could tell herself still one chance remained. But should her journey within extinguish the last of the fire, how then could she continue through life?

In her heart rose a traitorous, craven instinct that bid her turn back, refuse the final steps, and go onward as she had done, afore now. Though her efforts to change the future had failed thus far, she might try, again and again, allowing herself always to believe that next chance might prove the one where she could untangle the twisted threads of Fate without unmaking herself and those she loved. Why could she not continue thus, allowing for always one more chance? One more grasping hope to create the future she so sought ...

But then, she would forever know she had stood on the cusp of the

Truth and let fear turn her aside. Slowly, she gained her feet, and more slowly still, she climbed to the landing. As she crested the top of it, the sky turned to amber, seared by the blazing light of the setting sun before darkness would encroach all around her.

The bore beyond wove around the bend of a knot, making a gradual descent. What remained of the day's light failed to illumine the fibrous halls, forcing Pandora to ignite a torch in her hand with a snap of her fingers. Onward and deeper she delved, her footfalls resounding, heavy thumps upon the living insides of the great Tree. A sensation came over her, one she could not shake, that here, reality turned nebulous. Perhaps it changed for each desperate soul who dared this place, or perhaps it bent and twisted in languid motion, a dreamer shifting in their sleep.

The path wound round, and she began to suspect it had crossed itself, like some descending spiral. Bits of dirt and stone filtered in amid the living matter of the Tree, as if it were transforming into a cavern with each step forward she took. Her torchlight danced off the narrow walls, casting reaching shadows round each bend and giving the impression things waited for her, ever one more pace beyond her. Then, at last, the path opened out before her into a wide cavern. Roots dangled from above like a maze of stalactites, some knotted together in strange weaves, as though the Tree hugged itself in a desperate grasp, even it frightened by the place into which she intruded with brazen pride.

But if she was to be brazen, if she was to walk with audacity, let her do it honestly. Pandora strode forward, sweeping her right hand through the torch in her left until both held blazes, giving more illumination to the shadow-drenched cavern. Ahead, by the reflection of her firelight, she spied standing water, embowered by a circle of roots. She approached closer to the well, but it was empty. Besides her torches, she saw the clouded reflection of the tenebrous, root-clogged ceiling above. In the water, those twisted roots looked like the gnarled, arthritic fingers of matriarchs scarcely clinging to life.

Well, enough of this. She had not come here to muse on idle fancies. "Moirai!" Pandora cried, looking up from the water and whirling about the cavern, the spin of her flames sending the gloom recoiling at wild angles.

"She arrives," a woman's voice said from off to her side, and Pandora whirled once more to see a shrouded figure had appeared by the water's edge.

"She came," another figure said, now standing on her opposite side.

"She will be here," claimed a third, more youthful voice, and Pandora was surrounded by formless, hooded women.

Closing the fingers of her right hand, Pandora allowed her flames to wink out. As if in response, a brazier that had not stood there a moment ago burst into flame. All right, then ... Pandora extinguished her other torch, and more braziers sparked alight around the cavern, pushing back the gloom.

"Answers, she seeks," a figure said.

"... Though with mind closed," another continued.

"... Unwilling to see," the third finished, "that which already her soul apprehends."

Pandora shook her head, glowering at the implication of their words. Yes, she knew Prometheus had told her much and more of the Wheel of Fate. Yes, she *understood*, but when the shape of reality takes a form which cannot be borne, one is left with only the choice, however difficult, to try to make a better world. Prometheus sought to do so, with his gambit, but Pandora had not the patience for machinations spread across the breadth of history. "I reject your frightful Tapestry, Moirai, woven as it is without conscience or compassion. You spin the skeins of mortal lives without considering or consulting their wills and thus make mockery of choice, leaving us to dance to unseen puppet strings."

"The Tapestry ..."

"She does not ..."

"Refuses to ..."

"*See*," the youngest woman said. Abruptly, the figure stood beside her and laid a hand upon her shoulder. With the other, she pointed to the well, and Pandora followed her indication. Reflected in the water, she saw bands of luminance amid the cavern's reflection, though none existed in the real space the mirror echoed. She leant closer and realised the radiant strands erupted from *her*, spanning out in every direction, tethering her to distant endpoints. A million gossamer threads spooled out from her soul in that reflection, and as she watched, the image shifted, pulled back beyond the cavern. Her threads crossed others, wrapt around them, split apart and changed directions. Not millions, but billions upon billions of bands of light, forming an infinite web of connections.

"... The Tapestry ..."

Pandora recoiled, blinking away the sight, turning from the pool and its hateful revelation. "I did not come here seeking understanding of how lives connect to one another. I grasp well enough the interconnection of lives across the timeline, on account of which I delivered my past self into the torments I knew lay before her. My kin and I have shed oceans of blood and tears in the name of preserving your loathsome weave, for we could not have crafted another, better World." She swallowed, struggling to bridle her growing wrath. *Burn,* the Phoenix shrieked inside her breast. "You, I think, however might do so and yet *choose* not to. Are you not, then, the only ones in all the cosmos with free will and, at the same time, the ones who *abuse* that gift?"

"Of us ..."

"She thinks so much ..."

"Imagines omnipotence ..."

"Where none exists."

"In the throes of personal grief, she ..."

"Fails to grasp ..."

"We are, the most bound of all."

"The more revealed ..."

"The less one can change."

The claim slapped her in the face, stole her breath. It was impossible. Pandora refused to accept such. She refused to allow them to abrogate responsibility for the bitter state of this World. For if the implication their words held were truth, they were even less free than she was. Oracles perceived the future but could not change it and thus became trapped by their visions and were left thus impotent. Timewalkers saw the scope of history but could not alter it, for the timeline already accounted for their every thought, causality predicated upon the infinite chains that spanned the ambit of time.

And the Fates, who oversaw it all, who witnessed more than any other, watching it from some state outside time ... they ... They could not do aught save watch. Pandora crashed onto her knees, her palms slapping down into the loam around the well. After a moment, she forced herself to look up at them, those vile women who stood as symbols of all she loathed. "Can you not, on your loom, weave a better future than the one before us?"

"The future ..."

"Is perception."

"Illusion."

Pandora growled. "History then! Craft for Mankind a better history. Reweave the threads, give us a World without the need for such torments upon our souls as we now endure!"

"She does not understand."

"She does but rejects understanding."

"Clings to illusion."

"Weakness."

Oh, weakness she knew aplenty, and tears blurred her vision to hear this. For they made plain, they neither could nor would change the Tapestry. Perhaps, despite mortal conceit, they had not woven it in the first place but were rather a part of it, damned but to watch the unspooling threads. Perhaps, too, the predators Hekate feared, the Primordials from outside time, they would exist regardless. Did the presence of Khaos from outside the cosmos ensure that any World woven around it must needs be a World of suffering?

The Moirai had unequivocally denied holding omnipotence. In fact, they implied rather the opposite. That they, perhaps more than any others, lay mired in *impotence*. If they were gods, of any sort, they were useless ones. Mere facets of the Tapestry she had come here in the hopes of reweaving. She had known it a faint, distant hope, to believe that they might change Fate after hearing her argument. She had thought, if they existed outside time, perhaps they would not be bound within its causal chains. She had never imagined these creatures, whatever they were, would admit they had not the power to change aught, regardless.

"You will not help me." Though she swayed, she gained her feet. "Will not, or mostlike cannot."

"The Wheel of Fate must turn."

"The threads of the Tapestry must be maintained."

"This is the only World we are given."

Pandora nodded, though the truth all but choked her. For a moment, she shut her eyes. Faced with such revelations, she could see herself crumbling, all her resolve turned to dust. Hope could become ashes, flitting through her fingers. Already, the shadow of despair loomed above her like the impending tidal wave that would crash upon Atlantis. How easy to give in and accept the inevitable.

Was this how they convinced Athene to become Nemesis and enforce their foul Tapestry? With the inarguable knowledge that the only alternative was to allow the Khaos, the *Darkness*, to swell and swallow all that was or ever would be?

"No," Pandora snarled the word. "Whether I can change it or not, still I shall strive against this ill future. Better to fight in opposition of the apocalypse, better to save what lives I can, than to embrace this obscenity with open arms." One by one, she turned her glower on each of the Moirai. "Though your Wheel of Fate may preserve the cosmos, still it feeds the Khaos you hope to forestall, and thus you make yourselves slaves of that Khaos."

The women lowered their heads, perhaps in acknowledgment, perhaps in shame. Then they were gone, the braziers flickered out, and Pandora was alone, in an empty, darkened cavern.

❧

As Pandora emerged from the Tree, she flexed her fingers and extinguished the flames acting as her torch. The moment she stepped onto the landing, something crashed before her with a *thud*, and Pandora yelped, staggering backward. Nemesis rose from a crouch, moonlight glimmering upon her aureate panoply, naked xiphos in her hand. At the moment, her wings had vanished. Beneath her helm, her azure eyes had turned lucent, flaring with malice.

"Athene ..." Pandora began, hands up in warding. She had little desire to fight her granddaughter, and she had hoped, in revealing herself to Pandora when she had returned the Box, Athene had moved past the need for strife between them.

"Even now," Nemesis snarled, "having borne witness to sacred mysteries, would you blaspheme and strive against the will of Ananke. Such temerity warrants only a single response. We are, all of us, *bound* to the Wheel of Fate."

Pandora realised her intent an instant before the woman lunged, her xiphos darting forward like a striking snake. Instinct—born of her training with Prometheus—overtook Pandora and she twisted to the side, shoving Nemesis's arm with a manoeuvre from kalaripayat. The sword thunked into the Tree, and, even as it did, Pandora twisted aside and slammed a Pneuma-infused fist into Nemesis's abdomen. The blow sent the assassin staggering backward, but she did not lose her grip on her blade, instead tearing it free of the trunk as she stumbled.

"I do not wish to face you! You are my blood!"

Before Nemesis could make an answer, flames erupted along the night sky, and something shrieked toward them. On fiery wings, Kala surged up onto the landing, hurtling into Nemesis. The other Phoenix avatar collided with the assassin and sent her careening away, arms flailing to keep from pitching off the ledge and falling into the abyss.

"Stop!" Pandora screamed at Kala. "I can get through to her!" She grabbed his shoulder.

At once, he whirled, lunging for her wrist. Only the intense training with Prometheus allowed her to move fast enough to elude his grasp. But his attacks came with the speed of a whirlwind and the force of an erupting volcano, and Pandora was forced to give ground under the torrent, though time and again she turned away his strikes. As Prometheus had said, there were aspects of kalaripayat to his style, but only aspects. Still, maybe she could use it.

Predicting his next attack, she stepped under it and caught his wrist. At almost the same moment, Nemesis snared his shoulder. Before Pandora knew what was happening, Kala had reversed her hold and spun her around, slamming her into the wall. Something collided with her kidney and hefted her aloft, hurling her face-first into a branch above her.

Next she knew, she was lying on the landing, every nerve aflame with a riot of agonies. As her senses returned, she heard the gong-like clang of powerful blows striking metal. She pushed herself onto her elbows in time to see Kala slam repeated strikes into Nemesis's armour, each strike denting the cuirass or helm. The assassin was tossed around like a doll, beaten, flung into the trunk, all in the space of a heartbeat. Here stood the Destroyer, in truth, unstoppable, unfaltering.

"No!" Pandora wailed, and, on seeing the impending death of her granddaughter, the Phoenix burst to life inside her. A rising inferno erupted in her breast, even pain unable to survive its heat. "Kala, stop!"

She was on her feet as Kala caught the back of Athene's head and rammed it into the trunk with bone-splitting force. Nemesis collapsed in a broken heap.

Pandora shrieked and lunged, her arms in a conflagration turned upon her fellow Phoenix avatar. Kala twisted out of her attack in a dance-like flow, but she saw the momentary widening of his eyes on beholding the incarnation of the firebird in her. "What have you done!" Pandora bellowed. For all her training, she was still no match for this incarnation of the Destroyer.

Hands open, he assumed a fighting stance but did not advance. "I have removed a piece from the board." He hesitated. "And you, you hold within your breast the living inferno. It makes us kindred, of a sort, but no such bond will save you if you too serve the Unseen Order."

"I do not," she growled. "You, I thought, perhaps could have become an ally ... are not you friend to Prometheus? Yet you ..." She looked to Athene's corpse.

He started to rise, then a golden meteor streaked out of the sky, crashing at him. Kala rose from his crouch at the last moment, starting to dive aside, but the meteor caught him anyway and sent him hurtling off the landing. For an instant, his arms flailed wildly in the air, then he disappeared into the abyss beneath the Tree, obscured by roots and darkness.

A second Nemesis now stood on the knotted platform, where Kala had been a moment before. The woman turned, looked to her a moment, and then withdrew the Box from a pouch at her belt.

"Wait!" Pandora shouted, but it was too late, and a bubble of light engulfed the new Nemesis. It collapsed around her and she was gone.

In the distance, barely visible past the canopy of lesser trees, brilliant flashes rimmed Evenor Mountain, highlighting a vast, churning black cloud that had encompassed the peak. A storm, fiercer even than the eternal one encircling Olympus. She had seen this in the moment before it all crumbled ...

The land quaked and roared, louder than any drakon, the sound joining the waves of thunder from the storm, melding into a damning cacophony. The ground heaved, and Pandora was sent sprawling. The bucking land tore free of the roots around the Tree, pieces of it lurching upward whilst chunks of the ground fell away, vanishing into the darkness where Kala had fallen. Sections of root, still clinging to cyclopean stones and wads of dirt, lay dangling over the void. The Tree shook, as if in dread of the coming abomination.

The quake sent Nemesis's corpse tumbling toward Pandora, and she caught the body. Desperate, willing it not to be as she feared, she tore the bent helm away, though chunks of skull and brain splattered free in the process. The ruined face beneath that helm was not Athene, but a deep-skinned, dark-haired woman, perhaps Kandamian. "Vinata ..." Had to be.

Another tremor tore through the land, and her perch split in twain, a crack shooting up the Tree. This time, as Nemesis toppled toward the widening hole, Pandora allowed her body to plummet into the darkness.

This was the moment in which Atlantis would be rent asunder. Perhaps Mu was already destroyed. Now, her home, where she had so long ... Oh, Nyx's bosom! The younger Pandora was there, in the city, about to die!

Though her balance was precarious, Pandora fished the Box from her satchel. She need not move through time, only send herself to the polis, nigh to Taygete's Bridge. It would already have fallen, taking the Oracle Brizo, even as the woman had foretold so long ago.

All around, the deafening roar of the groaning land and the bellow of an apocalyptic storm on that mountain. The torrent of noise bombarded her senses, making it hard to concentrate. As if the heaving land ever trying to send her plummeting into the dark was not enough.

Frantic, Pandora twisted the gears and shifted the panels. She could ill afford an error now, for her timeline depended on someone saving her from the dying island. Pandora activated the Box.

7

HEL

19 Dark Age

In Eras swallowed by the engulfing maw of history, Hel's father stole the First Flame from the heart of the Elder God of Fire. She would, she supposed, never know the full depths of his experience, but she knew enough. Sitting upon her osseous throne in the shadowed halls of the necropolis of Kek, she had long mused on the how of it. For she knew well enough the why.

The Elder Gods were the apex predators of the cosmos, lurking in the fringes of the World, beyond the universe, beyond time, beyond space. In sick cycles of eternity, they devoured soul after soul, leaving behind only the dregs that might one day be reborn to repeat the process. Until naught remained and at last the fathomless abominations would consume the all that was or ever might have been. The agonies of Tartarus were but prelude to the timeless anguish every soul in existence would endure once the last Eschaton had played out.

The living and dead would writhe in eternal torment, become one with the endless Dark. All, unless Hel broke the Elder Gods. Unless, like her father before her, she took their power and turned it against them.

But Papa had never gone far enough, had taken but the smallest fragment of the essence of the Ever-Burning One. Hel would go farther; she would see it to the end.

The lampads had recorded fragments of the Ontos beneath the Eternal Glacier, though Hel doubted even the eldest of them still knew the lost secrets of fallen Eras. But she had seen it all. She had but to take that first step out into the void. Whilst any given mortal lay beneath the notice of the Elder Gods, Hel had no choice but to draw their eyes and ire upon herself. To challenge the might of beings so vast the cosmos could scarce contain their power.

Small wonder she hesitated, pondering her course over drawn-out years. Who could blame a person for delaying a battle they might well lose? Oh, but time kept creeping forward, relentless as the hunger of the eldritch horrors at the World's fringes. Sooner or later, she must make the choice: act or surrender to the crushing Wheel of Fate.

And Hel was not one to surrender.

Slowly, she rose from her throne. With languorous steps she walked through her empty hall—no one came here anymore, for she so rarely held court, remaining locked in her mind for days at a time—making for the stairs down to the lower levels. As Hades had done before her, Hel kept her prison-larder stocked with the souls of her foes. In the greater depths, though, below even the catacombs beneath the necropolis, in a cavern so immense it swallowed light like the night sky, she had once painstakingly carved a great summoning circle.

For months, upon hands and knees, she had chiselled away at basalt, tracing a ring of glyphs hundreds of feet around. The most complex, the most intricate, the most *desperate* working of the Art she had heretofore attempted.

Down the long stairs into the cavern she drifted, greeted by the demon's wheezing growls and the putrid coppery stench of it long before she reached the chamber. There, bound in fetters of mammoth thickness, knelt the skinless Old One, Aeshma. The creature lifted its head—if one could call a maze of horns lit from within by fell light a head—at her approach, and its malice washed over her like a burst from a sulphuric geyser.

IMPUDENT MORTAL! UPON YOUR SOUL SHALL I GNAW FOR EONS STRETCHING DOWN THROUGH THE END OF TIME.

"Impudent?" Hel mocked. "Coming from one who has spent the better part of a century on its knees before me, your bravado rings somewhat hollow, demon." The Old Ones were the spawn of Primordials. Demons, yes, but unlike their forebears, they were born in the World and thus tied to the Realms of the universe. Of whatever fathomless Abyss lay beyond the World, past the outer walls of Tartarus, Hel had learnt precious little, save that it was a Realm of Khaos, of absolute *Dark*. One day, perhaps, she would need to rectify her ignorance. If the Elder Gods had emerged from the Dark of the Abyss, had truly created the World of it, understanding that Realm was the key to understanding the cosmos in which she dwelt as well.

TIME HAS PATIENCE BEYOND MOUNTAINS.

"And you imagine still you shall await the chance at your vengeance across the breadth of time, when even mountains crumble? Your wretched mother may have birthed you at the dawn of time, *Old* One, but that offers no guarantee you shall witness the end of it all." Aeshma was the misbegotten get of Achlys, the Shrouded One as the lampads called their Elder Goddess of Mist. The father, if the demon had one, Hel had not determined, though Aeshma had taunted, on occasion, implying a power vaster even than that of his mother. "The Hekatónkheir ... Python ... I hear even many-headed Ladon have perished. You may hold more power than they did, but still, you are no Primordial. Death may yet close its jaws upon your throat."

In truth, she knew she wasted both her time and her words with these visits and petty taunting. But for millennia the demon's shadow had hung over her head, haunting her nightmares, chasing her waking mind into dark recesses. It had worked dread and terror over her across the stretch of her long life and even beyond, into her death. How could she deny herself the perverse satisfaction of twisting the dagger that had wounded its pride? How could she not repay the anguish it had rained down over her for so many years?

"Long have I pondered whither to turn my gaze and upon which of the hateful Archons I ought to move first."

MOVE UPON AN ARCHON? Now the Old One's laughter rang in her mind like a chorus of discordant cymbals and gongs. *YOUR MADNESS KNOWS NO BOUNDS.*

"I suppose I could have chosen any of them," she continued, ignoring the demon's mocking. "There was a temptation to bring down Pan, of course." The Sylvan, the dryads called it, and part of Dionysus's power—now her power, that which had allowed her to summon Aeshma into this circle—had come from that one. Hekate owed the Sylvan suffering, it was true. But other choices also had appeal. By directing the flow of dead souls to the Rimefells, she had weakened her kingdom in the Underworld. Unless, of course, the Rimefells became her new kingdom. "Surely even you must taste the delicious irony ... of me using you to bring low your mother."

But more vicious laughter answered her. Aeshma did not believe she could do it. Even now, the Old One had no idea of what Hel was capable of. It would learn, though. Very soon, *everyone* would learn.

"IT IS MADNESS THAT TAKES YOU," Persephone chided, sitting upon a bone stool in Hel's private library. "You might sooner bridle the sea or lasso the stars than bind an Elder God. They are the greatest forces in all the cosmos."

Hel crossed her arms over her chest and stared at her friend. "Do you ask yourself where I have gone, on those bouts where I would vanish for months—or longer—at a time over the past decades? Down countless winding roads I trod, to reach the farthest corners of the Spirit Realm. Keuthos and I walked through the accursed brightness of the Radiance, enduring the blight of its endless sun as we carved colossal sigils there. Beyond, in the Skystone Isles of the Stormpeaks, my Hel-wraiths weathered the tempests to work our Art. We chanced the ceaseless infernos of the Ashlands to engrave seals where no disciple of the Shrouded One would ever dare venture. In the Mortal Realm, where the Veil bars lampads from walking freely, there too we worked.

"Even unto the place which lies betwixt the worlds, on the edge of Tartarus, where I needed to conceal myself from the dark dragon that coils beneath the cosmos. There, too, I made my sigils. And do you know why, dear Persephone?"

Shudders wracked the other ghost and Persephone hugged herself. "Madness ..." she whispered again.

Hel snorted and shook her head. "The madness of defiance, as with the shears of my will I shred the Tapestry of Fate and spit in the faces of the Moirai. I have but to enact the final seal, in the seat of the Shrouded One's power." She did not name Achlys, even now, for fear of drawing the eye of the Elder Goddess. The last thing she needed now was such attentions falling upon herself, on the cusp of her plan's fruition. "My wraiths will do it and begin my reign."

"I do not understand," Persephone admitted.

Hel waved it away, for there was no reason to burden her with the details of the Art. "What matters is this: The Shrouded One has endowed the Winter Queen with a tendril of her power. Mist wraps around the soul of the queen. That tendril is a tether that, if we can seize it, even an Elder God cannot sever. Through the queen, I reach the goddess."

Persephone blanched. "You plan to war against the Winter Court, your erstwhile allies?"

Hel bared her teeth in a vicious grin. She had long ago fulfilled her oath to the lampads. Now ... now they would serve.

8

ATHENE

201 Golden Age

$\mathcal{A}$thene rose from a crouch to look around. She found herself in a vaguely familiar valley, though she could not place quite where or when she had seen this place before.

You are in Ogygia, just before your naïve grandmother will attempt to end the life of a teenage Zeus, who hunts her on behalf of his father.

Kronos had sent Zeus to hunt Pandora? When? Why? Athene shook her head.

She intends to unravel the threads of Fate by slaying the man long years before he can ever send her on her journey. Her success in so perverse an endeavour would rend causality asunder.

The destruction of history. Athene growled, shaking her head at the arrogance of those so quick to think they could cast aside all that had been or would be on their whims. She stretched her back, and her wings burst forth, though she had not intended to summon them. It would take some practice, she imagined, to gain full control of the ambit of her new abilities. For now the wings would, perhaps, help serve to intimidate a foolish girl who needed her path adjusted.

Assassin of Fate though you be, in some instances, a nudge may prove more efficacious than a blade.

As if Athene would have murdered her own grandmother. As if she would have become responsible for the creation of an irredeemable paradox that might destroy history.

She found Pandora attempting to build a crude snare of some sort, and Athene almost laughed at the absurdity of it. If her father had, at this stage, even a fraction of the Potency he possessed in Athene's earliest memories, he'd mostlike rip the trap to shreds and kill the idiot girl for her trouble. Pandora had absurdly underestimated her foe, and by stopping this ill-conceived attempt at murder, Athene would mostlike save the woman's life. Still, she found Pandora's hubris in thinking to break history thus more perturbing even than an attempt upon Zeus's life.

Pandora spun at her approach, eyes wide as she took in Athene's appearance. "Who are—"

Athene raced forward, grabbed Pandora's peplos, and shoved her, sending her hurtling away. The woman hit the ground hard, rolled several times, and lay moaning. Athene's gut jumped as the realisation hit her—Pandora did not yet have the power of Nike. Her sudden assault, meant to drive back a powerful foe, could have killed a hapless mortal had she landed wrong. She would need to pull her blows here.

A beat of her wings sent Athene flying to where Pandora lay, and she touched down in a crouch beside her. At a glance, she could see the woman yet breathed, Moirai be praised. She half expected their castigation in her mind, but they said naught. Was she only fulfilling the circles of history that had always unfolded as such? Either way, she needed to make her point well enough. She heaved Pandora to her feet once more, staring into the dazed Heliad's eyes. "You would think to thwart Ananke?"

The woman gaped at her, and Athene wondered what strange thoughts must have darted around her mind in such a time. Pandora stole a glance behind her and tensed. Athene could see why, for they stood close to the edge of a cliff that plummeted down to the rock-strewn sea.

Cast the timewalker into the void and let the tides of history carry her whither they may.

Such an idea left Athene queasy. But she had not sworn this oath to the Moirai, to all Mankind, to balk now. If such an act would have killed Pandora in the past, the Moirai would never had ordered it. The woman *must* survive this in order to become the woman Athene met later. So Athene grabbed her by the back of the neck, hefting her aloft and, thus carrying her, walked to the cliff's edge.

Pandora shrieked, drawing a knife from her belt. Its blade clattered off Athene's cuirass, useless. Athene snatched the woman's wrist, twisting until the knife tumbled from Pandora's fingers. Pandora's response was to kick Athene in the shin. Her sandal clattered on Athene's greave, no more effective than the knife had proved, yet Athene had to admire the woman's grit. Here she was, utterly powerless in the face of a foe far beyond herself, and still she fought. She could almost imagine her grandmother trying to bite her, should she come close enough to her mouth.

Yes, there was something glorious in the woman's refusal to surrender. Tenacity beyond mere stubbornness, Athene thought, as she set Pandora down upon the ground.

"Please," Pandora began. "Please don't—"

Admiration or not, Athene had not forgotten the Moirai's words. She beat her wings, the sudden gust sending Pandora flying off the cliff, shrieking and flailing as she surged toward the waves.

And Athene trusted she would survive. History demanded she survive.

AFTER USING the Box once more, Athene appeared on a hilltop, beneath a star-strewn night sky. The disorientation had begun fading more quickly with each use as her body acclimated to the strain of shifting through time and space. Athene rose, looking around, and noted her wings remained.

Pulled by strings of the heart that, for a moment, might seem more adamantine even than threads of Fate, a misguided servant might well say too much.

"What?" Athene asked. Sometimes the Moirai's obscurity made her role harder to suss out. "What am I doing here? Where am I?"

Should your grandmother learn truths before the crucible of time has tempered her awareness, the strain might turn her brittle. Thus, history demands separation before words spill forth untrammelled from the broken dam of a servant's love.

Bemused, Athene took to the air, and, guided by instinct given to her by the Moirai, she flew across a land she soon recognised as Phoenikia until she reached Byblos. From high above, she looked down into the courtyard of the royal palace and there saw Prometheus, deep in conversation with Pandora. Whatever Prometheus's oath to Moirai in times past, whatever connection he held to them, he plainly did not serve the Unseen Order, and Athene had no time to unravel the complexity of his machinations or true loyalties. This man was meant to be the first, greatest servant to the Moirai, but they doubted him and feared he would reveal too much out of the yearnings of his heart.

That, Athene could not allow, no matter how she sympathised with his motives.

She tucked her wings and fell into a dive, shrieking toward the pair, then crashed into the courtyard with enough force to split the cobbles. She landed in a crouch and slowly rose, turning her helmed gaze upon the pair who might well violate the flow of history and crack the seams of the cosmos.

"Fucking bitch," Pandora moaned, having fallen to her arse when Athene hit the ground. Grit, indeed.

"No," Prometheus growled. Athene's grandfather had fallen, as well, though he'd caught himself upon his hands and knees. In an instant, he pushed off the ground, flipping sideways through the air and landing on his feet in front of Athene. Lightning-fast, his open-handed strike surged at her chest, and Athene barely managed to block it on her vambrace. His next strike came even faster, and all she could do was block blow after blindingly fast blow, giving ground under his relentless assault.

Many of his moves were unfamiliar, unlike the pankration arts she'd learnt from Artemis, and thus difficult to counter. In desperation, she allowed him to land a blow in exchange for scoring a kick to his knee. As he toppled, she caught his arm and twisted it around behind his back.

"Pandora, flee!" he yelled.

Growling, Athene slammed a fist into his face. She did not like the thought of hurting her grandfather, especially given all he had done for her, but she had no choice now. His mistakes brought this upon him, or so she told herself.

"No!" Pandora cried, but she did as Prometheus had asked, and ran from Athene.

"Vinata," Prometheus growled at Athene.

He mistakes you for the first Nemesis, the Moirai spoke in her mind. Even Prometheus did not know there were two of them. When she was certain Pandora had fled, she shoved her grandfather by the arm.

Wary, he rose, wringing out the pain she'd inflicted, even as he circled in a half-crouch, other hand up in warding.

Your purpose is fulfilled here.

Athene wanted to speak to him. She had a thousand questions to pose this man, chief of them how much he knew of Fate and all it held in store for her. Could she reveal her identity to him now?

It is not for him to know all things. Knowledge enough already compounds into the weight of mountains bowing his shoulders. So any more of the truth would only serve to burden him; Prometheus, too, was caught and bound by the Wheel of Fate, no freer willed than Athene or anyone else.

She backed away, one hand behind her back, setting the Box as the Moirai unconsciously guided him.

"Vinata ..." Prometheus said, hands shifting from a fighting pose to one of conciliation. "The Unseen Order is not what you think it is ..."

"Or perhaps you are the one misguided, refusing to see Truth."

The man faltered a moment. "You are not Vinata."

Damn. Had he recognised her voice? Before she could do more damage, Athene pressed the Box open, and its swallowing bubble of light engulfed her.

9
____

KIRKE

200 Golden Age

$\mathcal{A}$mbrosia, of course, had become the life of Titans, changing their blood to ichor. Changing their World. For who, released from the peril of mortality, would go back? Given the chance to live forever, a Titan would go to any length to maintain that immortality. They would steal, lie, bribe, or kill.

And as the population of Titans rose around the Thalassa Sea, demand for the draught increased until Damkina alone could not attend to such needs. Thus, from among the Goetic Circle candidates, had she trained three apprentices, the Hesperides, who alone besides Damkina knew the secret of brewing Ambrosia. Isolated on their island, in their hidden garden, they crafted the most sought-after good in all the Mortal Realm.

Secrets, of course, tended not to last forever.

So, alongside Enki she sailed for Ogygia, where a rising power amid the Titans lived. One Atlas, whom some claimed the strongest of all Titans. Not so many years back, Men had developed biremes and, with them, managed longer sea voyages. It had allowed for the rediscovery of

Hesperides Island, and Ogygia beside it. Atlas had taken the smaller island as a fertile haven for his crews of Phoenikian war bands—pirates, in truth—whilst he sought to expand his naval empire.

Enki hurled an anchor over the edge of their boat, then looked to Damkina, who nodded. On the voyage over, she had thrice considered asking if this step was truly necessary, even knowing exactly what his answer would be.

History must unfold.

Ever, ever unfolding. Atlas would seize Hesperides Island, enslave the Hesperides, and spark the Ambrosial War. Many years later, he would force the Hesperides to train his daughters, the Pleiades, to brew the Ambrosia. And somewhere along the line, the Hesperides would disappear. By allowing this to happen, Damkina was condemning her former apprentices, women she liked, to centuries of captivity and, she assumed, eventually quiet executions. Or by denying history, she could instead condemn the whole World to Khaos.

So she would weep for them. And she would allow Ananke to wrap its coils about them, as it did to everyone.

At her nod, Enki vaulted the gunwale and landed in the surf, prompting Damkina to follow. They sloshed ashore, then climbed the hill where the pirate lord had built his fortress. It was a wooden palisade enclosure that, to the people of this Age, must have seemed intimidating, though it was but a shadow compared to the great city Helios had built for himself in the east. Or for that matter, mighty Thebes to the north.

Unlike Helios or Phoebe, Atlas had no Art to assure his power, nor the established power base Kronos or other Titan warlords had attained. What Atlas had was a small fleet crewed by loyal, fearless sailors. The Titan was more about strength than grandeur, and his ambition—and yeah, proximity—made him the obvious target for Enki's manipulations. Of course, Atlas had also publicly declared Prometheus his brother, and Damkina truly hoped the Firebringer would not be in attendance today. She had no idea what she'd say to him if she saw her grandfather now.

They made their way up the hill to the fortress, and seeing only two Titans, Atlas's captains let the gates swing wide. Atlas himself came out to meet them, a massive grin splitting his even more massive face. To get that large, Damkina had to wonder if he'd tasted Man-flesh once or twice, but somehow controlled the addiction it would produce.

Enki and Atlas exchanged pleasantries, and he brought them into his private rooms. Private, but not unoccupied, for a trio of naked women lay sprawled around the room. One had a sheet draped over her hips, but the other two seemed to have tossed their modesty into the darkest hole they could find and proceeded to hurl debris on top of it just to make certain no one would ever dig it up again. The whole room was redolent of wine and sex and something else. Poppies?

With a grunt of satisfaction, Atlas collapsed onto a heap of pillows and motioned for Enki and Damkina to join him. The big Titan winked at Damkina and patted his knee. As she knew it for a jibe rather than in earnest, Damkina decided to offer him a rude gesture instead rather than curse him with arthritis in the offending knee.

"The Thalassa World changes quickly," Enki said when he had taken a seat across from Atlas. A girl crawled over and offered him a bowl of wine, but the man waved her away. Like Damkina, he kept his hood up, little eager to show his face.

Damkina settled nearby and snatched the wine bowl from the girl before she could take it away. No sense in letting it go to waste.

Atlas grinned and spread his hands, trying to impress with his bounty. Whilst plundered wine and lots of willing sexual partners did have a certain appeal, Damkina had to admit, he was hardly rolling in wealth, either. Maybe it was because he distributed spoils fairly among his men. They sang his praises, that was certain. "Indeed, ship designs improve each year. We can range much farther and faster than we could when I was a youth, and you"—he pointed a finger at Enki— "I have to thank for many of these improvements. So ask what you will of me? Food and drink, companionship, Kandamian gemstones, all can be arranged!"

"Which of those treasures compare to the golden draught which turns Titan blood to ichor?" Damkina said after sipping her wine.

The big Titan chortled. "Well, indeed, and when we see a ship carrying it, we take it. But such are few and far between; hard to find in a sea so vast."

"Sooner or later," Enki said, leaning forward, "someone shall try to control the source."

Atlas huffed. "Be that as it may, no one has deigned to inform me where I might steal that. Would make life easier, I suppose, if people told you where they planned to hide their treasures."

Damkina lowered her gaze to the swirling surface of her wine. What were three more deaths upon her conscience now, anyway? In the scope of her long life, she lost others she had loved dearer than these apprentices, and for less reason. All her thoughts of going back, of correcting her myriad mistakes and crafting a better life, they had been but childish fancies.

History must unfold.

"But, my friend," Enki said, "it is known already that the source of Ambrosia is the Hesperides, brewed on the great island just across the channel. It would little surprise me if Tethys does not seek to claim the Ambrosia within the season, and I've no doubt Kronos too knows the location." Because, of course, Kronos was one like Enki, though Enki named him a misguided Gnostic rather than one of the Unseen Order. And Tethys, well, they had already agreed they would go to Thebes next to let slip rumour of what lay upon Hesperides Island. Given the woman's Telkhine allies, Damkina would not want her as an enemy. She could only imagine how bitter the struggles betwixt Deep Ones and Atlas's pirates would become.

History must unfold.

Damkina found, despite her mantra, despite her knowledge of what must happen, that she could not look up from her wine. At least, not until she'd thrown it back and tossed aside the bowl.

Once a few great Titans knew of Ambrosia's source, it would take little time for more to learn.

With but a few words, they had thus begun the Ambrosial War.

IN THE DANK caverns beneath Olympus, long before Zeus would build his palace, Damkina walked with Enki, her torch adumbrating the chamber of the Oracle Mirrors. As Enki made some adjustment to one of them, Damkina strolled the circuit of the room, letting her torchlight fall on one quicksilver surface after another. She knew, if she looked deeply, she might perceive past or future, or spy upon distant places. Yet, she dared not look, for she had seen enough of the shape of time to know she had no desire to see more.

Even, she had taken to warding her mind in an effort to block out prescient dreams. Damkina had witnessed enough, and now she preferred to trust the future to Enki. She had seen incipient hints of the rise of the Destroyer, known he was meant to save the World from Khaos … but every hint she saw of him was one of carnage, of death unimaginable. No, she did not want to see such things.

"I thought this place belonged to Zeus?" she said. "Or, I mean, I guess Kronos, since Zeus is probably just a brat at the moment." Not that he'd grown out of such, but whatever.

Enki rose from where he'd knelt beside one of the mirrors. "To Kronos and his Gnostic Cabal, yes. Potent tools, these, and ones mishandled by cretins who fail to grasp that not only is their struggle against the Wheel of Fate futile, but that their success would mean the damnation of all Mankind. Only the Wheel and the Hidden God behind it can forestall the swell of Khaos."

"So what are we doing here?"

He beckoned her over to the mirror he'd tinkered with. "Kronos possesses the calm control that accompanies countless Ages of life. But even his control is not impenetrable. He thinks he needs to look into the future and that, seeing the shape of it, he will be able to avert it. So I will give him his wish and show him his final ending. And when he looks, calculation and patience shall give way to fervour and desperation, becoming the instrument of his undoing."

As he bid, Damkina looked into the mirror. Through Kronos's eyes, she saw.

Frozen stones, a shadowed hall that failed to keep out the bitter, howling wind.

Kronos walked toward the intruders, a man and a woman. He kept his hands behind his back to still them, though dread of the closing circle crept upon his heart.

"Mimir," the man said.

The woman, though, gasped. "Kronos." Pandora! Kirke's grandmother was there, in that rime-laden place, looking upon Kronos.

"So comes the herald of my death," Kronos said in Elládosi. "Down through the Ages I have wandered, wracked by enduring dread for the doom long ago beheld in the mirrors we wrought." He moved to close the gap between them, wrath kindling. "They were our vanity, those mirrors, our relentless desperation to forestall the weavings of Fate. We thought that if we could behold the future, we might find the means to avert it. And when that failed, we fought with such obdurate valour against the ineffable. And every step yet brought me to this protracted moment, to gaze down into your golden eyes and know my end had come round at last."

"I have not come here to kill you," Pandora whispered. "I just want to understand."

"You," Kronos spat back, "timewalker, would flense away the armour of your ignorance, bit by agonised bit, until you are left agog at the untrammelled horror you have laid bare. You are the razor with which Fate shall flay us all."

The image flickered, blurred.

When next it was clear, Pandora was turning, looking behind at a new man who had appeared, perhaps a Kandamian by the look of him, save for his emerald eyes. He rose from a crouch and advanced, gaze locked upon Kronos. "Gnostic."

Damkina felt the dread within Kronos redouble.

Another flicker.

The stranger's blade bit into Kronos, tore him open crotch to chest, in sudden violence that had Damkina wanting to shriek. Another swipe. A head lopped from its shoulders.

Darkness.

"*Pandora!*" Damkina said.

Enki nodded. "Even now, she dwells on Ogygia, having given birth to a child." To Damkina's *mother*. "And soon, once Kronos has seen this, he will be desperate to find her and that accursed, beautiful Box. He will invade Ogygia." Damkina blinked away the strain of it, for what must be, must be. "Now I must make for Thebes."

"Why?" she asked, still dazed by the vision. "Tethys is already embroiled in the war. What need to prompt her further?"

Enki held her gaze, his eyes too knowing. "Because Tethys must be there, at Ogygia, to save Prometheus's lover from Kronos."

It struck Damkina, then, that Mother had grown up in Thebes. As, of course, she must.

IN A READING ROOM, Damkina sat with Morpheus, eating olives and annotating scrolls. The boy had become a man and given the way he had clung to her heels in the wake of Enki's display and departure, Damkina had raised him almost as her son, though neither of them had put such into words. Too, his oneiromantic abilities had surpassed all expectations, and she wondered how long before his abilities went beyond her own. From the future, she knew he would become one of the most famed oneiromancers in the whole of the Era. Already, he had ascended to the Inner Circle and taken on an apprentice of his own, a Kimmerian named Hypnos.

It was strange, Damkina had thought at first, thinking of one she'd raised as a child now shaping another, younger mind. Such whirring thoughts had forced her to re-read the same passage on her scroll thrice already, so she set down her quill and looked to him. "How goes the training?"

Morpheus quirked a brow before her meaning seemed to settle on him. "Well enough for the most part, though he nigh lost himself wandering the dreamscape last night."

Damkina frowned. No one, not even the wisest of oneiromancers, knew whence came dreams or how deep into foreign worlds the mind might burrow. There was a sense that, somewhat akin to the fathomless depths of the Roil, one could wander so far one might never return. And too, there was ever the fear that nightmares could prove something more than the conjurings of one's own mind. Mother had warned of oneiromancers lost in somnambulistic prisons, unable to ever wake again. She had received such warnings from Morpheus, passed on to Kirke, who in turn had given them to Hekate and Hypnos. Which, she supposed, left one to wonder if such oneiromancers ever existed, or if that fear was one more sourceless product of the circularity of time.

"Daughter," she heard Helios say from the main hall. "What are you doing here?"

Damkina held up a finger to forestall any further comment from Morpheus. Her father had many daughters, but Kirke had been among the eldest, and was not yet born. So which sister ...? Even as she drifted to the room's threshold, she caught a familiar voice, though not one she'd heard in centuries.

"Isn't it obvious?" Artemis asked. Damkina paused in the shadows, tension thrumming through her muscles at seeing the Phoebid here. "I've come to learn the greater mysteries at long last, Father." The Artemis she saw now seemed different, fiercer, or at least more prideful than the one Damkina had last seen. She had never gone far into studies of the Art, and Damkina doubted the woman had managed any sorcerous works. But here she was, trying to prove something to her father.

And behind her stood a painfully young Hekate, fresh-faced and fiery-haired, her golden eyes glinting in the firelight.

"What makes you think the Circle seeks new members?" Helios demanded.

Damkina rolled her eyes. Father had always disdained females, and the last thing he'd wanted was one of his daughters involved in his secret pursuit of the Art. But, even if Artemis would fail here, Hekate *needed* this place. "Oh, come off it," she said, throwing up her hood and stepping from the threshold out into the main hall. "The Outer Circle has space for two more novitiates, and in walk two seeking the positions. Praise the Moirai and move on."

Her father grunted, plainly displeased, but waved Artemis to follow. No doubt he wanted to offer her oh-so-helpful fatherly advice.

Damkina looked to their new Hyperborean novitiate now. "Keuthonymos, induct our new recruit."

The young man fair leapt to his feet. "Yes, mistress." He raced to Hekate's side, grabbed her hand, and dragged her away toward the library.

When they were out of earshot, Damkina allowed herself a sigh, aware Inanna was watching her. Rather than return to the reading room with Morpheus, she slipped off into her private chambers. With the door closed, she leant against it and shuddered. There was something bitter-sweet and gut-wrenching about seeing her mother like this, alive again. Young and naïve, and with so much pain ahead of her. And unless Damkina missed her guess, about to conceive Kirke with Helios in an orgy.

For a while already, Damkina had let slip hints that she might join Enki in his wanderings around Gaia. The Circle was well established, and with Hekate inducted, her last reason for being here was accomplished. It would pain her to leave Morpheus behind, but not quite so much as it would hurt to be here and see herself born—which made her wonder, for the first time in a long while, how such had felt to Pandora.

Perhaps she'd give Hekate a fortnight to settle in; that, and make certain Helios did not seek to drive off their initiates.

Then, after two centuries, the time had come for her to quit this place at last.

DAMKINA WOULD NOT HAVE JOINED in the Sea of Oneness regardless, but on learning her mother was taking part, she fled the Lodge into the city. There was something perverse about being present for one's own conception—at least she assumed this would be the night when Helios would get Hekate with child—and she could not stomach the thought. Instead, she headed into Byblos and began to prepare supplies for a journey. When she had made what arrangements she could, she joined Enki in his manse outside the city walls.

By lamplight, the ancient sorcerer pored over clay tablets graven with strange runes, scribbling notes on a papyrus scroll nearby. He did not look up at her entrance, and she was not certain what she even wished here, save to be away from Byblos. They had spoken, before, of seeking out new potential sorcerers in the desert enclaves of Kumari Kandam, or perhaps geomancer shamans within the Jungles of Nysa.

Following the end of the Ambrosial War, Enki began going more oft by the name Mithra. "It is closer to my original name," he had said.

"There is a certain appeal in knowing Matarśivan, Kratu, and those who remain of our brethren know I am about."

He meant, of course, that he taunted the other immortals, all but daring them to strive against the inevitable. Through rare cracks in his implacable facade, Damkina sometimes perceived hints of his cruelty. By and large, he took the suffering of others as a necessity of history, neither good nor bad, and certainly not a source of pleasure. But ever so oft, she got the sense that others, his kindred, had betrayed him, and this he took as a personal affront.

To Damkina, he was still Enki, and she was not certain how long it would take for that to change. "Have you wine?" she asked, because it seemed as good a way to strike up a conversation as any. Well, and yeah, because she needed to be riotously drunk this night, though she had no desire to share her flesh with him or anyone else.

He set down the quill before looking to her. "It is this night, then." Then he nodded. "There is wine in the amphora in the kitchen. Fetch it and bowls, as it suits you."

The Phoenikians had yet to develop vintages that compared to those she favoured in later days, but sometimes one did not need to savour wine. Sometimes, one just needed a way to blunt the razored edges flensing one's mind, and it would do for that. She returned with the wine and sat on the floor before Enki, then poured into two bowls. Then she drank both before pouring one for him, as well. "You feel it?" she asked when he sipped at his.

"The wine?"

"The *weight*."

Enki set his bowl down and stared at her. "Of knowing the future, of bearing witness to history as observer, as watcher, yes. We are forever watching the revolutions of the Wheel." He grew silent a moment before taking up his bowl once more. "There are few who have felt it more deeply. But we must remain Unseen, and the Wheel of Fate must forever turn."

She looked to him. Maybe ... she wanted him to be something else to her, to offer her more than the sporadic comfort of flesh and the sense of purpose he gave her. But Enki—Mithra, she supposed, now they were leaving the Circle behind—seemed incapable of being that to her, and she supposed it was better to content oneself with what one had than mourn things not meant to be. He did not love her, she knew, so she strove not to give her heart to him, either, though Damkina was forever flinging her heart out in the hopes someone would catch it. Some lessons could not be learnt, not when the soul defied the mind.

"I think I am done with the Circle," she said.

"Our purpose here is achieved," he agreed.

And purpose was, in the end, all she had left.

"By now," he said as they walked the outskirts of the Empty Desert, "young Hekate has stolen the Sefer Raziel from the Circle we founded." Damkina said naught—it had been destiny, of course—and he continued, "History, most oft, needs but a nudge to stay on course. Your mother finds herself pursued by Hypnos."

Now, she frowned. Morpheus's apprentice showed such promise as an oneiromancer. That, and, given that Damkina had all but raised Morpheus, Damkina had felt a slight kinship to Hypnos. Already, she had a sinking suspicion of what would follow.

At her frown, Mithra answered her unspoken query. "I cannot allow Hypnos to capture or kill your mother."

"Morpheus will not be well pleased if you kill him." It was paltry objection, compared to the life of her mother, much less the necessity of Fate. It was, however, all she had to object with.

"Which is why you shall bring the most promising member of the Circle to meet me in Nineveh. It is time for him to gain new purpose."

In the Badian Steppes, in a small camp, Ningal found them, buying horses. Mithra planned to ride for Nineveh, and Damkina was bound to fetch Morpheus out of Byblos. A year away had given her time enough to clear her head, and she had grown to miss the boy she had helped raise.

She had not, however, missed Ningal, and yet there stood the woman, a snake draped around her neck like a scarf. Even the way the Anunnak sashayed toward them seemed serpentine, and there was a fierce, predatory gleam in her eyes.

"Did. You. Know?" Ningal fair spat at her father.

"I know many things. Others, I glean when it becomes needful."

That sneer grew so fierce, Damkina imagined some ker or demon inside the woman, though they stood beneath Hyperion's glare. Naught so malicious ought to cross into sunlight; it seemed profane to think a person capable of wrath running so deep. "Did you know I would lose another daughter to your churning Wheel?"

Inanna was dead? Damkina faltered, uncertain how to react to that. She had liked the younger Anunnak, had seen a grand future ahead of her, even if she had a bit more pride than talent. When Damkina had left the Circle, the woman was alive and well.

Mithra looked aside a moment, as if seeking his answers from the infinite blue of the sky or the vast horizon beyond the camp. When he moved, it was so sudden, his passage so swift, Damkina might have taken it for a sudden gale. He swept across the dozen feet between himself and his daughter in the pace of a heartbeat—less—and hefted her off the ground with one hand upon her jaw. "What I know, Daughter, is that you murdered Ninurta and stole the Tablet of Destiny, betrayed it into the hands of our foes, all in spite of your kindred. Had not I foreseen your survival of this day—thus confirming Fate's will for you—I would reward your perfidy as befits such a crime. Even so, your husband too knows what you have done to his brother and will not cease to hunt for you."

When Mithra let her fall, Ningal collapsed to her knees, rubbing her neck. "So 'twas spite on your side, then, to let her die, having foreseen it?"

"I never said I foresaw Inanna's fall." Mithra seized his horse's mane and leapt onto the animal's back. Riding bareback, now before the invention of saddles, had been one more thing Damkina struggled to reacclimatise to, though Mithra had not deigned to share designs with civilisation, as yet.

"And I can see how it so grieves you," Ningal spat. Indeed, if Mithra agonised over learning of his granddaughter's demise, he hid it well.

Damkina swung onto the back of her horse, casting a pitying look at the woman. No mother should bury her daughter. But still, she saw little she could do for the woman. So she rode for the port towns along the northern shore, thence to sail for Phoenikia.

❧

NINEVEH WAS, at this time, the greatest city in Neshia. An eight-mile-long double wall encompassed the settlement, broken by gates in each of the cardinal directions. Ashlar stone composed the bottom twenty feet of the wall, with another thirty feet of mudbrick built up atop that. Between the height and thickness of the wall and the many towers that warded it, Damkina imagined it must be the best-defended city in this Age.

Small wonder, since bands of Neshian warlords out of the Badian Steppes raided the countryside like swarms of locusts. The fertile lands of the Tigara River brought prosperity to the numerous villages along its banks. That prosperity attracted greedy, grasping hands, forcing the villagers to call for the protection of Nineveh on a regular basis.

On the western horizon, fingers of smoke curled. Some poor settlement put to the torch before Ninevehan defenders could reach them, she assumed.

With Morpheus by her side, Damkina passed through the north gate. She had a shawl wrapt around her face, but the gate guards dare not question two Titans, and so they strode unopposed down through a bazaar redolent with spices and the scent of meat too long in the sun. Morpheus paused to browse at some baubles Damkina thought might have come from Nysa.

The young man had taken it ill when she had told him Enki had slain Hypnos. Before that, he had begun hunting Hekate in her dreams and had only grudgingly agreed to give over his pursuit of her. Indeed, she learnt Nephthys had intended to call up keres to hunt for Hekate, and Damkina had talked her out of that, too, warning it was too dangerous.

Morpheus agreed to come for her sake and hear out Enki, though he had scarce spoken to her on the voyage across the Thalassa. Nor was she certain whether he yet haunted Hekate's dreams, searching for her, seeking his vengeance for his dead apprentice.

On returning to the Lodge, Damkina learnt Hekate had wrought great carnage there. Before that, even Artemis had, possessed by a bear spirit, slain Inanna. Already, the Circle Damkina had built was rived with cracks. It would not endure the remainder of this century. This, she tried not to dwell on, for there was a sadness in inevitable decay of all creations, the more so for having already foreknown of such things.

She did not press Morpheus to hurry. Whilst he no doubt cared about Nysan trinkets almost as much as he did for the seagull droppings that had painted the harbour district, she allowed the man his petty revenge. Petty vengeance was, after all, vastly preferable to the more dramatic kind Damkina had visited on more than one unhappy wretch who had vexed her.

When he'd had his fill of mulling over things he had no intent to purchase, Morpheus allowed her to lead him on toward the Sesan Bathhouse. The man quirked a brow at her, for the attendants would never allow him into the women's baths or her into the men's. Damkina strove to hold her expression neutral. She was not certain she succeeded in that, but whatever.

She flashed the doorman a hand sign Enki had taught her, and he waved them on with a stern nod. They followed not the main corridor to the baths, but rather stairs down, to where the fires beneath the pools heated the water. Despite the chimneys designed to filter smoke out through grates in the alley, these underground chambers stung her eyes and induced a fit of coughing. The two blind slaves tending the fires had shawls tied around their faces but no doubt went to sleep each night sore-throated and miserable.

Past the fire pits and around a bend was a storeroom where piles of wood lay in wait for whenever the fires dwindled. While neither of the slaves could have seen what she was about to do, still, Damkina cast a furtive glance over her shoulder to ensure they were alone. Satisfied, she pushed a brick in the wall triggering a mechanism to pop open the concealed door. This led to another passage, and here, Damkina took up a torch which spread its flickering light down the corridor. The way stretched on long enough Morpheus must have begun to grow apprehensive, but to his credit, he held his tongue and did not tarry.

Eventually, they came to a bronze-banded wooden door that creaked open at their approach, which, Damkina had to admit, unnerved even her, though she'd come here before. The hall opened into a stark, circular chamber decorated with naught save a circle of round carpets on the floor and a handful of torches atop bronze stands. A man sat on one of the mats, a cowl over his face. Only one of the torch poles was lit, flinging bands of light and shadow around in haunting chiaroscuro. Water streamed from the walls in thin curtains that, in the torchlight, looked more like flowing shadows than liquid. Something chittered high above. Bats, perhaps, though the light failed to reach the recessed ceiling overhead.

"To what strange place have you brought me?" Morpheus demanded, though he followed her into the chamber. With awe and disquiet plain upon his visage, the oneiromancer slowly turned about, taking in the play of light and dark created by the falling water. He looked next to the hooded man who yet remained with his legs folded beneath himself. "Who are you?"

Now, Mithra rose, throwing back his hood and revealing his face. "One who found a promising psychic and saw his gift nurtured that this day might come." Damkina envied him his apparent ability to distance himself from any pain over the death of his kin or the rift opened betwixt himself and his daughter. Or perhaps, so driven by his mission, he did not feel such things.

"Psychic?" Morpheus said. "You mean one with the Sight."

"That and more, yes. Be they termed witches or shamans or wizards ... they are those blessed with aberrations of the mind that allow them to see and touch fragments of the Ontos concealed from the somnambulant masses. And among those few, we find the ones most primed to become servants of the greater Ontos."

"Servants?" Morpheus asked.

The torches strained and flickered, as though blown by a heavy gust. When they stilled, around the room's periphery now stood six figures in dark clothes and monstrous face-concealing masks. Morpheus started, falling back a step, hands raised in warding.

Mithra, however, took a step toward him with arms spread wide in welcome. "We walk in the shadows that fill the spaces between moments. We are Unseen."

"We are Unseen," Damkina repeated in unison with the assassins who had stepped across the Veil and entered the Mortal Realm. Not for the first time, her heart clenched at the fear of what would become of Morpheus if he should reject this offer, for Mithra would not suffer anyone who knew even this much of them to live. And yet, Morpheus had still lived at the time Kirke was banished to Aiaíā, so he must have accepted. He *must*.

And he did. "Tell me, then, of the Ontos."

Because for some, the thirst for answers outweighed all other concerns. And Mithra had the answers to every question that had ever mattered.

10

ARTEMIS

399 Dark Age

*H*er sailors, on arrival in the polis of Athenai in the dead of night, found the city all but deserted. The people had fled, perhaps across the strait to Korinth, or perhaps into the wild hills of the island. Only the most recalcitrant of the aristoi had remained on the acropolis, along with Olympian priests and priestesses still convinced their gods would arrive to save them.

The Babilimian warriors had looted whatever they could carry back to their ships, and Artemis had watched them, torn somewhere between pleasure and despair at the sight. *Had all this always been inevitable?* Mithra's Wheel of Fate meant everything was always inevitable. Why, then, should this moment prove so damnably bittersweet?

When their triremes lay heavy with plunder, Artemis noted as her warriors set fire to Athene's grand city. *This is a pyre for Apollon,* she told herself. *It is a memorial to all who died for Olympus's whims.*

Yet seeing the city burn brought little satisfaction.

WHILE THE ATHENIAN civilians had gone into hiding, their navy, Artemis soon learnt, had not fled. Rather, they had joined with the Korinthian fleet and gathered at the tiny island of Salamis. Their position at the northern end of the Strait of Korinth made access to the mainland impractical unless she was willing to sail around and expose her flank to attack. More than that, though, the massed warships of the Elládosi stood in open challenge to Babilimian naval superiority. Athene had, no doubt, heard of Artemis's command on the sea and sought to provoke her into attacking.

And it would work.

She stood at the bow of her flagship, Perspicacity allowing her to gauge numbers of enemy vessels even in the predawn blackness. They lurked, aware of their gathering foes, but waiting. "Send word to the Kemetian fleet," Artemis commanded. "Have them sail around and block the southern end of the Strait."

Artemis was through running from any confrontations. If her enemies sought battle with her, they would find it, and only as their ships sank toward Pontus and their lives flashed before their eyes would they realise the hubris of their choices.

"BRACE!" Artemis bellowed the instant before her trireme's ram crashed through the hull of a Korinthian bireme. A cacophony of shrieking wood followed, the snapping of oars, the roaring crunch of planks bursting, all covering the screaming of men sent down toward the Deep Ones. A hail of splinters rained over her vessel and Artemis raised an arm to ward against shards striking her face or eyes.

She felt the impact in her teeth. As the initial shockwave subsided, her marines began to leap onto the broken bireme, fearless in their pursuit of enemies of the god-king.

All around, ships from both sides lay ablaze, tossed by the turbulent waves. Upended vessels slowly sank into black depths while columns of smoke choked the sky, blocking out the morning sunlight. The Elládosi had, the moment she entered the Strait, managed to drive the first line of the Phoenikian fleet into the second, that fool Ariabignes outmanoeuvred like a child. Well, Artemis had seen his body floating by, obviating any need to demote the man.

Artemis squinted through the haze of smoke, gazing from one ship to the next, hunting her prey. She trusted her marines and commanders to have this well in hand. What mattered now was ensuring Athene did not escape from this battle. The god-king had sent word he wanted her brought before him—even providing the orichalcum chains with which Artemis could accomplish the deed—and, though Artemis would have found it easier to kill the woman, she would not deny Mithra's will.

There, on the far shore, stood a figure taller than those surrounding them. Artemis allowed Pneuma to flow into Perspicacity to enhance her senses. Her vision turned eagle-like, keen even across the distance and the haze of war clogging the air. Athene stood in full panoply; her face concealed beneath the cheek plates of a Korinthian helm. But it had to be her! That height, the fringes of her bright white tunic flapping beneath the edge of her pteruges. It was Athene, Artemis was certain of it.

With the roar of a dying behemoth, the mast of the sundered ship split, its plummet cutting off Artemis's view of her mark. Without so much as a thought, Pneuma flooded into Alacrity, enhancing her reflexes, dilating her perception of time. The mast fell as though passing through treacle. Blazing arrows slowed mid-flight, became a shower of miniature shooting stars passing over the battle.

She would not lose this chance. With a single bound, she leapt astride her flagship's gunwale. She allowed Pneuma to flow into Potency, then, unshouldering her bow, leapt again. This time she hit the side of the still-falling mast, ran along it, and allowed more Pneuma to flow into Lightness. Her next bound sent her soaring, almost seeming to fly. She nocked, aimed at the man beside Athene, and loosed. Unable to allow her attention to follow the arrow's flight, she focused instead on landing on a distant Athenian bireme.

After tossing her bow to her other hand and pulling her knife, she crashed down amid the flabbergasted crew. An oarsman tried to rise. Her blade opened his throat even as a slap of her bow caught the man across from him full in the face. She kicked another oar, cracking it and send the haft slamming into the chests of its two rowers. From the way one dropped, his lungs might have caved in.

Marines surged for her, valiant—or desperate—enough to face a Titan in close combat. She parried a xiphos on her vambrace and rammed her knife into the marine's armpit. At once she jerked her blade free, planting it in the throat of another attacker. A third she caught by the chin, hefted him off his feet, and brought him down skull-first on a bench with enough force to shatter both wood and bone.

They were too slow. By the time they knew what was happening, Artemis had carved her way through two dozen marines. Closer to shore, maybe sixty feet away, the blazing wreckage of a trireme stood half-submerged. Once more allocating Pneuma to Lightness, Artemis vaulted the gunwale, kicked off it, and bounded onto the sinking ship.

The shattered hull jutted at almost forty-five degrees from the water, and she caught herself only by snaring a loose line. Her sandals slapped against the steep incline, struggling for purchase upon the sea-drenched, broken decking. The heat of the flames washed over her exposed face and skin, scalding, but she had no Pneuma to spare for her comfort. Sweat and sea spray dribbled into her eyes as she cast about, looking for an angle.

Another leap sent her hurtling from starboard to port, closer to the shore where her prey awaited. She clung then to the gunwale, foot finding a hold in an oar gate. Artemis struggled to climb—

A whoosh by her head was the only warning, and she released her grip the instant before a javelin impacted the rail where she'd clung. She slipped, hit the deck, and skidded along on her back. Overhead, mounted on a pegasus, Athene soared. Artemis caught a splintered plank as she slid by, but it broke away in her hands, sending her careening toward the churning deep. Her bow tumbled away, vanishing. At the last instant, she snared tangled rigging hanging from the mast. The sudden stop jerked at her shoulder, drawing a grunt of pain from her.

She had no time to focus on the ache, though. An instant later, Athene's sandalled feet crashed into the angled mast, the wood groaning on her falling weight. Artemis caught a glimpse of burnished greaves just before a spear surged for her face. She kicked at the deck and sent herself skidding away, beneath the opposite side of the mast. A rower's bench had burst up through the deck, and Artemis kicked off this, released the rigging, and flipped around in the air to land on the mast beside Athene.

The woman whipped the spear around in a wide arc, forcing Artemis to drop, falling over backward to avoid it breaking across her body. She kicked out, caught Athene's shin between hers, and the two of them toppled off the mast together. The spear offered a satisfying clatter as it fell. Then the pair of them were grappling, skidding toward the sea. Growling, Athene reared up. Artemis just twisted away from a blow of a gauntleted fist that punched a hole through the deck. Athene snared the planks and—as Artemis was still entangled with her—brought them both to a sudden stop.

Artemis's Pneuma-infused blow took Athene on the jaw, sounding like a gong against her bronze helmet. The impact bent the metal inward, no doubt pushing in against the woman's jaw. Artemis hit it again, and a third time. Athene lost her grip and they were sliding once more, crashing through debris and lines. They passed through a curtain of flame, and Athene recoiled from the pain. It gave Artemis enough chance to get a foot against the woman's gut and kick away. Artemis flipped around, flooding Pneuma into Lightness and allowing herself to float backward.

But there was nowhere to go, naught she could catch onto, and she began to drift down toward the sea. She needed to get it over with. Teeth gritted, she released Lightness and plunged into the darkened water, feet-first. The shock of it stole her perceptions a moment. Above, blazing ships created a burning mirage across the surface. All around, sinking wreckage and drowned bodies. A shadow rushed by her and Artemis's heart lurched into her throat with sudden dread.

Deep Ones—she had long since adopted the Phoenikian name for sirens. Poseidon must have sent his forces to aid his faltering fellow Olympians. Frantic, Artemis swam straight up.

Webbed fingers snared her ankle and jerked her back down, face-to-face with an opal-eyed, shark-mawed horror. Only belatedly, as his fangy mouth closed in upon her face, amid the flowing platinum locks, did she recognise Poseidon himself. With a shriek—and a blinding cloud of bubbles—Artemis shoved at Poseidon with all the Pneumatikoi she had.

Not enough! His grip was adamant upon her. She lunged with her knife, but he was faster in the water, and so much stronger. Something seized onto Poseidon then and jerked him away. Artemis caught a brief glimpse of Sirsir, a Deep One sworn to serve Mithra. Through Marduk, she had met Sirsir twice, though she had never thought to owe him her life. The two sea gods caught one another in a whirling blur, and Artemis swam for the surface once more.

Her lungs were exploding in her chest. Her vision had begun to turn cloudy.

Then she burst into air, gasping down hungry breaths, blinking against the sudden brightness of the sun and the numerous burning ships all around. The moment she caught her wind, she cast about until she spotted a nearby ship. Not caring whose it was, she swam to it, snared the side, and began to scale it. From the language shouted onboard, these were Phoenikians, her troops. No doubt they stood in disarray having lost their commander, fool though Ariabignes had proved.

On realising someone was boarding, the crew brandished spears at her. "That's the admiral!" another man shouted before she had enough breath to order them to stand down.

Artemis heaved herself over the gunwale and crashed hard onto the deck. All she wanted was to lie here for a few hours. Athene. Athene. Athene, godsdamned Athene! She would not escape this day.

Gritting her teeth once more, Artemis rolled over and pushed herself up on hands and knees.

Someone gasped, and Artemis followed the crew's gazes skyward, where a pegasus was circling above them. Athene's steed had returned, and it seemed Zeus's daughter too thought they were not done this day.

"Get me a bow," Artemis commanded, struggling to her feet.

A man handed her one, and an arrow, and she nocked. Artemis had to leap aside from another hurled javelin. "Forgive me," she whispered, not to Athene, but to a steed against which she bore no ill will. Artemis loosed. Athene banked, no doubt thinking Artemis had shot at her. But her arrow took the pegasus in the throat—Artemis winced at it. The animal convulsed, and Athene was sent tumbling end over end.

The Titan slammed back-first into the deck with enough force the planking cracked. Tossing the bow aside, Artemis stalked over, checking that the fetters still hung at her back. Athene had discarded her ruined helm, the bruising on her face plain as she struggled to rise. Artemis assumed Pneuma had allowed the woman to avoid broken bones from that fall, but it winded her, nonetheless.

With a snarl, Artemis leapt onto Athene and swung a fist at her head. The woman caught her in a pankration hold and bore her down, twisting her around. A stubborn, useless flutter of pride at her former protégé's prowess arose and was stifled in Artemis's breast. She twisted and wriggled until she managed to ram her elbow against Athene's temple. The impact dazed her foe, and it was all Artemis needed to spin the woman around onto her stomach. Fingers nested in Athene's hair, she slammed the Olympian's head against the deck. Then, while Athene was stunned, Artemis grabbed the orichalcum chains and slapped one closed over each of Athene's wrists.

Not only did strength drain from her foe in an instant, Athene buckled, swayed, and fainted.

Like Artemis, only Titan Pneuma had even been keeping her on her feet.

Even that, Artemis reflected as she collapsed in a heap beside her prisoner, was barely enough. "Get us away from the battle."

"We can still win," a Phoenikian protested.

Artemis looked to Athene's unmoving, broken form. "We have won."

INTERLUDE: PROMETHEUS

Asura Era, Dark Age

Mighty Kali's shattered corpse lay upon the pyre, her dark skin crackling as the flames rose higher. Matarśivan watched, jaw clenched, as his hopes burnt away. Inside his breast, Surtr danced, urging him to seize control of the flames and immolate the whole of the gathered Aditya throng. His Flame would have him become one with the carnage and revel in the unmaking of the cosmos.

The Adityas had gathered, mourning their champion, though he suspected they did not yet realise they ought to mourn *everything*. Kali's lover, the Oracle Manyu, knelt beside her, resisting all who tried to pull him away. Perhaps he intended to cast himself upon the pyre and join his beloved. And Matarśivan had not the heart to stop him.

For a moment—a precious, ephemeral instant—he had believed Kali could slay Vritra, as the Adityas now named the dark dragon. It rampaged across Kumari Kandam and the World wilted at its passage. It slew Adityas by the score, and Asuras too, should they draw close. The Adityas' enemies had thought to control the unfathomable forces of Khaos, but they had failed to do more than aim its initial assault.

They could not stop it now, and Matarśivan knew it would feast and feast until its frenzy called forth more tendrils of Yaldabaoth. Until the Archon Lord tore apart the World and feasted upon all Prakasa. Until Light forever winked out.

Matarśivan had *failed.*

The Fates had shown him the Ontos, and even with foreknowledge of what must impend, he could not avert the future. The end of the world had been inevitable, and Kali's fall—even if her immortal soul endured—was the death knell of the cosmos.

If there was more time, Kali would have been born once more, spun out by the Wheel of Life into another incarnation to live and, in so doing, draw up yet more Prakasa for the Archons and their lord to gorge upon. She would have come again and had another chance, but he could not wait, for no more years yet remained in history.

He had reached the end of all …

The end …

Matarśivan looked up from the pyre. He had never yet met Aditi's reincarnation as he had beheld in pyromantic visions. He had foreseen meeting her again, in other lifetimes. If there was more future, then … there must be some option yet before him. Some last gambit that would buy more time.

Yaldabaoth and its Archons would invariably come to claim souls, for no creature would deny itself food forever. No power in the cosmos seemed capable of slaying the Archon Lord. But what about a temporary victory over just *this* tendril of it?

Could any other warrior achieve it?

There was a thought, abhorrent, that had begun to form unbidden in his mind. So loathsome he had forced it down every time it reared its inchoate head. But if a future was to remain, if he was to preserve aught of the Prakasa and of Man, then he might have to do so with the most terrible of all sacrifices. Matarśivan would need to keep the Wheel of Life turning, feeding the eldritch horrors. But if he could buy Mankind time …

As the flames rose, Matarśivan stalked away, seeking solitude in the hills.

One of the Adityas caught his arm, and he turned. "Savitr."

One of Aditi's firstborn, in fact. "What are we to do?" the Aditya asked. "How do we fight such a being?"

The man had such imploring in his eyes, Matarśivan could not help but place a comforting hand upon his shoulder. A child of Aditi ... And Matarśivan would not let him face the end alone. He hoped his eyes conveyed the message, and perhaps they did, for Savitr nodded and allowed him to pass alone from the field.

Matarśivan needed the Fates for this gambit to have any chance of unfolding. Such a play was beyond his power to enact alone, though he could make scant guess what answer they would make him. His mistresses would decide, in the end, whether the last hope must fade into cinders or be kindled into a new Era.

When he was certain he was alone, he sat, legs crossed, and fell into a deep meditation. The Fates existed outside of time or space, and thus, he could reach them in a kind of mental projection not unlike pushing his soul into the Spectral Realm, though he had surrendered that ability when he shattered his Watcher ring.

It was quiet. The only sound his slow breaths as a void spread out around him. The darkness that engulfed him differed in flavour from the primordial Dark from which his foes had come, or at least Matarśivan liked to believe it did. The demons had come from Khaos, and he sought some semblance of Order. He dared hope the Fates different, in kind, from the demon gods who so lusted after Prakasa.

They awaited him there, the three hooded women standing about a well, the only object in this non-Realm. Perhaps they knew he would come. Perhaps they knew what he would say.

"The World ends," he said.

"It does," one of the Fates admitted.

"It has," said the second.

"It will," added the third.

If so, then perhaps it lent some weight of possibility to his plan. Matarśivan blinked in the darkness. Though he had no body here, still, his heart hammered at the thought of even speaking the gambit aloud. "The dark god Yaldabaoth rises."

"It does."

"It has."

"It will."

Did existence outside time skew their minds, or was it his linear perspective that was so flawed? Either way, their tripartite prattle tended to vex him, no matter how oft he consulted with his mistresses. "To keep it from consuming the sum of the World, we must feed it."

But it would take more than just the normal progression of the Wheel of Life, for Vritra's presence here indicated Yaldabaoth's hunger compounded over time. The rest of his words stuck in his mouth, foul and choking.

"We need a cycle," he rasped. "A cycle the dark god might accept, whereupon it could periodically gorge itself upon souls—ravage the World, yes—but thus sated, perhaps it would avoid consuming *all* the cosmos."

"It could delay," one of the Fates answered. Strangely, the other two held their peace.

"To drive that, I need a human soul, a catalyst to do what I cannot, and both cause the Eschatons and avert the total end by holding back complete annihilation." Such a delicate balance, and it *should* have been Kali. But what weal would come of lamenting a reality that could never materialise?

He scarce allowed himself to hope for the last aspect of his gambit. Of a soul born over and over and damned to such suffering, to lifetime after lifetime ... to become something so fortified through the crucible that it might ... No. He dare not give voice to that hope even in his mind, much less to the Fates themselves. To preserve the World and Man was all he could hope for. For now.

"This Man must preserve the cycle of history and keep the Wheel of Life turning, while offering these intermittent feasts to the dark god."

"Creator," a Fate said.

"Preserver."

"Destroyer."

Yes. One to create and preserve the Eschaton cycle, and to serve as a catalyst for destruction when needs be. A warrior, for they must fight against horrific odds to ensure the unleashed destruction would leave some hope for new life to rise again. And ... and an Oracle, like Matarśivan himself. For, if there was ever to be hope for something better than this abhorrent end, he would need someone able to apprehend the Ontos in order to strive against it. But that had not been Kali ... Mighty though she'd been, she had not the gift.

As one, the Fates reached into the well and, when they rose, between themselves they held a stone slab some foot and a half long.

"The Tablet of Destiny," one said.

Matarśivan took the stone, peering over it. "It's blank."

"Yes."

"A name."

"Carved willingly."

Choice. Oh, of course Matarśivan could not force this burden upon anyone. The weight of it could crush most souls, perhaps even his. Someone must choose to take the onus upon themselves.

When next he blinked, he sat still amid the hills in the night, with the slab in his lap. For a long time, all he could do was stare at the pristine stone. Whoever inscribed their name would bind themselves to his gambit. Not just in a single life, but in all their lives. They would shackle their soul to the role of Destroyer, and they would suffer for it as none had ever suffered in the history of the World.

They would fight and die, over and over, forged in pain and loss to become something more than mere Man. A force that could fight the battle Matarśivan could not.

Oh, he ought to carve his own name, he knew. To mark himself with the destiny. But he had neither the strength to pull it off nor ... the ability to die. And the Destroyer must die, time and again, until his life became the sum of so many champions.

Matarśivan could not do this, for he could not die. And that, he knew, served as a convenient escape from his inability to bear the burden, though he bore far too many of his own strains already. The Destroyer would need a guide, in lifetime after lifetime. He would need someone to keep him on his path. Someone to make sure the cycle unfolded as it must and thus protect against a yet worse fate.

Slowly, Matarśivan rose. He needed a Man ravaged by pain and desperation. One as broken by loss as Matarśivan himself had been when Aditi fell. Someone ... like Manyu.

So he would go, show the man the Tablet, and ask him if he would carve his name. Ask him to fight Vritra, even knowing he must die trying.

Ask him to become the first Destroyer.

And preserve this fragile World.

PART III

We have all heard the term Elder Gods, of course, and perhaps Primordials, but as the sacred text reveals, the most apt name for these entities—which predate time—seems to be that of Archon. For they do, in fact, each rule over one of the primeval elements that compose the cosmos, the text makes this clear. Nine Archons, each claiming lordship over a spirit world, all of which exist within the so-called Spirit Realm. As to the exact nature of these beings, that is, perhaps, the most important mystery the Circle might ever delve.

— First Chronicle of the Circle of Goetic Mysteries

11

PANDORA

400 Dark Age

The collapsing light bubble deposited Pandora beneath Taygete's Bridge, amid a scene of utter anarchy. People fled in all directions, driven by animalistic need to save themselves, yet already realising no safe haven awaited any of them. A massive rift rent the island in twain, the two halves lurching away from one another, the sea rushing in to fill the gap. By the hundreds, people tumbled from the uneven land into the opening maw of destruction before them. A wave of guilt, as encompassing as the rising water, swept over her. For Pandora had sworn to save this island once, then sworn to save the World, and she had failed in both. The future could not be changed. It could, however, be fought, and fight she would.

She gained her feet and saw a woman—her younger self—on hands and knees, crawling after her lost satchel and the precious Box. With a Potency-fuelled leap, Pandora bounded the gap to where the woman tried to reach and scanned the area. There, on a flagstone that had once led to Taygete's Bridge, the satchel lay precariously dangling over the canal. The stone shelf had settled maybe twenty feet below street level, seeming to cling to the wall by sheer tenacity, and Pandora had no idea if it could take her weight.

But this had to work. It *had* worked, because she had been saved back then. Another great leap sent her over the edge, flying toward the loose stone. As she landed, the surface groaned beneath her. Debris rained over her in a torrent. With one hand, Pandora snatched up the bag's strap; with the other, she punched into the dirt wall. An instant later, the flagstone cracked and tumbled down into the surging river.

She would not die. Not like this. Not without accomplishing just one more thing.

Flames licked her fingertips as she flooded Pneuma to her arm, infusing Potency with as much power as she could. She heaved and, even with one arm, managed to send herself careening skyward to land back upon the main street. It was pitched at a steep angle, and she skidded down toward a crevice, so she had to leap again to reach the relative safety of a flat section of cobbles. Even this perch would not last long, though.

All around, geysers spewed vapours and seawater, adding to the chaos erupting across the once glorious city. She yanked the Box free of its satchel and tossed the bag aside. How strange to hold two of these!

And where was the younger Pandora? Where had ... Oh! The ground had given way!

Pandora raced forward, skidding to a stop when she saw the spot where the other Pandora knelt upon a flagstone, some six feet below street level. She set the Box, then hoped down beside the younger woman and offered her a hand. When the woman accepted it, Pandora yanked her to her feet, and their gazes met.

The younger woman gawped.

"We don't have much time," Pandora warned her. And still, the younger woman seemed unable to form a coherent thought. How innocent she had been, back then, before so much of this had unfolded and stolen that from her. How far she yet had to go, to stand here, but a few steps away. A swell of pity rose in her breast, but she could not afford it now. Instead, she released the other Pandora's hand and grabbed her bicep. "I know, I know. I remember what it was like. Try to focus, though." She squeezed, pulling the other woman out of her wild musings. "Focus, Pandora. You're trying to save Prometheus, yes? Only a son of Zeus will be able to set him free. You understand? A son of Zeus." The younger woman nodded, and Pandora handed her the Box. "I've set this for you, all you have to do is open it."

More fulgurations burst in violent frenzy around Evenor Mountain. What in Tartarus was unfolding in that place? The whole island was tearing itself apart, had already become two islands, and still some nightmare happened up there.

They had no time, though. "Go, Pandora."

The younger woman nodded and popped the top.

Even as the light bubble began to form, a thought, a memory rose in Pandora. "Oh, wait!" she shouted. She could not forget! "You must convince Nike to fight alongside Zeus, against Kronos, or Pyrrha will die!"

The younger Pandora vanished in the collapsing bubble.

The stone on which Pandora stood cracked, sending her free-falling, down toward the river. Shrieking, she reached into her satchel as she fell and popped the Box, not even caring when or where it sent her. Just as surging water reached up to seize her, the bubble swallowed her, too.

A WAVE of disorientation seized her, almost akin to those she'd felt when first using the Box. Perhaps she was relying on it too much, and it had begun to strain her mind and body? She shook off the daze and found herself crouched in a familiar lounge. Before she could sort through the maze of her memories, footfalls upon marble drew her eye to see a Titan woman plodding into the room, wine sloshing from her goblet as she did so.

The woman's eyes widened at the same moment Pandora recognised her: Enyo. Ares's lover had proved as deranged as the man himself, when Pandora had known the two of them during the Titanomachy.

"Nike?" Enyo asked, a slight slur to her voice. "The fuck have you been all these years, huh?"

Bitter revelation smacked Pandora with all the force of the cataclysm that would one day tear this island apart. Rising, a disheartened laugh burbled from her chest, unbidden, though perhaps it kept her from weeping. Moments from now, her younger self would stumble into this room. Enyo would recognise young Pandora as Nike, bring her to Zeus's attention, and Pandora's life would be over. With hers, so too the lives of her whole bloodline and so many others. Of all the World—as the time-line collapsed and Elder Gods began an eternal feast upon every soul in existence. Eternal torment for all the cosmos, or Pandora could surrender another piece of her soul, and become the person she had never wanted to be.

"Bitch, you laughing?" Enyo tossed the cup aside. "Why have you not come to Olympus, as the king bade all Titans, to pledge fealty? You in league with these scheming Pleiades?"

Enyo stumbling upon Pandora would have been the future, if not for the fact Pandora had slipped on the Titan's spilled ichor. How cruel was that ouroboros.

History is merciless.

She and Prometheus had mused on it, ever and anon, and always it came back to that same refrain. It little mattered what sort of a person either of them wished to be, for time was not wont to give them choice.

She found she could muster naught save a glare for Enyo and a sad shake of her head. "Would that we had not met this night."

"Pshaw. Tell it to Zeus, bitch. Assuming he lets you get in a word afore he makes you mouth his rod and beg his forgiveness." Enyo snared her shoulder, trying to drag her before her master. No doubt the sick Titan fair salivated at the thought of seeing another woman humiliated and tortured thus.

Flames erupted along Pandora's hand, and she slapped that hand across the Titan woman's face. Enyo flailed, seized in a paroxysm of pain, though in her shock, she mounted a poor defence. Pandora slammed her other, Potency-infused, hand into Enyo's throat. She had expected the woman to flare Pneuma to harden her flesh, but she either could not or was too drunk to do so. Pandora's fist drove so hard into Enyo's throat her spine burst out the back of her neck. Her body crumpled, golden ichor seeping from her wound, mocking Pandora for the murder she'd just committed.

Trembles shot through Pandora's body. That pain in her chest rose again, a sudden tightness, this time borne upon a tide of self-loathing that choked the breath from her. Monstrous though Enyo was, Pandora had not wished to slay her. Now, at last, she could truly understand the choice Prometheus had made to perpetuate the Eschaton Cycle, to fuel it with the Destroyer. In surrendering pieces of herself, of himself, they perhaps preserved a tiny shred of hope for the rest of Mankind.

Laughter mingled with tears and she knew she could not stay here. In a matter of moments, her younger self would walk through the doorway, fall upon the floor, and scream in horror of what had been done here. What *Pandora* had done, after all. Zeus would seize upon the excuse to execute the Pleiades—to later be reborn as the Queens of Mu who invoked the Leviathan—and she and Prometheus would flee this symposium for Ogygia. But once unleashed, it would not take Zeus long before he decided to summon Prometheus and demand an answer to his prophecy. Was this the beginning of it all? No, as ever, searching for the beginning of an endless circle was a gesture of futile vanity.

Pandora was a murderer now.

And now, she must be again. If she could not stop the Eschaton, she would at least mitigate the worst of its carnage. That, for now, meant cutting the head off the Unseen Order. Mithra and his Anunnaki must die. Whatever else unfolded, she would not allow them to claim any throne out of the charnel house they had wrought of Gaia. The Order would rule no future Eras, this, she promised herself.

With fingers still trembling, with an eye twitching from the turbulent movements of her soul, she set the Box.

12

HEL

20 Dark Age

A cluster of lampads had gathered upon the banks of the Gjöll, watching the procession of the dead across the gold-thatched bridge. In their pale, wispy cloaks, the eidolons turned all but invisible in the Mist, hidden from Hel and her wraiths, where they crouched upon the bridge's sloping roof.

Silent, motionless, she and her elite watched as Khione and her followers drifted amid the fallen, shepherding souls toward the Winter Court. Such had been the arrangement Hel had made with the queen years back, and it had served well enough. Until now.

The lampads were, Hel had no doubt, flush with hunger, the craving a hollow in the pits of their frozen souls. Hypnos, who had stalked Khione and her kindred many a time over the past months, confirmed not all the shades who crossed the bridge made it to the queen. Idly, Hel wondered if the Lady of Winter knew Khione sampled delights meant for her table. It mattered little though; whether Khione pilfered souls with the queen's blessing or knowledge, either way, the lampad's last days were spent.

Hel—or Hekate, really—had given Khione reason to loathe her. That acrimony in turn bred the same in Hel herself, and the wheel spun and spun until one of them would be ground to dust beneath the churn.

"Rise ..." Hel whispered, and as one, her Hel-wraiths flowed over the roof's edge. A fall from this height would leave mortal bodies splattered across the frozen landscape but would little harm a wraith, even if they had not the Pneumatikoi of Lightness to slow their falls. They leapt, drifting down like silent, falling leaves.

So intent were the lampads on their impending feast, they never bothered to look skyward. Had they done so, they might have beheld the damning shadows closing in upon them. Instead, the Hel-wraiths landed among them, skeletal claws plunging into pale lampad flesh. The shades the lampads had guarded shrieked, fleeing in all directions from the erupting bedlam.

Hel lunged at Khione, but a wall of solid Mist arose before her, miring her limbs, thick as quicksand. The vapours moved, as if with a will, to bar Hel's access to its children. The lampad noblewoman had recovered from her shock too quickly and disappeared into her natural element. A growl of frustration poured from Hel, then she burst into a spellsong. Cloying Mist tried to climb down her throat and forestall the magic of her voice, but Khione's power was not fast enough. The air quivered, and the Mist parted in a hemisphere around Hel.

And still, Khione was nowhere to behold.

"Keuthos!" Hel snarled. "Where is she?"

Her friend had snared a female lampad by the back of her neck and driven her to her knees before him. Hel could not make out much beneath Keuthos's hood, but he craned his neck one way and the next, peering through Mist too thick to find their prey. "She will warn the Court."

Hel growled once more. "Let them be warned, then." When she was through, no one would hide again from her wraiths. Least of all in Mist. "I ..."

A psychic current seized her soul, thrummed through her form, bombarded inside her head. *Pyrrha ... Hekate ... Answer my plea ... Come to your daughter. Pyrrha ... Hekate ... I await you ... Just beyond the Veil ...*

Wrath, bitter as rime, seared in her, instinct demanding she devour the soul of any with the temerity to dare invoke her name. Yet the woman's voice had said "daughter," and for that reason alone, Hel tried to choke down the paroxysm arising in her. The summons, the call upon her soul, it would prove a distraction hard to ignore.

"Escort the prisoners to Kek," she commanded Keuthos through gritted teeth. Whichever of her daughters called her now, Hel would answer, this one time.

BENEATH THE EARTH, Hel found a corpse, rotted and useless for all but a momentary jaunt into the Mortal Realm. In possession of that body, she crawled from a tomb of dirt and rock and, halfway free, looked upon Kirke's gawping visage. Her daughter was little changed from last Hel had seen her. Hel, however, must look a sight of horror, her host taking on the aspect of ruined form. The thought brought a rush of vicious pleasure to Hel, for why should not Kirke, alive, suffer the wracking of her heart on looking upon her dead mother? All the living should suffer, even as all the dead dwelt in torment.

"M-mama?" Kirke gasped. Hel yanked herself free of the earth and rose, meeting the Titan's gaze with hers. "Mama ... Nyx's bosom, what happened to you?"

The name of Nyx might well attract attention Hel could little afford at the present junction, and she hissed to hear it. "Do not ... speak the names of the Elder Gods ..."

Her daughter nodded, well versed enough in the arcane to grasp Hel's meaning.

"Why ... call me ... here ..." Hel demanded. "I ... sit now ... upon the throne of the Underworld ... I have a great many ... things in motion ... and no time for concerns of the Mortal Realm ..."

Kirke swallowed, looked apt to burst into flight on realising how severely she had erred in making such a summons. "I need the Box back."

Of all the things Kirke might have demanded, it had never crossed Hel's mind she would ask for that abominable gear in the machine of cosmic mockery. "Why ...?"

"Because I'm going to change the past and make a better future for all of us."

Hel chortled, even knowing how much the laughter of the damned discomfited the living. "You ... cannot ... change the past ... nor the future ..."

"The Box, Mama. *Please.*"

Hel had neither the time to argue with the child nor the will to spare her the suffering she sought to bring upon herself. "Then ... I will tell you ... where to find what you seek ... One ought to be free ... to learn such lessons oneself ..."

"WHY NOT JUST CONSUME OUR souls and be done with it?" the female lampad Keuthos had captured demanded once Hel had returned to Kek after Kirke's summons. Encountering her daughter, seeing her alive, it had taken a greater toll upon Hel than she would have liked. For the disquiet the woman had engendered, Hel hated Kirke, should have devoured her presumptuous soul and had done with it. Hated her ... should have hated! Wraiths hated everything.

With an effort of will, Hel regarded the lampad. The Hel-wraiths had gorged upon souls, but not enough to dissipate their prisoners, demonstrating impressive self-control Hel would need to reward. The enervated lampads had been unable to offer much resistance as the wraiths dragged them back toward Kek and the ritual chamber Hel had prepared in the catacombs.

Now, she looked up from her preparations at the lampad, wondering if weakness had driven the prisoner daft or if she merely watched the wilful persistence of hope refusing to die even in such straits. The seven Hel-wraiths, sorcerers even in death, were busy each attending to their smaller circles within the great ring of sigils Hel had created, and yet a susurration of laughter passed among them.

A shame Khione had escaped this fate. Even the Moirai would have appreciated the delectable irony of seeing the lampad bound to Hel again, and this time in a true fusing. With only seven lampads, she had only one for each of her Hel-wraiths and thus would have to forgo the ritual. Every time that thought arose, it engendered a flush of irritation she quickly suppressed, reminding herself the power she would siphon from Achlys would far exceed whatever her minions claimed from the lampads.

With a chisel cut from the bones of one of the Stygian monstrosities that swam through the nether rivers, Hel finished carving the last sigil before answering the lampad. "Seven of you and seven of my servants ... We could have consumed you to the pith and sent the dregs of your soul crawling back to the Wheel to spend eons scraping for enough strength for rebirth. This we could have done upon the banks of the Gjöll. Yet we escorted you across the treacherous spaces of the Roil, here, to a chamber carefully prepared for the most intricate of sorceries. Hmm ... Yes, we did that so we could then eat you. Is that what you think, you fatuous worm?"

Another wispy cackle bubbled up from the gathered wraiths.

"In the days of Dark Faerie, Men worked the Art to fuse the souls of their kind with those of primal beasts spawned upon the Moon. Thus did they create the therianthropic bloodlines even in those with the barest glimmer of shamanic gift. All in their desperate attempt to break the hold of your Elder Race upon the Mortal Realm."

She doubted any of the prisoners held here were old enough to have witnessed such glories, but even if they had, time would have mostlike swallowed the memories into its fathomless gulf. Either way, the lampad prisoners stared at her, guileless and yet still wise enough for fear to crease their faces.

"Such glorious blasphemies were thought lost, and yet vestiges remained. Enough to repeat the procedure ... with some alterations."

From the looks on their faces, her words settled upon the prisoners like leaden weights. Eyes widened and hands went to gawping mouths. Some of them whimpered, and one pleaded for death rather than the end she had in mind for them.

Yes. A shame Khione would miss this.

SIBILANT INCANTATIONS THRUMMED through the etheric currents of the Roil, setting Hel's psychic senses aflame. Her Supernal words echoed in her mind, melding into the river of invocations her wraiths uttered, drowning out even the agonised wails of the lampads. Almost drowning them out, perhaps.

The lampad before Keuthos shrieked as the wraith sank talon-like fingers into her shoulders. It was not physical pain she dreaded, though, Hel knew. In time with the profane rhythm of the cants, her soul-made-flesh peeled away, torn into ephemeral ribbons. The strands of her essence flowed about Keuthos, coiling around his limbs. Pieces of the lampad whirled as though spun by unseen hands. All around, the scene repeated between the other Hel-wraiths and lampads.

Somewhere, in the deepest recesses of her mind, a twinge of pity sparked within Hel. This she smothered with a grimace. What use for pity in a World such as thus, where souls were drawn from the Wheel for the sole purpose of offering a feast to ever-hungry gods? Empathy was an indulgence offered betwixt one morsel and the next. And Hel would rather be predator than prey.

At last, when naught remained of the captured Mist spirits, the incantations fell to silence, leaving the chamber pregnant with the import of the moment. For now, she had created something new, something which even the blighted Elder Gods had never conceived.

Before her knelt seven wraith warriors, infused with lampad souls bound into the cheires plating their arms and etched cuirasses beneath their shrouds. Mist seeped out from the chinks between the plates, melding with their ephemeral garb. Shadowed hoods concealed their faces, but she knew them each, bound as they were to her.

Weakened though she was by her sorcery, still Hel drifted among her changed servants, laying a hand upon each, savouring the frigid chill of their armour. Keuthonymos and Melinoë first, then the others, one by one.

"Arise, my empousai," she said. "My *Mistwraiths*."

For now she had champions with all the powers of wraith and lampad combined in one form. Now, they would wander free across the expanse of the Rimefells, invisible predators not even the native spirits could dare stand against.

After blessing each of her servants, she returned to Keuthos. "Go now to the Fimbulvinter mountains and complete the last seal. Take Phobetor to watch your back." Now she looked to the others. "The

Winter Court will already make ready for war. Let us then take the fight to them."

The time had come to bring low an Elder God.

HEL'S LEGIONS of the damned flooded out of the Corpsewood and swarmed for the silver spires of the Winter Court. Having learnt of Jason from the shade Medea, Hel took her petty revenge upon the man who had betrayed her grandniece by assigning him to lead the vanguard. With Medea by her side—the witch had never practiced sorcery and thus avoided becoming a wraith—Hel waited and watched as the lampad forces expended their energy upon her ghost army.

Any given lampad was more than a match for most shades, but then, Hel had mustered over twenty thousand shades. To the nobles of the Winter Court, her forces must have seemed an endless flood.

By her side, Medea chuckled when the pale blue flame of a lampad immolated Jason's wretched soul. "Perhaps there is justice beyond life after all."

Hel snorted. "Justice, like conceptions of fairness, is an illusion the living comfort themselves with so that they do not have to face the inherent iniquities of the World. What we can claim is not justice but vengeance. Power, Medea, is all that ever mattered. With power, you can revenge yourself against those who have wronged you. With enough power, mayhap we can even avert the end woven for us into the Tapestry." And such aims justified any act.

The elder lampads—lesser gods—those who had existed for Ages and grown flush with ancient powers, waded amid the shades like farmers scything wheat. With blades of ice or etheric flames they hewed and burnt, laying waste to bands of dead warriors. Ever so oft, she saw a lampad pause to feast upon a soul, but doing so left the gorging spirit vulnerable, and more than one caught a javelin in the face for their trouble.

Hel felt it as Melinoë approached, vaporous and shrouded. "Now ..."

"Not yet." Hel would rather the greater lampads expended more of their Pneuma on the ghosts before she unleashed the empousai. She had two hidden plays to make—or three, she supposed—and each of them would need count.

So they waited, watched as a hundred melees unfurled. As souls were eviscerated and sent screaming into the Dark to be consumed by predators more dire than any of the gathered eidolons. As she watched, a female lampad sent a cascading explosion of icicles erupting along the ground in a wave that engulfed dozens of shades. Lances of ice burst through chests of those at the fringes, whilst those in the wave's path were encased with the wave.

Was that Milucra? No, but a spirit god, for certain. One so ancient she had perhaps even seen the days of Dark Faerie. The Winter Queen now sent forth her greatest assets. A titter of anticipation shot through Hel at seeing such brazen displays of power. When one player moved the valuable pieces, the other must needs respond in kind.

"Empousai ..." Hel commanded.

And they came. Like clouds of congealing mist, they seeped unto the battlefield, unperceived at first, drifting amid the chaos like shadows. The lampad goddess must have felt their presence, for she broke off her slaughter of the shades and cast about. Too late, though. Nephthys and Inanna seized her arms with claws immune even to her glacial cold. From a puddle of Mist, Melinoë arose before the lampad, bearing an axe with blades wide as her torso.

From the distance, Hel could not see the lampad's face, could not watch eyes widen and dread rise up from the bowels to seize one who must have thought eternity her right. She could not see any of it. But she could well imagine it. That massive axe swooped down and cleft the lampad into two bloody halves.

Palpable shock and horror ran through the gathered forces of the Winter Court, no doubt aghast to see the greatest among them cut down with such sudden violence. Melinoë fell to devouring the rapidly dwindling dregs of the lampad's soul, and the remaining Mistwraiths set to slaughter.

Soon, every last lampad would bow before Hel. That, or face oblivion.

13

———

KIRKE

704 Bronze Age

Even trusting to a cowl was no guarantee Aeëtes would not recognise Damkina as Kirke, so she relied on a glamour she had learnt in her millennia training with the Unseen Order. Still she kept her face veiled with a velvet himation, wanting no chance of disrupting the timeline by allowing herself to be recognised. Given she had also developed the ability to step across the Veil—an aspect of umbramancy the Order had perfected—she could easily come and go and thus slipped into Qulha Palace in Kolchis with ease.

For three years, Aeëtes had stewed over the fate of their sister, Pasiphaë, whose body and mind were destroyed in the birthing of the Minotaur and subsequent abuses Minos visited upon his wife. Three years of agony and dread. Misery, fermenting long enough, poisoned the soul. Such states left one primed for manipulation.

Still, it had come as a surprise when Mithra bade her induct her half-brother into the Art, and specifically the greater arcana. Damkina had all but forgotten it, so, so many years ago, when Medea and Jason had claimed her brother had been trained by a sorceress. The name had meant naught back then, nor had she recognised it, when Raziel had bestowed the same name on her after the fall of Nyx.

Whilst she could not suppress the roil of disgust that churned her gut at the thought of lying with her half-brother, neither could she deny the demands of Fate. *History must unfold*, she told herself, as cloistered in secret meetings, through flesh and instruction, she inducted him into the greater arcana. In an earlier Age, she might have sent him to the Circle of Goetic Mysteries, but Enodia had seen the Circle broken, and with few sorceresses left on Gaia, now it fell to Damkina.

And if, after such liaisons, she spent hours scrubbing herself in the bathhouses and, more than once, retching, well, such was just one more minuscule price to pay for the continuance of the cosmos. Day by day, night by foul night, she saw the shadows deepen in him, power and damnation rising in equal measure.

"First he must suffer the treachery of his flesh and blood, the loss of his heirs, and the shattering of his pride," Mithra said. The Unseen One met her in the shadows of the Penumbra, the hidden roads by which the Order could walk *around* the Mortal Realm. Time had acclimated her to the perpetual gloom and malaise of this Realm, true. Mithra, though, he seemed never the least bit perturbed as he moved through the netherscape. Regardless, he had warned them all to remain wary of the eidolons that prowled the ether, who would happily feast upon their souls. "Only then, once the edifices of his ego are rendered unto dust, can he become the needful tool of the Unseen Order."

First, Damkina nodded at his words, accepting all that the Moirai must have in store for her brother. Only later, when she was alone and nursing a goblet of wine, did she stop to think on the depths of meaning in his claim. Was it coincidence Enki recruited Morpheus to the Order after the loss of his apprentice had nigh broken the oneiromancer? Was it coincidence that Raziel saved Kirke from Nyx, at the lowest moment in her life, when the weight of compounded millennia had already crushed her will?

She found it rather difficult to sleep that night. Or for a great many nights thereafter.

POSING as a wine merchant some few years later, Damkina mused once more over the question of moulding the broken into new tools. Maybe that was why Mithra had set her this task in Thebes. Though it pained a little, still, even Damkina had to smile at the merciless irony of the Moirai, when she sold the tainted wine to Megara.

For so long she had been indignant and, in time, even livid at Athene's accusations that she had induced Herakles's madness leading to the death of his children. As Kirke, she had professed her innocence over and over, and Athene never accepted it. Yet here she was, doing the crime of which she'd been accused, thousands of years after being convicted of it in her sister's heart.

Fate was cruel. There was naught amusing about the whole thing. And yet, somehow, as Herakles's wife carried home the tainted Argosian red to surprise her husband with—and would he ever be surprised!—Damkina could not help but laugh.

Laugh and wonder, had Athene not rejected her back then, would she still be here *now*, inflicting this torment upon the woman's foster son? Had the scorn Athene heaped upon Kirke for a crime she did not commit help lead Kirke down the path to becoming the perpetrator after all? Well, Herakles too would be forged into a useful tool, broken before being remade.

He was not the Destroyer, Mithra had told her, for the Destroyer was one to bring about the Eschaton. Rather, he was an incarnation of the Destroyer soul, bound to live and die and suffer in ways that would temper his soul to prepare it for one of its ultimate incarnations. "And who shall that be?" she had asked.

"When the time has arrived, you shall be the first I tell," Mithra had promised, and she took it as an honour.

A DOZEN or so years after Damkina's time with Aeëtes, it came about that the Unseen Order needed to arrange for a birth, and Morpheus, having abandoned Zeus when ordered, had joined the Magi, the priestly class of Neshia. Morpheus had sought to recruit some of his former brethren from the Circle of Goetic Mysteries. Isis had scorned him, refusing to leave Kemet. Morpheus had told Damkina that Isis had become obsessed with the idea of resurrecting the dead, mad as such seemed. Heka, however, had left Isis's court with Morpheus to join the Magi, and it was the first Damkina had seen of him in some years.

Heka had joined her and Morpheus for a drink in her manse in Nineveh. When they had each downed a goblet, Damkina had brought Morpheus alone back to her sitting room. She collapsed upon a plush, velvet-lined seat that resembled more throne than chair, watching the other oneiromancer.

After a glance around the room—no doubt checking the Penumbra for spies, as well—Morpheus looked to her. "We are Unseen."

"Always," she rejoined. "And unseen we must be in moving the pieces around the board." A moment she held his gaze. "I want you to send King Aspadas a dream that his daughter's child will destroy his empire."

"You want him to murder his own child?"

"No." Damkina shook her head. "Aspadas has a soft spot for his girl and could never stomach her death. Rather, he'll marry dear Mandana off to King Kabujiya of Kissatu."

"So he trusts his tribute king to keep in line, yes?" Morpheus quirked a smile, and Damkina could imagine what he was thinking. Kabujiya was the son of Kurus, a staunch ally of Nineveh, whom Aspadas's father had well rewarded for his loyalty. A choice the Ninevehan kings would one day regret.

"Desperation coupled with familial bonds makes for impaired judgment," she agreed. "And Mithra has foretold that, one day, the issue of Mandana will indeed seize control of the dynasty. In the meantime, have the Magi spread a prophecy that a Babilimian will one day become heir to the Ninevehan dynasty. When the time comes, the fulfilled prophecy will ensure Kurus II has the popular support."

Morpheus quirked a wry grin, then swept an elaborate bow in response. "We are Unseen."

"We are Unseen," she agreed.

❧

THROUGH MITHRA, Damkina learnt that Herakles and other demigods had sacked the city of Ilium. Laomedon and all his sons, save one, were slain, and his daughter was taken away as a war prize to Elládos. Intent on currying favour with the faltering Phrygian kingdom, Nineveh had sent Magi to Ilium. Mithra had insisted Damkina be the one to find Laomedon's last surviving heir, Priam, comfort him, and make certain he became a strong enough ruler to keep his city from falling.

Well did Damkina understand why. For Priam's son Paris would spark the Ilian War with Elládos, and that, she knew, was history. *History must unfold.* It was Mithra's circular justification for all things; wearisome, and yet no less needful, given the Ontos. So Damkina spent months advising the young king, helping him maintain his dynasty. She had not planned to slip into his bed, but then, enough wine tended to make such things seem like better ideas than they oft were, especially when it had been long since one had felt a gentle touch.

Less so, still, had she expected to find herself with child. But then, here she was, heating a draught in her alembic to rid herself of the damn thing. Most oft—sometimes she forgot—Damkina took precautions to avoid such situations ahead of time, but there were ways to solve the issue after the fact. The potion was best left to simmer a few hours, so Damkina wandered the halls of the royal palace of Troy, ill at ease, dour, and in no mood for company. She imagined her expression made that plain enough, because everyone who saw her ran as though the keres had burst out of the Dark and come seeking souls.

The thought brought a bitter smile to her face. Yeah ... Nyx damn her for growing so careless. Ambrosia reduced fertility, but it did not eliminate it. It was not even as though she loved Priam. But he was handsome and kind and in need, and she couldn't help herself. Despite thousands of years of life, she could never help herself. She made her way back to her room, and with a huff, she collapsed upon a rug before the hearth. There was some irony, for she recalled being in this position before, long ago, on behalf of Athene. Hephaistos had forced himself on Kirke's sister, and Athene had bade Kirke brew a draught to rid herself of his unwanted get. Athene hadn't been able to go through with it, though. In the end, she'd relented, had the babe, loved him.

Should Damkina do that? She wrapt her arms about her knees, staring into the dying embers. She could have the child, raise the babe, as she had not gotten to raise Pandora. Thousands of years had passed now, and never had Damkina allowed herself to conceive again. But she could ... She could have someone who would need her for her.

She could ...

By Damkina's bedside, Priam stroked the babe's brow, whispering soothing nothings into her ear. The child had Kirke's auburn hair and her father's dark eyes, this little princess of Ilium, bastard child though she was.

"Have you a name for her?" Damkina asked, reaching for her daughter.

"Indeed," Priam said. "I would call her Kassandra."

It was a pretty name, and Damkina approved. Only much later, as she dozed in convalescence, did she recall where she'd heard it before, millennia prior, from the lips of Artemis.

14

ARTEMIS

399 Dark Age

From the deck above, Artemis watched Athene out of the corner of her eye. The fallen Olympian sat upon a vacant rowing bench, her orichalcum fetters threaded through an iron ring designed to chain slave rowers. The woman had been stripped of her armour, left with naught save her torn tunic, which, from the look of it, had acquired some new stains in the day she'd spent on the lower deck. Considering the Elládosi under her command—and Athene herself— had killed thousands at Salamis and Thermopylae, Artemis could little blame the crew if they had splashed her with filth and waste.

The quartermaster swiped a backhand at Athene as he passed, but the blow never landed. Marduk had caught the man's wrist, holding it firm. For a brief instant, outrage flashed over the man's face before he must have realised he had nigh turned his ire on the god-king's son. "We do not torture prisoners for sport," Marduk said, releasing his grip. Artemis's betrothed did not let his gaze linger upon the quartermaster but rather swept it over all the crew close at hand in warning.

Much though part of her wanted to strike Athene—indeed, a

burning need to beat the woman senseless flared in her soul—Artemis loved Marduk all the more for the compassion he'd shown the Olympian. However little Athene deserved it.

On a whim, she took the ladder, passing Marduk as he returned to the upper deck. Her beloved did not mention what had transpired below. Below, she felt Athene's eyes on her as she made her way through the banks of oars to where her erstwhile friend sat bound. The quartermaster had wanted her forced to row, to make up for the depleted crew numbers, but Marduk had overruled him, saying it would only lead to disruption.

Grim faced, Artemis settled down upon the opposite bench, staring hard at Athene. She wasn't even certain what she'd come here to say, but the urge to say *something* had risen, ever and anon, since she'd captured the woman. Maybe she wanted to scream at her, to demand she open her eyes and recognise that Artemis had been right all along. A uselss part of her wanted to beat the stubborn delusion out of Athene, as if by sheer temper she could force the woman to cast aside the blindfold she wore to hide the truth from herself.

"Look what you have become," Athene said before Artemis could decide what, if aught, she had to say here. "A lackey to a foreign power, rendering murder among those who worshipped you."

Artemis scoffed at that. "Spare me the hypocrisy, Athene. You have slain your portion and more over the centuries and wrought suffering aplenty among the innocent and guilty alike. Now you fight and kill in the name of a *madman* who clings to power with a death grip, strangling the land you claim to protect." She leant across the space between them and seized a clump of Athene's dirty, matted hair, pulling her face closer. "The god-king commands you be given the chance to repent, which is the sole reason I've not yet killed you for what you did to Apollon."

Athene flashed her teeth and, for a heartbeat, Artemis thought she intended to fight back, even unable to use her Pneuma as she was. "Tell me ..." Athene spoke through gritted teeth. "Tell me of the Unseen Order that tugs your strings even as you profess your actions as your own."

Gaping, Artemis lost her grip on Athene without realising it, recoiling. "H-how do you ...?" How could she possibly know of Mithra's secret order? How could she understand those who moved in the shadows of the World, maintaining the spinning of the Wheels? Or ... was Athene not a mere tool of the Gnostic Cabal but a willing accomplice to their insanity?

A new thought dawned, impossible and terrible, and so gut-wrenching Artemis lurched to her feet. Themis had warned her Ningal mostlike lurked upon Olympus, manipulating Zeus. Was it possible Athene could be ... But this woman was the same one Artemis had known almost since Athene was born, and she refused to countenance the implications of the course her mind took.

Still, she could no longer stand to look at the woman's visage and stormed away, fair leaping her way up the ladder in her haste.

THEIR SHIP ARRIVED IN UGART, and from there, they had to cross overland until they could reach the Ufratu. Along the river, they took a ship to Babilim, and, upon arriving in the city, Marduk and the Immortals escorted Athene before his father. Artemis had not been summoned which, though it sparked a twinge of resentment, she struggled not to dwell on. Once, long ago, Mithra had taken the time to show her Truth. Perhaps he would now do so for Athene as well, and if so, he might have thought Artemis's presence a distraction for the woman. This, Artemis told herself as she bathed and changed.

She was enjoying a bowlful of pomegranate seeds when Phaethusa, who had returned on one of the other ships, came bursting in and threw her arms around her. "Was it hard?" the Heliad asked.

Artemis doubted she meant the fight. "Hard not to kill her, or hard to endure the leagues in her company to bring her here?"

"Any of it? All of it." The woman's golden eyes glinted with sympathy.

Artemis let the bowl clatter on the low table and rubbed her face. "The ones we love best are those who can cut us the deepest, I think."

Phaethusa nodded, her expression that of one who knew all too well the truths of which Artemis spoke. For a moment, the woman worked her tongue over her teeth without speaking, then she started. "Oh. The royal guard just brought me report of a Heliad woman spotted in the city."

Artemis sat up straighter. "Kirke?" Was it possible, after all these years, their sister had finally deigned to show herself? She had to assume Lampetia would have come straight to Phaethusa. Kirke, though, always went her own way, and sometimes she imagined even the Moirai struggled to predict that one's path.

Phaethusa shrugged. "Not sure. Should I go find her?"

"No," Artemis said. "I'll go myself." She could use the distraction from whatever unfolded betwixt Mithra and Athene. "I'll catch up with you later."

In the city between two markets, admiring the canal-fed gardens, she found not Kirke but Nike, of all people. The sight of the woman after so many centuries caught Artemis off guard, and for a moment, she gaped. Then she swallowed. Last she'd seen Nike, they had been friends ... but it had been before the war against Olympus. "They told me a Heliad woman had come here," she said. Nike spun to see her, eyes wide. "Of all those I imagined might have come, I never guessed it would be you." Though the woman seemed surprised to see Artemis, she in no way seemed intent on causing trouble. Decision made, Artemis strode forward and pulled her into an embrace, if an uncertain one. "After Ilium, I did not know where you had gone. I looked for you, though. I guess ... I should have known you only ever show up in the midst of conflict." Artemis managed a half-smile. "Goddess of Victory, indeed. Damn, but I'm glad you're here."

"You are?"

Artemis nodded. "Of course. You've come to help me bring down Zeus, have you not?"

"I never held much love for the tyrant of Olympus," Nike said with a hint of hesitation.

Gaia and Thoth be praised for that! "Come, then," Artemis said. "We've much to discuss. I'm only recently back from the war in Elládos, and I cannot long linger here. Before I return, I should introduce you to the god-king. And, of course, to my betrothed." She grabbed Nike's arm and pulled her for a tour of Etemenanki.

Inside, Nike gawped at the Hanging Gardens, though they stood below the construction and had not yet witnessed the true splendour. The two of them fell into easy rapport, and while Artemis had still hoped she might have found Kirke at last, she remained elated at reconnecting with Nike. The woman had an earnestness about her that endeared her to Artemis. Besides, Artemis could think of few better allies.

When she spotted Phaethusa, she called her sister over and introduced Nike to her, then ordered the servants to serve up a feast worthy of her guest. They brought mey wine and lamb stew, followed by figs and dates and succulent delicacies from around Neshia. Artemis noted, as they ate, that Phaethusa watched Nike with obvious reservation. If her half-sister remained mistrustful of a new face, Artemis could not blame her, but they would need to talk later.

Nike ate like a starving woman, so intent on the food she had not noticed Phaethusa's behaviour. Indeed, Artemis caught Nike stifling a yawn. "You must have had a long journey to reach this place."

Nike shook her head. "I'm fine."

"No, we have heated baths to rival even those of Atlantis." Artemis lurched to her feet, grabbed Nike's wrists, and forced the woman to rise. "No one knows better than we do how much relief a steaming soak offers to weary bones and aching muscles." After the long miles along the Ufratu, bathing had been the only reason Artemis had felt herself once more, though she'd have happily bathed in any lake or stream, as well.

She guided Nike through the palace to the bath hall, Phaethusa trailing along behind them. Over her shoulder, Artemis cast a look of warning to the woman. *"She is my friend,"* she hoped her eyes stated plain as day.

The hall was decorated with a mosaic in a dozen shades of blue, all meant to relax the mind as well as the body. The moment they entered the women's baths, servants arrived to help them undress. Nike's servant blanched at the woman's battered garb. "New clothes for my dear friend," Artemis said before the servant could embarrass anyone.

"This must be ... disposed of," the woman replied, determined to make Nike uncomfortable. For which Artemis resolved to have a word with the servant's mistress as soon as time allowed.

The pool lay cut out of a raised stone platform, and more servants guided them up the steps. A curtain of steam rose from the heated water, filling the air with a pleasant haze. Nike slipped into the pool without the slightest hesitation, which had Artemis raising a brow as she eased her way down. In her experience, plunging right in worked in icy winter streams, not half-boiling bathhouses. Phaethusa followed, trying to mimic Nike's imperviousness to the heat and, from the look on her face, not quite managing it.

"Nice to hear you are betrothed," Nike said. "I always ... wished happiness for you."

"And one could do worse than the son of the god-king," Phaethusa said.

Nike glanced back and forth between Artemis and her sister. "Is that ... how you came into the service of Mithra? Through his son?"

Damn it, Phaethusa. "No, I met Marduk later. After the fall of Ilium, I was ... lost. I gave my loyalty to Mithra, and he swore one day Olympus would pay for its myriad crimes."

After a moment, Nike seemed to accept that. "Tell me about this Marduk," she said, looking at Phaethusa as she spoke.

Artemis decided it best to answer. She wasn't certain how Phaethusa had gotten off to a prickly start with Nike but so wanted these women to like one another. Both meant much to her, and she despised the thought of enmity growing between them. "He commands the Immortals. I would call him the finest of warriors. His mother was a great sorceress, though she died in childbirth, long back. Mithra will, of course, rule for all eternity, and he has groomed Marduk to serve forever as his right hand and general. Where Zeus would have regarded Ares in such a position with unabating suspicion, Marduk holds Mithra's complete trust."

Nike grunted in relaxation, enjoying the bath hall. "All good things. But I meant to ask, rather, about *him*. In what, five thousand years or so, you never showed inclination towards marriage. Now I learn you are engaged. I doubt it is because the man is good with a sword."

Phaethusa snickered. "Maybe he is good with another type of sword."

Not looking at her half-sister, Artemis splashed an armful of water at her. "He's ... introspective. Others have called him brooding, but it is more they do not perceive the depth of his ever-churning soul. He has a fierce intellect that challenges me at every turn without ever crossing the line into arrogance."

"Oh, he's prideful enough," Phaethusa chimed in.

Artemis frowned. "On the battlefield, perhaps. And not without justification. I recall him knocking you upon your arse whenever you tested his mettle. But I meant to say he respects the intellects of others."

Her sister huffed. "Of you, anyway."

"And his father?" Nike cut in.

Artemis mulled over the question a moment. "I thought I had taken more than my fill of men claiming divinity." Her voice had dropped, for even here, she'd not like to risk her words getting to the wrong ears. "But Mithra ... When you hear his words and finally sound the depth of his meaning, only then will you begin to question if a man might, indeed, be also a deity." That, or at least he knew the Ontos, and the weight of knowledge created within him a divine aspect.

"Or mayhap," Nike said, "Mithra serves more as the means by which you might claim the vengeance you so desire against Zeus."

Artemis frowned. "You seem exhausted, Nike. I can arrange chambers for you to rest before you meet the god-king."

"Yes. Thank you."

❧

ARTEMIS ALLOWED Nike some hours to rest. When the woman rose once more, she took her out for a proper tour of the Hanging Gardens. "I wanted to introduce you to the god-king, but he sits now in council with his advisors. Though we sacked Kronion, our losses at Salamis and Thermopylae proved greater than anyone expected."

"Why did Mithra strike them in the first place?"

Though she could not have said why, Artemis decided it best to choose her words with care. "Word came from Elládos that some of the poleis had refused the tribute of earth and water. It made war inevitable, but in truth, Zeus would mostlike have forced the issue no matter what the poleis said. Either way, Sparta and Kronion refused to join the empire."

Nike was frowning now, though she lifted a sprig of jasmine to her face, enjoying a scent that would have had any other person smiling. "So asking for submission was but formality, as if to give justification for the slaughter that would invariably follow."

"No." *Well, perhaps.* Artemis leant against a tree and folded her arms over her chest. "Mithra has no intention of harming those who offered the tribute and thus became his vassals."

"Even if he doesn't harm them, Zeus will name them traitors and visit a worse-still fate upon them. You have left the common people caught between two damnations with no means to save themselves."

Artemis shook her head, unable to deny Nike spoke truth, and all the more vexed for it. "There is a corruption riving through the core of Ellá-dos, and it spawns from Olympus. I will see it burnt out."

Nike ripped the jasmine flower off its branch and crushed it, then let it tumble from her palm. "And those whose lives are cut short may take comfort in the world being made better for others."

Artemis winced. She heard something. Footsteps crunching softly on the grass. She jerked her head to the side to see Marduk drawing nigh, smiling as he laid eyes on her.

"Marduk," Artemis said. "This is my old friend, Nike."

Now her betrothed at last seemed to take note of Nike and swept a bow. "I would count any friend of yours as my friend." He turned back to Artemis. "Father commands you attend him in the war council. He would speak of the ships."

Artemis nodded. "I was giving Nike a tour of the palace. Perhaps you could fill in for me."

Marduk fell into another bow. "It would be my pleasure. Lady Nike."

Nike shot Artemis an ominous look. Though Nike had admitted having no love for Zeus, Artemis wondered if Nike would join her war after all. She was the last person Artemis wanted as an enemy in this.

15

ATHENE

2400 Bronze Age

*M*ired *in the infinite expanses of self-delusion, caught within traps of the mind generated by fragments of Truth, the Gnostic seeks to infect another with his delusion.* The Moirai's voices held a cadence of urgency, such that, as Athene rose, looking around familiar peaks, she at once set off in the direction in which they guided her. She was upon a lower slope of Olympus, though, from the look above, some time before the end of the Titanomachy. The perennial storm had not yet gathered and no city of self-aggrandising temples yet graced the summit.

She came to a cave, access to it limited as the stairwell that had once reached it had fallen away with time and the shifting of the land. A single beat of her wings hurled her across the gulf, but rather than head in, Athene paused on the threshold examining the strange reliefs carved into columns on either side of the entrance. Beyond the columns, unusual geometric traceries, the likes of which she had never seen before, stone cut into intricate lattices bifurcated by parabolic arcs.

As Athene moved within, voices echoed.

"But I offer you my hand," a man said. "I offer you the unvarnished Truth, and with it the hope we might change Fate at long last."

"I—" Pandora began, then spun as Athene's armoured foot clanked upon the stone. The Heliad had a kopis in hand, holding it like she had at least some idea of how to use it now. Did she have the power of the Phoenix at this point?

The platinum-haired man behind Pandora she thought must be Kronos, though Athene could not even remember the look of her paternal grandfather. "No!" Kronos blurted, making a break for it. For a single instant, knowing he was of the Gnostic Cabal, Athene thought perhaps her purpose here was to put an end to him. But history recorded that her father had cast him into Tartarus, mostlike not long hence.

"All you've seen," Kronos bellowed at Athene, "and still you are *blind*! Blind by choice, mired in your self-delusion, a pawn to the Unseen!"

The irony was that, were she to try to reason with him, she might have used the same words. The Gnostics, in their desperate, self-destructive desire to escape the rule of the Wheel of Fate and the Archons, deluded themselves about the alternatives. Before she could answer the Ouranid lord, Pandora lunged at her, swiping with that kopis.

The attack was, if not clumsy, hardly a threat, and Athene blocked it with a casual swipe of her vambrace. The impact sent Pandora's weapon skittering across the chamber. From the force of Pandora's blow, Athene was fair certain the woman now had become Nike, which meant she was less likely to kill her grandmother by mistake. She caught Pandora's shoulder and rammed a knee up into her gut, sending her flying back further into the chamber. The woman rolled and skidded along the floor, almost tumbling down into a chasm that had rived the floor, and Athene suppressed a wince. Driving Pandora into a ravine that might well have stretched a thousand feet deep was not, in fact, part of the plan.

The threat remained Kronos—or her meeting with him—and already, the Gnostic was escaping down a side passage.

Athene looked to Pandora, who had gained her feet and looked to, perhaps, be considering following Kronos after whatever illusory secrets the Titan had promised her. Another beat of Athene's wings closed the distance betwixt her and Pandora, and she shot a punch toward the woman's head. Pandora blocked it with enough force Athene's arm stung even through the vambrace. Athene fell back, stunned at the raw Pneumatikoi the Phoenix bestowed. She had heard it was vast, but considering Pandora scarce seemed to know how to use it ...

Athene, however, did know how to use her body as a weapon. She struck again, and when Pandora tried to block once more, she caught the woman's wrist and twisted her arm behind her back. Athene slammed her other hand down between Pandora's shoulder blades, sending the woman flying, to spill once more across the floor, though Athene had taken care not to knock her toward a chasm this time, but rather toward the entrance.

As Pandora sprawled, a newcomer trod in, his eyes like emeralds. That was the man Athene had fought on Atlantis and driven away from Pandora, the one who had killed the first Nemesis. The stranger stepped around Pandora, blocking Athene's view of her grandmother. Perhaps he believed Athene might, in fact, have slain the woman. Certainly it was best if Pandora thought her life in danger; Nemesis would lose her ability to sway the woman's course if Pandora's fear of her waned.

"Assassin," the man said.

The Destroyer is beyond you ...

Or perhaps he just needed another chance to go flying off a cliff. In slaying Nemesis, he had already proved himself an enemy of Fate. And Athene had already defeated him once. Her wings sent her hurtling toward him. But the man dodged each of her blows with dancer-like grace, twisting aside from every lunge with a minimum of effort. After several such evasions, he blocked her arm and his other hand shot out, slamming into her cuirass. The impact drove all wind from her lungs, caved in her breastplate, and hurled her across the chamber.

She collided with a pedestal at the centre of the room, smacking her head, then flailing to keep from falling over, one hand clutched her bruised sternum. When at last she managed to draw a breath, it was laced with fire and pain. Whilst holding Pneuma, she didn't think she'd ever felt anyone hit so hard, not even a Cyclops.

The stranger extended his arms and leapt at her, wings of flame erupting from his back and immolating his shirt even as he streaked toward Athene. Realising her peril, she grasped the Box and activated it. Light welled around her before the stranger landed, collapsing into a bubble and shifting her away from his descending attack.

§

THE BREAKING WAVE of light deposited Athene onto cobbled streets, and she fell into a heap, hand to her chest, gasping in pain. What in the dark of Tartarus had that man been? He had powers like unto Nike, but far, far more refined.

Time comes round, and we return whence you came.

"What?" she rasped, still breathless, as she looked around. She was in an alley, so it was hard to be certain, but she thought this might be Babilim. Had they brought her back here? Was that the Moirai's meaning?

Enough is done to ensure the Tapestry holds. For the Box, but one task remains in your hands. It must be restored to its rightful owner.

"And that is?"

Pandora, the one for whom it was first made.

Athene growled in pain and frustration. So the Fates had just sent her careening through time, thwarting Pandora at every turn, only to aid her now by giving her the damn Box in the first place. It vexed, though it made a perverse sort of sense, she supposed. To uphold the timeline, they had needed to ensure the timewalker could not gain knowledge that might allow her to alter choices upon which existing history remained predicated. Given that Athene knew the first Nemesis—this Vinata—had attacked Pandora at least once, it was also possible a Nemesis had steered her on other occasions. Perhaps Athene would never know the full truth of it all.

Perhaps she did not need to know.

Weary and pained, she climbed to her feet and plodded down the alley, her steps guided by the invisible nudges of the Moirai, telling her which way to turn. They led her to a tunnel beneath Etemenanki—the royal palace. There, in the depths, they bade her wait, and wait she did.

Soon after, around the corner came Marduk, escorting Pandora. Athene's grandmother now bore orichalcum fetters—the same ones that had bound Athene not long ago, she thought—and the commander of the Immortals was dragging her along by the bicep. Athene did not know what the woman had done, but if the Moirai wanted the Box returned to her, they could not intend for her to remain a prisoner or be turned over to the god-king. Perhaps, not so unlike Prometheus, Mithra too was driven by human whim and weakness, and thus the Fates could not trust any one servant with all the needs of Fate.

"Nemesis," Marduk said, wary. Perhaps he had dealt with the other Nemesis in the past. It was a strange feeling, everyone so oft mistaking her for a dead woman. Would Marduk have known her well enough to recognise her voice, as Prometheus had? Having never met Vinata, Athene could make no real effort to sound like her.

Athene stared hard at the god-king's son. "I must speak with the woman. Alone."

"She is *my* prisoner, held on charges of attempted deicide. I shall bring her before my father." Deicide? Had Pandora tried to slay Mithra? It was not so long ago that Athene admired the woman's brazen tenacity, though this seemed a step too far.

She cocked her head to the side. "Would you defy an order from the Moirai themselves?"

Marduk grimaced and Pandora hissed as though he was hurting her. All at once, he shoved her toward Athene, who caught her and kept her from tumbling to the tunnel floor. "I want her back the moment you finish with her."

Athene glowered at him in silence, watching him as he stalked past her. When the prince had gone, Athene dragged Pandora away until she came to a storeroom. She hurled open the door, dragged Pandora inside, and released her to go light a lamp. That done, she peeked back out the door to ensure privacy, then shut it.

"Are you here to kill me, at last?" Pandora demanded.

Athene remained facing the door, though her helm would already have concealed her expression. Small wonder she could think that, given their many confrontations. What would Pandora say, Athene wondered, were Athene to claim everything she had done had been to save both Pandora and all life upon Gaia? "No," she said.

She turned back to Pandora, then.

Her grandmother took a hesitant step toward her. "Why do you serve the Fates? Why this wretched determination to hold fast to a timeline in which so many are condemned to futures they would never have chosen?"

"You hold choice up as the inviolate standard to which all must bow. Were the will truly free, surely then the self-interested masses would have sent the world spiralling toward oblivion long before now. You are quick to rail against a timeline whilst forgetting that, so long as it exists, so too does life."

Her grandmother was already shaking her head before Athene finished speaking. "Life is beautiful *because* of our wills. Choice is the fulcrum upon which the meaning of our lives swings. Even if all is written, at least grant it is written by choices already made rather than deny the very existence of free will."

Athene clenched her fist, her gauntlet squealing in protest. The woman did not understand and, short of Mithra showing her the Ontos as he had to Athene, she was not certain she could be made to understand. Or perhaps Pandora, like the deluded Gnostics, was too dogged in her determination to prove free will, even if that will meant naught save the damnation of the World. Perhaps, then, she would refuse to see even when the Truth pranced naked and unblemished before her eyes.

"If you did not bring me here to execute me, then why delay my reckoning with Mithra?"

Athene looked up at that. "Execute you? Such were never my orders nor intent. I am bound to tread the river of time and follow its course." Maybe, If Pandora knew the truth ... Athene grasped her helm. "But I would not slay my own blood." She pulled free the mask, revealing herself at last, and let the helm clatter upon the floor.

Her grandmother gasped on seeing her, then fell into wordless stuttering. Athene could almost see the whirring gears of her mind, as complex as those of the Box. She must have struggled, trying to parse the order of so many events. The Moirai had not forbidden her from revealing herself, but somehow she doubted they wished for Athene to explain all she knew. No, the Fates had sent her here for one reason, and that was to restore something which Pandora had lost and would need again, were she to uphold the Tapestry of Fate.

So Athene withdrew the Box from her satchel and proffered it to Pandora. Though the woman continued to gawp, Athene pressed the Box into her open hands.

For those fetters, a key lies dormant within the depths of your satchel.

And indeed, when Athene reached for it, she found the means to unlock the orichalcum chains that bound Pandora. Once she had freed her grandmother, Athene stepped back. She didn't know how soon Pandora might activate the Box and did not want to get caught in that bubble and swept away to another time.

Pandora looked to her, her gaze growing firm. "I will never give up. I will never stop fighting this."

Athene fought not to smile. As if that, too, was not already accounted for by Ananke. "I know."

As Athene watched, Pandora set the Box and vanished back into the time stream.

AFTER REDONNING HER HELM, then glamouring herself to invisibility, Athene climbed the stairs inside Etemenanki until she could reach the god-king's chamber. Only on the threshold did she allow the illusion to fall away. She had no desire to encounter either servants or Immortals here, but she needs must speak with Mithra about all that had unfolded.

As she raised a hand to pound upon his door, it swung wide, revealing Marduk. The prince glared at her. "Where is the prisoner?"

"That is for me to discuss with your father."

Marduk sneered. She could little blame him for being vexed, considering she had taken Pandora from his custody, then appeared without the woman. But she had not come here to speak with the prince, regardless.

"See to your betrothed," Mithra called to his son from inside the room. At that, the prince wavered a moment, then edged around Athene with a huff.

Was Artemis wounded? Athene scarce knew what to think about her erstwhile Olympian sister. So much had happened in so short a time, she'd had no time to dwell on any of it. Artemis had slain Themistokles and so many others, had brought Athene before Mithra in orichalcum chains. And yet, Mithra had shown Athene the Ontos, and Artemis served the same master. Did that make them ... allies once more? She could not see how to push down the rivers of bad blood that had cropped up between them.

"Enter," Mithra called, cutting through her musings.

Athene slipped into his chambers and looked upon the god-king. Burns marred his face; his beard had grown threadbare from whatever had scorched him. Nike's pyromancy? He bore numerous bruises, including a black eye, and favoured one shoulder. If Nike had striven to slay him, it appeared she'd gotten damn close. Assuming such a thing as *close* yet had meaning, given the absolute course of Ananke she now understood. The path before everyone was forged of adamant, immutable; the potential for deviation was but an optical illusion, a trick of perception.

"The Moirai commanded me to release Pandora and restore the Box to her."

Whatever he had expected, it had not been that. Though brief, hidden almost instantly, shock widened his eyes, and she saw it. The god-king served the Moirai, but they did not tell him everything, any more than they did to Prometheus. An unnerving thought occurred then: did they *know* everything? "If so commanded, then you have done well." He rubbed his jaw. "The situation escalates rapidly. I needs must take the army to Mu to deal with the queens there and their intent to raise the Leviathan."

"Leviathan?"

"The Elder Goddess whom the Magi name Tiamat, yes."

She knew, then. "It will be the Eschaton. They are that powerful?"

"They are the reincarnated Pleiades. Through dark sorcery, one called up the souls of others, moved them into these bodies to reunite themselves. It is a dangerous practice, this controlling of the movements of souls, but yes, it made them powerful indeed. And the Eschaton will be needful, to forestall Typhon's consumption of the cosmos. The Hidden God will see the Dark sated and driven back into quiescence. The Leviathan is but a tool toward that end."

Athene understood. Mithra intended to provoke the Queens of Mu, to use the war between continents to drive them to such desperation that risked the destruction of the World. Only through the carnage could they hope to survive.

"Hunt down the remaining Gnostics, Nemesis. Their role in history is all but played out. We cannot allow them to continue to interfere. The Wheel of Fate must spin. Ningal, the daughter of Enki, she ... You must find her and end her machinations. She can shift her face and thus eluded your predecessor."

Oh, Athene was fair certain she knew where to find her. Artemis, of all people, had lit the spark of doubt within Athene. It seemed a reckoning with Athene's stepmother was long overdue.

INTERLUDE: MARDUK

400 Dark Age

Marduk found Morpheus in a wide tent set with plush cushions and enough luxury one might forget, for a moment, they camped not two miles inland from a blood-strewn battle-field. The Magus was smoking a copper pipe, its putrid smoke filling even the airy pavilion with an astringent reek that made Marduk's eyes water. Morpheus looked up at his entrance, his gaze lidded, bleary. In these mind-bending herbs, the man must seek answers ... or perhaps solace. Marduk knew little of Morpheus's past, but what man lived for millennia without amassing oceans of regret? Yes, the same peril of memory Artemis had spoken of must sit heavy upon the ancient Titans.

Though uninvited, he settled across from the Magus, legs folded. When the silence stretched, Marduk scratched his beard. "Well, your arrival came timely."

Morpheus blew out a puff of smoke that hazed the air between them. "There are ways an oneiromancer might induce waking dreams and thus draw upon needful insight even in times when sleep might prove elusive ..."

Was that how the Magus knew he was needed? "And what do these dreams show you now?"

"Questions, unvoiced ... worming their way to the surface ... maggots gnawing the living ... They squirm 'neath your skin ... tiny burrowers ..."

The image drew a grimace from Marduk. Did the man already know why he had come? Not long before he'd parted with Artemis, she'd asked him whether he had ever consulted Morpheus about the visions he saw, aye, like the waking dreams of which Morpheus now spoke. Always, this Magus knew too much, said too little. "I see things, conjurings of my mind that I cannot explain, for they seem to have so little to do with aught I have lived or might know."

Morpheus flicked his pipe with one finger before drawing another puff. "The World is not what it seems, O Prince." The oneiromancer chuckled at his private jest, though Marduk saw naught amusing. "Some of us, we are blessed, *cursed*, with the psychic sensitivity to apprehend pieces of the Ontos—the Truth behind the illusion. The Sight, some name it, though this sensitivity could well be things felt, heard, or intuited without reliance upon the eyes. Perhaps your mind opens to perceptions beyond the ken of the mundane."

"You imply I see past or future ... or distant events having no connection to me?"

Morpheus snorted. "That's as could be, but then ... perhaps what you see is you all along, and you have simply ... forgotten. What is gone ... what is to come ... all of it spun by the Wheel of Fate. Time is ... part of the grand illusion of which I spoke ... don't you think?"

"I think you speak in riddles and I shall mostlike leave this pavilion more confused than when I entered."

The Magus quirked a smile, then offered Marduk the pipe. "So certain, are you? What if you could summon a dream ... a memory ... a portent of things to come ...?"

Why should Marduk wish to induce such a state? Had not he come here seeking a way to block out these phantasms? Yet, with tremulous fingers, he reached for the copper pipe the Magus offered. He grasped it, felt its warmth. "You think I am like you?"

"No ... I think you are ... like you. You just don't know it yet."

Heart racing, sweat beading his brow, Marduk raised the pipe to his lips.

§🐍

Drenched in blood—no little of it his—Ninurta paced around the twitching form of the Zû. The demon bird was twice the size of the largest of elephants and had torn through the livestock of Ninevehan farmers, carrying away cows in each talon. That was not, however, why Ninurta's father Enlil had ordered him to slay the Old One. The Zû had stolen the Tablet of Destiny, and Father had demanded its return.

He allowed his Pneuma to seep into his mace. Hints of barely contained lightning crackled along Sharur's fluted head, the only illumination on this night. Ninurta had blasted the Zû out of the sky, and wafts of smoke yet rose from the demon's ruined wings. Overhead, storm clouds still rumbled, blocking out the moon and stars, leaving the night almost pitch black. Raising his coruscating mace for light, Ninurta knelt before the eagle-head of the demon, not close enough it might lash out and tear into him with that hooked beak.

"Where is the Tablet, demon? Long have I hunted for you, long searched for that which you stole ..."

Its mind brushed against his in answer. An awful, choking darkness threatened to swallow him as though he plunged into a pit of tar and was being dragged into its suffocating depths.

Gone ... Reclaimed by the Cabal ...

The Gnostics! Father had taken the Tablet when the sun came to this Era, he had told Ninurta. But he had not held it long ere the Zû had come. "I had not imagined those benighted fools deranged enough to summon a demon to do their bidding." Ninurta rose, hefting Sharur to smash this thing's skull and make an end of it.

Something struck him in the back of the head and had him collapsing in a heap before the demon bird. His head felt hot, sticky, his skull cracked. Ninurta sent energy there, tried to stymie the blood loss. He'd not reinforced his flesh or bones, had not thought any danger left. He managed to turn, to look at the figure approaching.

A woman in a dark cloak. Sharur's light went out when he'd dropped the mace, the flow of his Pneuma to it cut off; Ninurta couldn't see much of aught now. The woman threw back her hood, stared at him, expressionless. "Ningal?" he tried to mumble, but his heavy tongue would not shape the words. In his sister-in-law's hand dangled an open sling. She'd felled him?

Ningal knelt, retrieving Sharur with her other hand. "So long spent driving monsters from Kumari Kandam, making the land safe for Mankind." She clucked her tongue. "You deserved better, Ninurta. But I cannot have you finding the Tablet ..."

Realisation settled upon him, then. Ningal had called the Zû, had used the demon to betray them to the Gnostic Cabal. Why, he wanted to demand but could only moan. Had she ... been the one to betray them to the Cabal even in ancient times?

She seemed to understand. "Ereshkigal." Her daughter, Ninurta's niece. Dead, in the days of darkness. "And yet he would have me bow before the Wheel of Fate and preserve it?" She grunted. "Sorry, Brother. I'll see to it your father gets the mace back. You'll be known as the hero who slew this demon; it will be the last one you tally, I fear." Ningal hefted the mace. It did not crackle in her hand. It did not need to.

MARDUK MUST FIND KINGU, he knew, for whatever the Deep One intended in skirting the Kandamian army, it would spell disaster. So he tracked the spirit south, along the river and into the jungle. With the sun blaring against the cerulean sky, he suspected the Deep One would have gone into hiding, perhaps somewhere beneath the river. Marduk had no easy way to be certain he did not bypass the watery creature, but he must try, must trust in whatever insight his fevered mind had begun to conjure. If he failed, too many men would die for it.

How had he seen such a vision of Ninurta? The legendary hero, famed for driving demons out of Kumari Kandam, and Marduk had seen himself as that man. What strange phantasms did Morpheus's smoke conjure? But he'd seen Ninurta bind lightning through Sharur ... Could Marduk learn to do such a thing?

Along the riverbank he trudged, trying to feel the World, to sense aught amiss that might indicate the presence of something Otherworldly. If Morpheus was right, if Marduk had within him a psychic sensitivity, if his visions presaged that rather than madness, he had a chance. Of course, if Marduk was going mad, he supposed not much would help him now.

Bah! He wished Artemis were here. The huntress was so adept he imagined she might well be able to track a fish through water. Besides which, it had been too long since he'd heard her voice. He misliked having her away, fighting battles across the sea. He knew his father had sent her on a mission, but Father had not deigned to reveal it, and Marduk feared for her safety.

In time, he came to a hut alongside the river, elevated by stilts and reachable by a ladder. Before this hut crouched a man, a Muian, Marduk assumed, tending an oven dug into the ground. Beside the oven lay a stone-ringed fire, over which steeped a pot of tea. Whilst the man had the build and tattoos of a warrior, he made no threatening move at Marduk's approach. In fact, the stranger motioned for Marduk to come and sit before the fire.

This man ought to have been his enemy but seemed more inclined to talk, and Marduk was no savage to assault a man merely for his place of origin, whatever the times between their people. Not taking his gaze from the Muian, he settled across the fire from him. "I seek a creature that may have passed this way."

The man looked pointedly at the river. "Fish pass by oft enough, hence why I come here."

Marduk glanced at the hut. "This is not your only home, then."

"These days, I live most oft in the mountains; a quiet life suits, when times so permit." Marduk doubted the war permitted any such thing for the nonce. The man set beside himself a tray with two earthen cups, took up the teapot, and poured for the both of them. Marduk accepted the cup the Muian offered but did not drink. It was, he had learnt, unwise to accept food or drink from those who might mean harm, leastwise until one had seen the other party sample the same fare. "Given the choice, I while away my time in the mountains, gazing at the sunset with my wife, or watching for the birds in the trees. Ah, but then, sometimes one craves a fish."

Indeed, the smell of whatever catch roasted in that oven had Marduk's mouth watering. When his host had sipped at the tea, Marduk decided it safe to sample. After draining his cup and returning it to the platter, he fitted the Muian with a gaze once more. "Appealing as fish may be"—and he did glance at the oven— "it is not a fish I seek."

"Yet a full belly might make everything seem more manageable. Bide here but a short while, and you may share with me before you're on your way. Or make haste, if it suits you. That choice is yours. Choice, in the end, is one of few things we might call our own."

Marduk's stomach rumbled at the thought. A meal might indeed give him more strength to hunt down Kingu, though any delay meant his prey might move farther afield. Still ... "I can afford to linger, if only a little." He watched the man's face. Unlike any Muian whom Marduk had seen, this man had blue eyes, ones so blue as to seem sapphires. A strange warrior, indeed. "It is a spirit I seek, though, and I need to know if one came this way."

The man shifted, poking a stick in the oven to turn the fish inside. "There is an invisible world all around us in which spirits move."

Marduk folded his arms. He had the distinct impression this man toyed with him, and such a thing ought to have irked him. In fact, he found himself somewhat perturbed he was not more vexed than he felt. "I do not speak of the Otherworld or the liminal spaces betwixt here and there, as well I think you know, Muian. Can you help me toward my goal or not?"

"Oh, I would indeed help you, such as I am able." The stranger seemed almost wistful at that and turned to stare into the fire, watching it crackle and pop. A faint sigh escaped the man as he looked back to Marduk. "Is a choice made so long back we can no longer recall it not still our choice ...?" A sad smile. "There is a place, close by, where shamans claim the Otherworld waxes and Mana runs strong. Follow the river to the next bend, then seek for a recess within the nearby mountain slope. Where the land falls away and a lava tube bores into the Earth, there you might find some of the answers you seek. Whether they will avail you, in the end, I suppose time will tell."

Marduk didn't know what that meant. Nor, in truth, was he certain he wished to know. Something about this strange man, about his words, it had a chill rising in him. He could not shake the sense that the shadow of an unseen predator had begun to loom over him. That, when at last Marduk might glance upon whatever doom lurked nigh, it would prove far too late to avoid it.

DESPITE HIS MISGIVINGS over the Muian stranger, Marduk stayed to sup on roasted sprat with the man, then followed his instructions. As the warrior had claimed, beyond a bend in the river, Marduk soon spied recesses in the nearby mountains. Within one such recess, he was able to climb down to a lower space. The tunnel that bored into the mountainside might have been invisible had not he already known it would be there. The rough-walled pyroduct wormed downward as though some fiery serpent had slithered along such a path in bygone days, and Marduk misliked the feel of the place. It had the hairs on his arms and neck standing on end, had his gut clenching. Was this the waxing of Mana—the Muian word for Pneuma, he thought—of which the stranger had spoken?

Moreover, did such dread come upon Marduk because the Muian had claimed this place ran close to the Otherworld, or did he feel this because the man had spoken the truth? Marduk doubted even Magi would have wished to tread here, much less an ordinary man like himself. Still, if something down that tunnel might aid him in finding Kingu ... Yes. For what better place for a denizen of the Otherworld to lair than within some sepulchral depths close to its own Realm? Marduk wondered, if he could see—as was said some few Magi could—the invisible reality alongside their own, what would he behold? Terror? The gut-churning realisation that things watched Men, just out of sight?

Bah! This place was affecting him, and he allowed his mind to torment him. After lighting a torch, Marduk started down the tunnel. His sandals echoed upon the stone, but other than that, and the muffled crackle of the flame he bore, an eerie silence settled over the pyroduct. As if he moved into a void, free of life, free of motion. As if he crawled ... into a grave.

He followed the tube for a quarter of an hour until he lost count of how many times he thought to turn back. Ever, something pulled him forward, some unnameable need for answers to questions he could not quite articulate. Then, of a sudden, the lave tube breached into a chamber. Enormous mounds of broken, worked stone lay strewn across an open space far wider than his meagre torch could illume. That torchlight glinted over remnants of shattered arches and crumbled buttresses, of buildings that had collapsed in upon themselves.

Was this ... Murias? Magi legend spoke of an ancient mountain city of soaring spires that had once flourished upon Mu, in the time before time, days called Dark Faerie. They claimed an Elder Race had built glorious, strange cities, one upon each continent, and from there sought to dominate Man and Titan. Marduk had assumed such things half fancy, but this place looked—and smelt—like something from outside of time, steeped in eldritch import. He could well believe something inhuman had built this fallen city that, if legend held true, had once touched the sky. The thought of seeing it whole filled him with both longing wonder and, at the same time, atavistic dread. Even he, a Titan and thus of an Elder Race, feared to look upon the workings of whoever, whatever had built Murias.

Mayhap he ought to turn back. Could Kingu have come so far? Would the spirit linger in such a haunted place? Marduk doubted it, but … Perhaps it was better to push onward to be certain. He wended around the piled heaps of a ruined city, imagining what each mound might have looked like, rising from a mountainside. Try though he might, he found his mind scarce up to such a challenge.

Torch out to one side, he paced through the ancient city, nerves fraying, unable to shake the sense that something momentous impended … As if he had trodden into the lair of a hoary monstrosity that might, at any moment, awaken from a millennia-long slumber. With his free hand, he gripped the hilt of his akinakes, drawing what small comfort he could from its solidity, running his thumb over the engraved pommel.

Then, amid the ruins, he came upon an unshattered pedestal, standing tall in the midst of what had, perhaps, once been a breezeway. He could guess no explanation for how this one edifice had survived the cataclysmic ruin that had fallen upon the rest of this chamber, and yet, there it stood. Upon the pedestal rested a stone tablet, graven with glyphs in some language he could not recognise. There were eight lines carved into the stone, one of which had begun to emit a faint blue light as he drew nigh.

Marduk balked, his steps faltering. What in the name of the Hidden God was this thing? Why did it react to him thus? Impelled by an urge he could not explain, Marduk strode forward, reached for it. His fingers brushed over the cold stone, and his mind reeled …

*K*ALI HAD LEFT *behind her a void, deep as the infinite dark between the stars, vast beyond all measure. To say her death had torn a hole into Manyu's heart was to name a mountain a pebble. Her loss ravaged him, stole his breath, threatened to leave his insides pitching away into oblivion. Shadows tinged everything, the World was shrouded by an omnipresent gloom that radiated from her.*

Perhaps from him.

Matarśivan's flickering fire sent the shadows swirling, leaping in profane mockery of the torrents of agony that washed over Manyu. The Rishi had brought him up into the mountains, to a cave, away from the battle against the horrors that followed in Vritra's wake. The demon dragon was sucking the land dry. Whole forests withered, turned to dust, and blew away beneath its colossal thrashing. Fields collapsed. And people, Adityas, Men, even Asuras, they vanished into the same dark void that had taken Kali.

Manyu wanted to care but he had so little left inside. When he left here, he would go after Vritra. The dragon would slay him as it had slain Kali, and he would be returned to the Wheel of Life. Perhaps then he might one day walk beside her once more. "Why did you bring me here?" he asked, for the sound of crackling flame abraded his nerves even more than the silence. Existence had become torment, every sound, sight, and sensation a fresh torture.

The Rishi sighed, turning those sapphire blue eyes back to the flame. "Long have we known one another, Manyu."

Manyu grunted. "I know what you would say. You shan't dissuade me from my course. I will face the dragon."

"I know." Matarśivan looked back to him now. "Loathe though I am to raise a pyre for another friend, I know you would not be denied this. Which is ... why ..." The Rishi shook himself. Manyu could not recall ever seeing him so lost for words. "I must ask you to do one thing first, Manyu, but it shall be your choice, and if you refuse, I will look for another."

"Speak it and have done." Manyu saw little reason to delay his ending.

Matarśivan grimaced, started to turn to the fire once more, then shuddered, denying whatever solace he had intended to seek there. "Afore I tell you the task, you must hear the stakes, old friend. I know your visions revealed hints of this ill future long back. I know you see things, hear things others cannot."

"What is this, Matarśivan? Was it not you who helped me hone those skills?"

"Yes ... but your psychic abilities run deeper than most Oracles. You have, at

times, seen glimpses of past lives, have you not?" He had, in disconcerting, unordered flashes. Matarśivan did not wait for an answer. "I ... Do you know why you have seen such darkness? There are powers lurking out in the cosmos, on the edge of the World, hungering for a way in, for a feast upon souls. Given the chance, they will gorge themselves, even unto the ruination of all the World. All the cosmos, swallowed by the Dark. A final ending of time and life, when no more reincarnations shall emerge, and no further chances at love or hope shall rise. This is the threat of Vritra, an extension of an Elder God against which we are less than insects."

The Rishi spoke with such certainty Manyu could not gainsay him, though his words evoked such atavistic horror as to freeze Manyu's heart in his chest. He wanted to deny such a claim, to rail against the sheer inequity of such an existence. How could the cosmos exist, how could Men and Adityas be given life and will and hopes and dreams, and it all amount to naught? It galled beyond endurance to hear that civilisation mattered no more to these beings than did the will of shrimp to Men. This could not be their fate.

"So ... we are all damned to this fate. Pretences of hope were just that— petty self-delusions."

Matarśivan leant forward. "You have seen the Earth dying beneath a tendril of this Elder God. When it finishes, every soul, living or dead, will be drawn to it. The whole cosmos snuffed out." He paused. "Unless ... we change it."

Yes, this fate, 'twas not to be borne. Manyu seized the Rishi's wrist. "You said there was a choice."

"Indeed." Matarśivan reached back and drew forth a blank stone tablet. "One person can carve their name here and take up the role of Destroyer." Matarśivan pulled his hand free and raised it, forestalling Manyu's objection that destruction aplenty unfolded outside. "You cannot stop the ending of this World. The Elder Gods will have their feast. But if you can slay Vritra, that tendril of the one intruding into the Mortal Realm, you can buy us time."

"What? Carve my name upon a slab, and I'll be strong enough to face that abomination? That's all?"

"No." Matarśivan closed his eyes a moment, seeming almost ashamed to ask whatever he was asking here. "It won't end. You will die in this fight. And your soul will be called up to fulfil this role again and again."

Because the Elder Gods would always be out there, just outside the World, hungry for their next feast. "This shall be a cycle," Manyu said, realisation hitting like a blow. "I make this choice now, I make it for my future lives, as well."

"I think, you will live as other men in the times betwixt Eschatons, but yes, you will thus bind yourself to the turning of the Wheel of Fate." He paused. "Manyu ... it does not have to be you. I can ask another Oracle; I can try to ..."

"No." Manyu waved that away. "Who would I be then, if I shucked this burden and let someone else take it up? Should I hide from the Truth now it is unveiled before me? In telling me what you have, in revealing the empty horror beyond reality, you have taken from me any hope of self-deluding peace. Yes, well do I understand what you ask of me, old friend. I will never be able to set down this weight once I heft it. Still, I was ready to die fighting Vritra. If there is even a chance I can take the abomination with me, how can I pass that chance?"

To his shock, a tear dribbled down Matarśivan's cheek. The Rishi wiped it away with the back of his hand, then drew something else from behind: a mace. Manyu had seen Tvastr working on this, had he not? When Matarśivan handed Manyu the mace, the weapon seemed to thrum with the potential for thunder. Its power coursed through him, multiplying his Prana. "The Oracle Manyu cannot stand against Vritra." Matarśivan fitted him with that sapphire gaze. "So become someone else. Become the one who will ignite the cycle and thus preserve the hope of life. Become the Destroyer ... Indra."

When the Rishi produced a hammer and chisel, Manyu—Indra now— began to carve his new name upon the tablet. To his shock, other names appeared beneath his carving as he worked, each character he carved expanding upon multiple lines. Eight names. The top one, the one he carved now, glowed, emitting a faint blue light.

"Behold the Tablet of Destiny," Matarśivan said as the last stroke fell, and Indra blew away the dust.

Fate closed its hand around him, grasped his soul. Hints of dead men's voices rang in his periphery. Indra rose, took up the mace. "With this ... I shall summon the lightning and subdue this devouring darkness." Even if only for a time. "I shall call my weapon Vajra, for it will give me the power of vengeance against Vritra." He spared a last glance to Matarśivan. "I go now to war. I hope I shall see you again."

"You will," Matarśivan said as he was leaving. Then: "But not in this lifetime."

MARDUK STUMBLED away from the tablet, collapsed onto his arse, and dropped the torch onto the dusty floor. For a moment, he could not breathe, so intense had been the vision. So real, so present he could not separate himself from Manyu. Had that been his life? The man he'd seen in the vision—Matarśivan—had that been the same man who had sent him into this buried city? He lacked the tattoos he now bore, but it was him, Marduk was certain. Which meant the sapphire-eyed stranger had wanted him to come, to touch this tablet, to *see* this, though Marduk had no idea why.

And that mace that Indra had borne, Vajra, that was ... Sharur. Marduk withdrew it from his back, stared at it. Indra too had felt lightning and thunder within this ancient weapon. But what was this vision, this Vritra? None of this had been in the histories the Magi taught. Something, perhaps, from beyond the time of the ancient darkness, even?

Wracked by trembles, he rose, snatching the torch, and made his hasty egress. He could not stand to linger a moment more in this place.

He retraced his steps to the hut by the river but found it abandoned. The fire's embers were cold, the oven cleaned out, and there was no sign of anyone nearby. The man had claimed he had another house up in the mountains. Perhaps, if Marduk searched for it, he might find the place.

Yet, the insistent force in the back of his mind had only redoubled after touching that tablet. It seemed to guide him onward, pull him toward ... something? Kingu, perhaps, for Marduk needs must still slay the Deep One to protect his people. If so, if his vision, unnerving as it had proved, had enhanced whatever sense was allowing him to track Kingu, then perhaps the stranger *had* helped Marduk, in the end.

Resolved, Marduk decided to follow his instinct—and the river—and continue his hunt. Whoever the stranger had been, a confrontation would have to wait.

THE RIVER CARVED its way through the coastal jungles of Mu. Ahead, a roaring cataract poured down the verdant slopes, throwing up a spray of mist across the vale. Peaks enclosed three sides of this place, with the only escape back the way he'd come, through the jungle and to the shore. Sharur's comforting weight strapped to his back, Marduk followed the riverbank, having to climb over water-slicked rocks to make the ascent. Had Kingu truly come this way? Could even a Deep One have swum up the rapids and eddies created by the numerous small drops in elevation? He had but instinct and dreams—hallucinations, mayhap— guiding him, and if someone else had told him such a thing, he'd have thought them mad.

Still, he found his feet carried him forward as if of their own accord, drawn ever by a frightful need to push further. Perhaps it was the work- ings of the Wheel of Fate or the will of the Hidden God, his hand upon Marduk's shoulder. Perhaps it was the sense of ineffable destiny he'd seen in Indra's seeking after a demon dragon. Regardless, he could not turn back now. This trek toward whatever end, he must see it through. These lives he saw were not his and yet so familiar; they guided his steps.

One foot upon a moss-covered rock, he paused, unable to shake the sense of something amiss here. He looked around, saw naught that seemed awry, and yet ... Marduk closed his eyes. The only sound the clamour of the waterfall, the rush of the rapids. Not a single bird cry, though the incessant chatter had dogged his every step through the jungle afore now. No chittering monkeys nor even the buzz of mosqui- toes. What would cause every creature to flee this place? Would they retreat from the presence of a Deep One, no matter how ancient or powerful?

Marduk snapped his eyes open, turned about once more, peering into the jungle. No sign of any fauna, Grim faced, he unslung Sharur before proceeding, its heft soothing to his nerves. Yes, something foul had disrupted the balance of nature in this valley. He looked to the sky; daylight waned. Marduk didn't think he much wanted to linger here once dusk closed its grip on this place. He could turn back now. The only thing pulling him forward was a niggling in the back of his mind, as if he thought himself some Oracle ... Had Kingu followed the river so far, to its source in the mountains?

He didn't know, couldn't know.

And still, he plodded onward, upward, climbing closer and closer to the cataract. The bruising of the sky came rapidly, even as he reached the falls, drawing close enough to see a recess behind them. A cave, perhaps shallow, in which a Deep One could hide from the sun. But why would the creature not bide in the river, then? Was it too swift to rest in? Marduk pushed forward, edging around behind the curtain of water.

He thought he heard a scrape of something rough over stone. So hard to make aught out over the roaring falls. Maybe his imagination played tricks on him. Sharur out ahead of him, Marduk pushed deeper into the gloom, peering one way and the next. The cave ran further back than he'd hoped, an incline descending into the bowels of the Earth, perhaps even burrowing into some nether Realm beyond the world of Man. He'd need a torch if he wanted to delve this place, though he was fair certain he did *not*.

A chittering echoed off stalactites, ringing through the cavern; this he had not imagined. In the distance, shadows moved, something large shifting its bulk. More clatter of—bone?—clanking upon rock. Not bone, he realised, when a single segmented leg moved within the rapidly receding line of sunlight—chitin. For the blue-tinged limb that revealed itself was arachnoid, and almost as tall as he was.

Heart hammering and a chill sweat beading upon his back, Marduk stepped back into the light. Was this what he'd pursued? Not Kingu, not a Deep One, but something yet more dire.

The creature advanced, its eight chitinous legs throwing up a gut-clenching clamour as it came forth, just far enough into the sunlight for Marduk to glimpse the thing in awful relief. Like a giant sea scorpion it seemed, save that it had the torso of a Man, albeit one whose flesh was encased in the same pale blue chitin as the rest of it. Its eyes gleamed in the dark, incandescent. The scorpion-man smacked together its pedi-palps, the clack of them worse even than the sound of its legs upon the stone.

Another demon spawn of Tiamat?

Though its mouth did not move, Marduk could have sworn the demon grinned at him. He felt it looked *into* him, as if every skittering appendage of this thing crawled across his soul. Instinct blared within Marduk, told him to run shrieking from this pool of Khaos. But if he did so, this thing would emerge in the night to stalk his men, crushing and poisoning and no doubt devouring their flesh. Was this why Kingu had come here, to summon forth this thing?

If Marduk balked now, if he gave ground, it would cost lives.

"Do you like the Girtablilu?" a voice asked from behind him. "Such they name the Old One in stories long back. 'Twas no mean feat to bring it here, I admit." Marduk spun to see a Deep One—Kingu, no doubt— emerging from the cave mouth, dripping wet, naked, armed with a blade that seemed carved of some alien spine. "Ah, but when the Queens are done, and the breach is torn wide, far greater spawn of the Elder Deep shall emerge into this world. Her taniwha shall come to hunt any remnants of your Giant bloodline who survive what soon impends."

Marduk eased his sword free, pointing its blade at Kingu and Sharur at the Girtablilu. "I know naught of what you speak, Deep One." Though, too, Kulullu had spoken of a war betwixt Titans and the spirits of the Otherworld. Whatever had unfolded in the dark of history, such knowledge was lost on this side.

"All the greater, then, your sin that your ilk should so ravage ours and yet fail to teach your offspring of the horrors you wrought. As if you can abrogate responsibility for crimes by burying them. Little does it matter whether you recall the days of Dark Faerie or the wars even before that. Either way, the price comes due, Giant prince. This Era ends this very night, though you shall not last long enough to witness the fall."

Marduk tried to withdraw, to keep them from catching him between them, but Kingu too circled, and the scorpion-man closed in. All Marduk could do was fall back until the cavern's edge lay behind him. Kingu had the right of it—so came his ending.

❦

Wherever Vritra passed, *death presaged it, the land drying into a husk. Indra pursued, mounted upon his seven-tusked elephant. He could see the serpent in the distance, its squamous black form miles long. Spurs rose from its back, and there, he saw the mound of horns bursting from its head.*

"Catch it," Indra whispered to his mount, and the elephant charged. Though it was no ordinary animal, still, primeval dread must have risen in the beast. Indra would not take it into battle, not this time. Not against such a foe.

Matarśivan had said Indra would not survive this battle, but Airavata need not share his ending. When he drew close enough, he leapt from the animal's back, surging Prana into his legs. His bound carried him across a fifty-foot arc, gave him time to draw Vajra off his back. As soon as he gripped the mace, it crackled with unshed lightning.

Indra landed in a crouch, bellowing a war cry. He rose, poured Prana into the weapon. Thunder ripped free of the clouds overhead. A flash of lightning.

That saurian bulk turned, bent to regard him with incandescent eyes, each big as his elephant.

With a grimace, Indra pointed Vajra at the demon dragon. A challenge. The last challenge, for each of them.

❊

HIS DARK CHORTLE echoing off the cavern wall, Kingu closed in upon Marduk, perhaps keen to claim the prey. The scorpion demon paced, its limbs clattering, but did not advance.

Marduk shook himself clear of the vision that had seized him. His eyes met Kingu's opalescent orbs. "I have slain fiends direr still than you or your Old One." Even as he spoke the words, he knew them for truth. He could not understand all of it, but he knew, he had been those men in his myriad visions. He had been so many men, so many warriors, down through the Ages.

Kingu bared shark teeth at him, affronted. The Deep One lunged, its spine-blade sweeping in with whirlwind speed. Of its own accord, Marduk's Pneuma surged, and he moved just as fast, parrying with his akinakes. Sharur closed in on the opening so created, caught Kingu in the side. With a thunderous rapport the Deep One was sent hurtling across the cavern, clearing the path betwixt Marduk and the Girtablilu.

The demon looked to him, perhaps aghast at his temerity in striking its master. The sound that erupted from the scorpion-man as it charged was less a roar than a cacophony of discordant shrieks. For a single heartbeat, the clamour froze Marduk in place. Then, flooding Pneuma, he raced at his foe and dropped into a slide, skidding beneath its stabbing legs. The Girtablilu slammed into the cavern wall, shaking the earth and tearing showers of stone free in its fury.

Still on the ground, Marduk launched forward, swiping with both his mace and akinakes. The two crossed upon one of those legs. Chitin exploded along with stinging, bile-coloured fluids that burst over

Marduk's face and torso. The demon howled, whirling around, forcing him to roll aside.

That barbed tail stabbed at him, lightning fast. A Pneuma-fuelled shove off the ground sent Marduk flipping through the air, legs cartwheeling to carry him to the side. He landed on his feet, came about, but the scorpion-man charged forward so fast all Marduk could do was leap aside once more. A pedipalp snapped at him, sought to hold him fast so the barb could impale him with its deadly venom. Roaring, Marduk brought Sharur down upon that claw. Another eruption of gore burst forth as he struck, obliterating another limb. He surged his Pneuma, tried to pour it into Sharur, as he'd seen Ninurta and Indra do.

Naught happened.

The tail jabbed in, fast, took him in the left shoulder, punching even through Pneuma-hardened skin. Searing venom burst into the wound. His akinakes spilled from his limp, useless fingers as tingling numbness spread down his arm. Rivers of agonies coursed through his veins with each beat of his heart. Convulsions took him.

POISON COURSED THROUGH HIS VEINS, threatened to stop his heart. On his knees, Indra glared at Vritra, and for a moment, the dark dragon regarded him as something more than mere prey. All around Indra stretched a withered landscape, the earth desiccated and cracked, brought to ruin at Vritra's passage. The spirits of the land too had perished, their souls devoured by the serpent, as would be all the cosmos. The incandescent eye of Indra's foe peered at him, lanced his soul, drawing up every painful memory of his life, supping on his regrets and faded hopes.

Unblinking, unspeaking, without the least communication betwixt them, somehow it mocked him. It taunted him for having lost Kali. It nettled him for his failures to protect his people, he the would-be king of the Adityas.

With agonising slowness, the serpent dragon reared higher, ready to strike. It drew out the moment of his destruction, savoured it, savoured too the dread and sorrow and shame it must kindle in his breast. But the dark dragon, for all its piercing insight, did not seem to glimpse what lay past all that grief—that ember of grim determination. Matarśivan had not mis-chosen—this, Indra swore. The Rishi had bade him take this step, accept this burden, because he knew Indra had something others did not: no matter the suffering compounded upon him, Indra would not bow. He would not break.

He surged Prana through his veins, burning away the poison. His fingers grasped around Vajra's hilt, and he hefted the mace one last time. And into the gleaming weapon Indra poured all of his roiling emotions. Into it went the shame and regret and pain. In went fear. Vajra became a conduit for Indra's wrath, for his tenacity, for his ... choice. He too had chosen to accept this burden.

Roaring, Indra rose to face his foe. Galvanic arcs leapt from Vajra, connecting him to the ruined land with coruscating threads. Parabolas of lightning spat their crackling spawn in all directions, repaying taunt for taunt to the hateful dark god before Indra. He was bellowing still, his voice melding with the deafening cacophony of earthbound thunder. Blinding fulgurations burst about him, white hot and furious.

Before the relentless storm, even the saurian god faltered.

Indra kicked off the ground, flying at his prey's head, leapt a hundred feet in the air. A vortex of lightning engulfed him.

❧

THE GIRTABLILU JERKED FREE its barbed tail, and Marduk pitched to his knees without the thing holding him up. In his periphery, he saw Kingu rising, stumbling toward him. The scorpion-man pranced about him, its gait rendered more awkward by its missing leg, though no less abhorrent. The demon closed in. That foul incandescence in its eyes seemed to seep from its mouth as well. Marduk could see himself being devoured, consumed by that infernal heat.

Poison was sapping his will, his Pneuma. Sapping it, yes, but not enough to break it. Destruction could be preservation.

The pedipalp surged in at his head. Marduk swept Sharur up, smacking the attack away. The scorpion-man recoiled, made fearful by the loss of two limbs already. Its momentary retreat gave Marduk space to regain his feet, though the ground seemed undulant beneath him, and he swayed. He wanted to retch.

As Indra had done, he flooded Pneuma through his blood, felt it burning away the poison. The tingling in his arm, the searing in his veins, it began to abate. Marduk gritted his teeth, felt the iron taste of blood trickling between them as he glared first at the demon, then at Kingu. The Deep One edged closer, but the look of uncertainty upon his visage was unmistakable.

Marduk spat a wad of phlegm and blood at Kingu's feet. "Perhaps ... you will be the one ... not here to see ... the end ..." He chuckled, though pain shot through his chest at it.

With a snarl, Kingu lunged at him, leaping into the air like an arcing bolt. Marduk caught him by the throat with his left hand. Kingu's eyes widened, unable to believe Marduk could use that poisoned arm. Marduk spun, whirling the Deep One overhead to slam straight down onto the cavern floor with a resounding impact. Bellowing, pouring all his pain and fury and Pneuma into the mace, Marduk brought Sharur down upon the spirit. Lightning surged, burst from the head in a white-hot flash, thunder echoing off the cavern. Flesh and bone and the rock beneath it shattered, burst in a spray of dust and gore. Lightning leapt against the ceiling and sundered stalactites, bringing them down in a series of rumbling crashes.

A chain of spiderwebbing cracks rent the ground. The pulped flesh of the Deep One seeped into those cracks.

Marduk rose, pointing the filth-caked mace at the Girtablilu, coruscating arcs still leaping about its head. Within the mace, thunder rumbled. The creature faltered, pacing sideways like some crab. Another chorus of chittering shrieks escaped it, then it began to retreat into the depths of the cavern, perhaps deciding it preferred the stygian darkness whence it had emerged to facing down Marduk. Either way, Marduk had not the strength to pursue. He let the Pneuma flow to Sharur wane, and the lightning winked out.

He limped from the cave, and out into the last light of the dying day. Had slaying Kingu saved his people?

As the rush of battle ebbed, his pain came rushing back in, choking him, threatening to drag him into unconscious depths. This, he knew he could not afford. *Continue forward,* he told himself and thus trudged back along the river. Making his way downslope in his current state was slow torture. Each slickened rock threatened to send him spilling face-first into a tumble. Each muddy incline, which he had climbed with ease to reach this place, had become an obstacle in his path.

Night closed in around him. A chill breeze swept down from the mountains. He wanted to pitch over, to collapse in a heap and let sleep claim him. He wanted to rest, for days—longer. The last trickles of his Pneuma were all that kept him on his feet.

He pushed further, into the jungle. He could not rest. Not with all Kingu had claimed. The Deep One had said the end was coming, something worse, perhaps, even than Marduk's father had anticipated. Worse than an Old One demon crawled out of the Khaos, worse than aught anyone could have known. Something akin to Vritra.

But the World had endured, which meant Indra had succeeded in destroying that abomination, even at the cost of his own life. If Indra was Marduk, then that meant Marduk, too, could face whatever was coming. He must face it.

At last, sometime past midnight, he breached the jungle's edge and came to look upon the dark water of the Muian Sea. Waves lapped the shore, promising ... something. A sense of foreboding so strong as to become crippling rose in his gut.

The tremors began. Quakes so strong they hurled him to his knees. With a roar loud beyond endurance, the land was rived, a colossal rent tearing open in the distance. The land split in twain, a seemingly bottomless chasm cleft from sea to jungle, swallowing sand and trees until even the mountains began to collapse inward, falling away into discordant depths. The churning ocean flooded over the fissure from both sides in cataracts that seemed potent enough to drain the sea.

Thunder crackled amid gathering clouds. Further out, Marduk gawped to see a mountain-sized wave rising from the depths.

And he knew Kingu had spoken the truth. The Elder Goddess, Tiamat, was come.

PART IV

And thus behold from chthonian depths,
  The scope of dread apprehension.
  Ere the end, with Ontos laid bare,
  Our prideful knees creak and bend,
  Leaving an echoing question.
  What frightful transgressions,
  Have this outré doom so wakened?
  — Translated excerpt from the Sefer Raziel

16

KIRKE

754 Bronze Age

*G*iving Kassandra over to be raised by Priam had sat ill with Damkina, had become a festering wound betwixt her and Mithra, one not soon assuaged. Nevertheless, Damkina had abandoned the girl to be raised in the royal halls of Troy and told herself it would be a better future for her. At least for a time. But Damkina knew well the fate before her daughter, almost as bitter as the one that had befallen Pandora, and that knowledge wormed away at her, cancerous and agonising.

She dove deeper and deeper into bowls of wine and, when that lost its power to blunt the edge of her melancholy, into brews of poppy and her alchemical creation to lose herself in dream. Those oneiromantic wanderings she scarce recalled.

Aspadas's son, Kurus II, had conquered Neshia, seizing the Ninevehan Empire and replacing it with one at his new capital of Babilim. The Babilimian Empire spread, and from the haunted vault of her dreams, Damkina watched Kumari Kandam fall before his sandalled feet. Soon, the Empire spread to encompass Phoenikia, for the emperor longed for the strong ships of that land and the for the spice trade they brought in from Nusantara. From there, she suspected he would set his sights upon Ilium; when Damkina had abandoned Kassandra, she had turned from Priam, too, and no lasting friendship existed between Babilim and the Phrygian polis. Kurus II mostlike intended to sail to Ilium and besiege it. Men had begun to call him Kurus the Great, and some thought he would take all the Thalassa World. Priam, with aid from Artemis, had become one of the greatest kings on that sea and thus one of the greatest threats to Kurus's supremacy.

Of course, Mithra and his Magi already knew that was not what would happen—Kirke had told him the future she had lived, long ago. That the Magi did not prepare Kurus II for an attack meant Mithra thought any loss of life necessary. King Krosius of Phoeba had made the mistake of invading Tyros, backed by an Elládosi fleet. Kurus's force had brought the Phoeban king back in chains.

The invasion of Phoenikia had perhaps, in Krosius's mind, be a preemptive strike lest Kurus move on Lydia next.

Shrouded, glamoured, and standing in the shadowed recesses of the great hall of Babilim, Damkina watched as the once-proud king of Phoeba was dragged across the tiled floor. Immortals flung the Lydian monarch to his knees before Kurus's opulent throne.

The great king glowered down at his fallen adversary, stroking his black beard. With the gold-trimmed frescoes above and the vast vaulting ceiling, Kurus looked for all the world chosen by some heavenly pantheon and infused with their power. Which was, of course, the point of the Magi in designing the hall thus. Kurus beckoned to Mithra at his side, and the Magus leant close, Damkina unable to hear what passed betwixt them.

Soon, however, word spread that the king had ordered a great pyre built in the courtyard. A shudder seized Damkina at the thought Kurus intended to have Krosius burnt alive. As if in a dream, she drifted out to the courtyard along with the rest of the court and the Immortals. She watched as the defeated king was forced to ascend the mound of his brutal execution and was bound there by a pair of Immortals.

As the Immortals lit the pyre, the Lydian took to mumbling under his breath, and whatever it was, Kurus held up a hand. "What does he say?"

Mithra translated for him. "He says a wise man told him no one alive is happy. That this sage had come to his court and dismissed all his gathered wealth as trivialities. But Krosius failed to take heed and sought ever more wealth and power."

"And lost it all," Kurus said. A moment, he glanced about his grand palace in Babilim. "Douse the flames!"

Later, Damkina thought to wonder if Kurus had intended to spare Krosius all along, for the man pledged his undying loyalty to the great king who had pulled him from death's doorstep. Pledged, and confessed the truth of his invasion. That his greed had been sparked by Zeus, who saw in Babilim a rising threat and sought to weaken them without open war. A tactic that had worked, to an extent, for though victorious, Kurus had lost men and ships both in his pursuit of Krosius from Lydia and into Phrygia. Certainly it left the Babilimian Empire ill prepared for war with Elládos or Ilium.

Thus did Mithra go to Ilium, not as a conqueror but as an emissary of friendship on behalf of Babilim. When he returned with Kassandra as a bride for Kurus II, Damkina had almost choked upon her rising bile. Her daughter, dragged a continent away from her home, was wed to the emperor of Babilim. No one had ever bothered to ask what Kassandra might have wanted.

In the Hanging Gardens around Etemenanki, Damkina walked with Kassandra. Overhead, storm clouds rumbled, threatening much-needed rain. A hundred times, Damkina had considered telling the girl she was her mother, but what would such accomplish, save creating an onslaught of questions to which she had no good answers? Or perhaps just one question, in myriad variation: why had she abandoned the girl to be raised by her father as the bastard princess of Ilium?

"Your dreams still haunt you?" Damkina instead asked, unable to bear the weight of confession when she could provide no answer to the question.

Kassandra whirled about, as if dancing to music she alone could hear, and swept an elegant bow before a sprig of jasmine. "Memories of might-haves flit upon darkened stages, mummery of things to come."

Yeah, sure, Damkina would take that as an affirmative. "I can help you learn to control the dreams."

"Help?" The girl's face crinkled as if she struggled to parse the concept. Kassandra never met Damkina's gaze, nor anyone else's, so far as Damkina knew. Prometheus had sought to help her, and Apollon too as Damkina recalled, but neither of those Oracles were oneiromancers. "What help lies in the face of revelations too bitter to swallow, when gazing upon Truth we realise, at last, we were never what we thought ..."

Damkina winced and drew her daughter into an embrace. Had she raised the girl, had she tended her oneiromancy from its first onset, might she have averted the madness that had seized Kassandra? She could never know that.

History must unfold ...

The refrain stuck in Damkina's throat like ... like a revelation too bitter to swallow. A chill wracked her, a wonder, as she turned to look upon her daughter's wild eyes. Just how much did the girl see?

❧

"CAN YOU HELP HER?" Damkina asked Morpheus, the two of them walking along the promenade beside the river, outside the city. Across the Ufratu, palm trees sprung up along the bank and beyond the cultivated fields fed by canals. The river was spanned by a stone bridge high enough ships could sail beneath it. The road from that bridge ran to the great gates and thence became the central breezeway. Babilim was an architectural wonder, she had to admit. Once, it had held her heart. Once, it had seemed home.

Damkina had striven to aid Kassandra in controlling her dreams, but her daughter's mind was cracked by the strain of her oneiromancy. Her Oracular gift had come too strong—until the woman lost herself beneath the enormity of it and was left wandering the sea of time, as though an aimless, formless shade in the ether. And Damkina's failure to pull Kassandra out of it chafed more than pride—it savaged her heart. Who was she, if she failed both of her daughters as a mother?

Morpheus, whom too she had once seen as her child, grimaced, holding his peace. The other oneiromancer slowed, drifting along the walkway as though caught in his own waking dream.

"Can you not aid her?" Damkina asked. Then another thought occurred. "Has Mithra forbidden you from intervening?"

That drew him up short. "Mithra sought a child of her bloodline." Kassandra had already given Kurus II a son, Kabujiya, named for Kurus's father. Did that mean Mithra had no further interest in Damkina's daughter? "He means her no ill," Morpheus added. "Only ..."

"Only *what*?"

"He said it was important that she bear more children to ensure the continuance of the royal line, should anything befall the young heir."

Damkina waved that away. Such was well understood in a dynasty, though she imagined Kassandra would have preferred Kurus direct his attention toward his concubines rather than toward her. "Then help her."

Morpheus sighed. "I'm not certain I can. Were her mind more stable, she might learn to control, to block the visions, but I fear her too far gone for such subtleties. Besides which, I cannot well cloister myself alone with the emperor's wife, to ward her dreams. It would be all but impossible to keep word of such a visit from spreading among the slaves, and you know how they would take such a thing. Rumour would spread like a flash flood through the city, and men would name Kurus cuckolded by his Magus." He looked to Damkina, ready for her objection. "From another room, I might enter her mind, redirect one nightmare at a time, but I could offer little lasting peace to her. Am I to spend the rest of my life set to no other task save helping your daughter sleep?"

"She won't live forever," Damkina said, petulantly.

Morpheus scratched his beard, discomfited, ill pleased at having to deny Damkina her request. Was it hard for him, his role? "There's something else you should know, Damkina," he said after a moment. "Your brother, Aeëtes ... Word came from Kolchis he abandoned his throne."

Damkina had ceased to think of Aeëtes as her brother when she stopped being Kirke. To allow herself to think otherwise, after what she had done with him ...

"They say, after he slew his daughter, the deepest of dolours took him, and he retreated into ever darker studies of the Art." Now Damkina had winced, both to hear of Medea's death and because she had set Aeëtes on the path of a sorcerer. She had destroyed him, her blood, because Mithra commanded it. Because it had always happened, a circle without beginning or end, and thus without reason save for its perpetuance. Circles within circles, the endless coils of the pitiless ouroboros.

She had done this, all because if she demurred, if she refused to uphold these odious loops, the whole cosmos would unfurl.

It was hard to swallow. "We are Unseen."

"We are Unseen," Morpheus agreed. She wondered if the mantra offered him more comfort than it did her.

ENRAGED that Zeus had prompted Krosius's invasion, Kurus spent the next decade preparing an invasion of Elládos. Mithra and the Magi, warning him such an endeavour was doomed, succeeded in forestalling his wrath, but Damkina knew it was only a matter of time before he forced the issue.

In the emperor's private council chambers, Damkina stood beside Morpheus, the both of them hooded and concealed, observing. Mithra spoke to the emperor, standing around a table bearing a map of the Thalassa world, with wooden models representing the forces of the strongest poleis. It was interesting, watching Mithra pluck the strings of one of the most powerful Men in the world like a well-tuned harp. The Unseen One strummed upon nascent fears to convince Kurus he had foes closing in from all sides.

"To ensure your supremacy of the World, you need a sign from the gods," Mithra said. "The people of the empire are immensely loyal to you, sire, but by demonstrating your divine favour, you instil in them a righteous zeal that will allow them to sweep away all foes. No man fights so fiercely as he who is convinced he does holy work."

Damkina folded her arms across her chest, almost feeling pity for Kurus. For even an emperor fell prey to the same weakness of the soul of which Mithra spoke. All Men, conscious of their mortality, sought to believe themselves blessed by something greater than themselves. It suited their fragile egos to think themselves set above other Men by virtue of their knowledge of truth. They forever sought to name themselves as *chosen*. Faith ever became the tool by which the powerful could induce the weak to praise their oppression as righteousness.

"And how can I prove I have this favour?" Kurus demanded.

Mithra had laid plain the fallacy of thought before the emperor, and Kurus had stridden straight into it, too proud to imagine himself but one more benighted fool. Men forever danced around the Ontos with their pale, self-important imitations of its Truth.

"Deep in the Empty Desert lies a ruin of the city of the gods. Within lost Gorias, find the sacred flame of the divine, and return with it, and even the tyrant Zeus may tremble before you."

Satisfaction spread across Kurus's face like an inevitable tide, the man already envisioning himself marching proud, hands ablaze with deific infernos. Did it ever cross his mind Mithra sent him to his death or that Gorias would become his tomb? Damkina rather doubted it. Given he used, abused, and cast aside Kassandra—named her a madwoman on more than one occasion!—Damkina was well glad the time to rid themselves of him had arrived.

KURUS, of course, never returned from Gorias, and in time, his son, Kabujiya II, took the throne. But Kabujiya had inherited his mother's gift of prophecy, and his visions, though they allowed him to annex Kemet, eventually drove him to madness. A shame, as the Order had hoped to produce in him a psychic of great use, heir to the throne of the vast Babilimian Empire. Worse still, given he was Damkina's grandson.

Damkina spent innumerable hours walking with Kassandra, trying to soothe nerves abraded by having seen what she could not handle. That was, she supposed, what it came down to. Kassandra had witnessed too much of the Ontos, and it had cracked her. Damkina's daughter had the potential to be, perhaps, an oneiromancer greater even than Morpheus. Greater than Hekate had been. Greater than any upon the face of Gaia.

There was a legend, the Flower-Faced Girl, said to be the greatest oneiromancer in all time. When Kassandra's burdens became too great, when the girl would weep, scarcely aware of the World for its burdens, Damkina would tell and retell the legend of Blodeuwedd. Little did it matter if the story held even a kernel of truth, for it seemed to comfort her daughter.

Kassandra, however, lost in her own reality, scarcely seemed able to connect with her son, and Damkina came to believe Kabujiya dwelt in a haunted existence he alone could see. By his late teenage years, he grew to see threats lurking in every shadow, even as he plundered the riches of Hy-Brasil. He took to opening the tombs of pharaohs in Memphis, infuriating the Kemetians. He sent men to plumb the Jungles of Kush looking for lost cities that had probably never existed. The emperor's unquiet mind only compounded on his return to Babilim, and one day, in Damkina's presence, he called his friend Prexaspes to him, for he trusted the man above all others. Kabujiya had begun reducing the number of Magi allowed in his presence, as if he mistrusted even his divine advisors, so Damkina supposed she was lucky he permitted her around. Perhaps, as a woman, he thought her little threat to his presence. Either way, it had become her role to watch the emperor in all of his meetings and, where she could, to mitigate the madder of her grandson's decrees. Thus, wary, did Damkina stand behind the throne for this by-and-large private audience between the emperor and his confidant.

For a time, the emperor paced about his hall, hands gesturing wildly at visions only he could see. At last he whirled upon Prexaspes. "Tell me, friend, what is it the people of the empire say of me? Do they conspire behind my back, whispering in the night about their *mad* king?"

So he knew. Even held within the surreal scape of his mercurial mind, he knew the people thought him deranged. Would such knowledge assuage his ailment as he sought to hold onto the public's approval, or would it exacerbate the condition as paranoia fed itself? Damkina feared the latter and did not think Mithra would be well pleased with this turn of events. Assuming he did not already know. The years had given her too much time to wonder if some flaw lay within her blood. Never had Damkina well fit with others, always risking drowning in the currents of life that others waded through without the least thought. Even so, Damkina had lived a life of some measure, as had Pandora and Hekate, others. But Kassandra, Kabujiya, it was as if the faults in Damkina—yes, the brilliance, but also the divergence in thought—were reflected back upon themselves through a chain of mirrors, trapping their minds in the infinite mazes of their thoughts.

Another wonder had long weighed upon Damkina: did the psychic perceptions come from the divergence of consciousness, or did they create it? Or, perhaps, was even that yet another ouroboros?

"They say naught save your praises, Master," Prexaspes said with well-advised caution.

The emperor took three long strides toward his friend, his fingers twitched uncontrolled at his side. "Speak freely!"

"T-they say you, perhaps, from time to time …"

"Speak!" The emperor flung his hands up in wild gesture. Like his mother, he did not meet the gaze of those he spoke to, rather seeming to stare into some middle distance perceivable only to him.

By now, Prexaspes had begun to tremble, and Damkina little blamed him. At her side, she clenched her fists, fearing what must soon impend. "They say sometimes you may overindulge in the wine, a little."

"Ha! Then their earlier claim of praises is a lie!"

"N-no, sire!" Prexaspes blurted. His eyes widened as he must have realised he had just contradicted his emperor.

"My visions give me the means to test the veracity of your claim, *loyal* friend." He snapped his fingers, and at once a small squad of Immortals escorted in a quivering boy.

"No …" Prexaspes moaned, though he did not approach either the boy or the emperor.

Kabujiya strode toward his throne and snatched a bow from beside it, even as the Immortals stepped away from the boy. "I shall launch an arrow in your son's direction. If you have spoken falsely of the people's loyalty, the gods will guide my arrow to his heart. If you speak the truth, surely then they will cause the arrow to fly wide, and I will know you remain a true friend to this empire."

With that, Kabujiya nocked his arrow.

"Please, sire," the man pleaded. "Please, I beseech you not to—"

The emperor drew and loosed, and across the wide hall, a boy of no more than ten collapsed in a heap. Damkina winced but forced herself to keep looking. Her blood had wrought this.

"Ha!" the emperor exclaimed. "Bring the chirurgeons and see if it struck his heart true."

Damkina, however, did not wait to find out. When she was certain no one was looking, she shadow-stepped from the Mortal Realm and fled the throne room with all possible haste.

"*This*," Prexaspes grated, "and after I slew his brother for him."

That made Damkina sit up straighter. She had invited the grieving father to join her, Mithra, and Heka for wine. They sat in a secluded hall decked with finery from across the Babilimian Empire, from the Phoenikian-dyed tapestries to the Nysan sandalwood table carved with tales from Neshian lore. They sat, they drank, and Heka and Mithra held their silence while Damkina consoled the man.

Surely Prexaspes knew they had called him here to bribe him for his silence about the crime, but he came and he drank, and Damkina allowed him to spill his laments in the confines of this private chamber. For here, and here alone, would he ever be able to air such grief.

"Smerdis?" she asked now, setting her wine goblet on the low table. She stole a glance to Mithra, who frowned.

Kabujiya had come to the Magi, saying he had dreamt Smerdis sat on the throne. And whilst the Magi had pointed out, justifiably, that this might happen many years down the line, even after Kabujiya had perished from natural causes, the emperor remained pensive. Thus, he had sent his brother to govern Asur on the sea separating Kumari Kandam from Mu.

Prexaspes grunted in assent. "He had me escort his brother to his posting. Only before we reached it, I was to drown him in the mouth of the river and make it look an accident."

And wait a short time to report it, Damkina assumed.

Damkina looked to Mithra once more. For generations the man had striven to create an Oracle king on the throne, and this madman was the result. Damkina's tainted grandson. Or had Mithra known how this would play out? It was a question she would never dare voice aloud.

History must unfold, she told herself, and for what paltry comfort the mantra yet offered. If Mithra had known, though, in sending her to Ilium to comfort Priam over the loss of his kin, if, perhaps through Morpheus's prophetic dreams, he had planned all this ... Was such possible?

For the first time, Mithra broke his sullen silence. "But Smerdis shall return and shall sit on the throne, even as the Oracle Kabujiya foretold."

"He is dead, I assure you," Prexaspes said into his wine.

Mithra looked to Heka, who waved a hand over his face. With the glamour, he looked almost identical to the emperor's deceased brother. Had she not known better, even Damkina could not have easily distinguished between them. Which meant, of course, that for the court, the sane, wiser son of Kurus the Great would come to oust his mad brother from the throne. It was, she supposed, for the best. Even if it meant her grandson would ...

Still, doubts lingered. Mithra had shown her the face of Fate and the shape of Truth. Had he not ...?

WHEN KABUJIYA WAS DEAD, supplanted by his sane brother, Kassandra came to look upon the corpse of her son, enshrined in his royal tomb beneath Etemenanki. A servant bore a guttering torch, casting sickly shadows over the body of Damkina's grandson, and over her daughter as well.

The years had worn the Oracle, or maybe her visions had done so. Grey streaked Kassandra's auburn hair, and worry lines creased her face. Damkina wanted to reach out, to take her daughter's hand, but the girl did not like to be touched, and Damkina had little comfort. Kassandra did not weep, at least not here. She did not, in fact, even look at the body so much as she looked past it.

"Your other son now sits the throne," Damkina lied, hoping Kassandra would take some comfort in even the false Smerdis.

"Blood seeps 'twixt fingers clenched too tightly. A line ended in pulsing wounds no false seeming can staunch."

Damkina clutched her hands to steady them. Kassandra knew. She knew the real Smerdis was dead, as well. Both her sons gone now, lost to machinations they scarce understood.

She had the horrifying sense she was losing Kassandra, too, that the woman drifted into the same darkness that had claimed her sons. Damkina could not forestall herself from laying a hand upon Kassandra's shoulder.

The woman shuddered, shrugged it off.

There was no comfort to be shared.

As Damkina had feared, Kassandra faded until, in the end, it was a but a shadow that passed from Gaia. For that shadow, still, Damkina wept. Long did she linger in the crypt below the palace when they interred Kassandra beside the body of her son. And when they pulled her from that place, a piece of herself she left buried there as well.

❦

A dozen years later, Mithra bade Damkina and Morpheus attend him when he went to court. Of course, she knew he would have some machination or other; he always did. Still, she never would have guessed it when, with a song she could never imitate, Mithra stripped the glamour from Heka before all the gathered throng.

"This traitorous Magus has deceived you with his Art!" Mithra cried. "He has slain both the emperor and his brother and now wear's one of their faces to usurp the throne!"

Heka, for his part, gawped, as if in utter disbelief Mithra could betray him. Even at the moment when an Immortal's spear pierced his chest, his visage revealed more shock than horror. Damkina imagined it mirrored her own.

When she looked, she saw four more Magi waiting in the fringes, making their numbers an auspicious—and no doubt intentional—seven. The rest, it unfolded before her like a play, the entranced audience swept up in the dream it induced.

"The heirs of Kurus the Great are no more!" Morpheus proclaimed. "Treachery has brought low the line of kings, and now our vast empire teeters upon a precipice. Leaderless, we shall become prey to the encroachment of the Elládosi!" The oneiromancer Magus turned about, playing to the court, taking in their reactions. "A choice now lies before us: whether to surrender all we have accomplished and fall back into our disparate states ..." He waited for the import of his words to settle upon the crowd. He spoke not of freedom from the chains of the empire but of the loss of prestige they would all face as their great empire became a husk. Pride, so oft, proved stronger than wisdom. "Or to appoint a new king, of a new line."

"Who?" some noble among the court demanded.

Morpheus turned, slowly, as if considering. As if he had not walked down this hall with every word rehearsed and polished to maximum effect. All Damkina could think was, *"Why was I alone not told of this?"*

"I can see none better than he who uncovered this conspiracy," Morpheus said at last, spinning to indicate Mithra. "One who, like the perilous rulers of Elládos across the sea, has Titan blood in his veins. Who better to protect us in our darkest hour but an Anunnak god-king?" He dropped to one knee before the chief Magus. One by one, at irregular intervals no-doubt calculated to seem spontaneous, the other four Magi bent the knee to Mithra. And slowly, so too did the court.

Damkina was not conscious of having knelt before the new emperor, and yet, she too was on one knee staring up at him.

ॐ

"I TOLD YOU, ONCE," Mithra said, now occupying the emperor's luxurious private chambers, "that you would be the first to know the identity of this Era's Destroyer."

Damkina swallowed, unable to keep from fidgeting with her cloak. A thread had begun to fray on one end, taunting her and demanding she pluck at it in every free moment. "Yeah. So the Eschaton draws nigh at last."

"A few centuries yet, but the boy shall be Titan and thus have time to grow into his powers."

"Shall be?" She forced herself to drop the damn cloak. "He's not even born yet, then."

"Not yet. We knew your blood would give rise to a powerful Oracle ..." He held her with his intense gaze and she fought the urge to squirm.

His meaning slithered in upon her, wormlike as it burrowed through her soul. "Kassandra. Her sons."

Mithra did not bother to answer that. "They were flawed, unfit to be vessel to the Destroyer's soul, and it was incarnated in another Elládosi. One that will perish soon, in the impending war against Ilium." He spoke with such certainty of things to come. Once such conviction had balmed the wounds Fate had inflicted upon her; she began to think herself but a pawn upon this board. Mithra's surety about the future felt more like chains than salves, now. "Who better," the man said, "to serve as mother of the Destroyer than the most trusted, most valued ally of the Unseen One."

A dream rose up then, though she had striven to fight against it, had not wanted to know a future if she was to have no control over it. Heat flushed her neck, her cheeks, her ears. "I ..."

"You can give birth to the next iteration of this Earth." By birthing the destruction of this one. But she knew it all for necessity. Such was Fate, and Fate was the preservation of life on Gaia. It was the aversion of total Khaos and eternal damnation. It had to all mean something, all her sacrifices, all her pain.

Civilisation rises and flourishes, but in time, corruption grows. When the World threatens to crumble beneath the weight of its darkness, the Destroyer arises to usher in a new Era. Life continues, and the Wheel keeps spinning. History must unfold. These things, he had told her, and she needed to believe them.

So the mother of the Destroyer was, in the end, as Mithra claimed, the one who gave the gift of life to Mankind. How could anyone deny such an honour?

Heart pounding, she let fall the shoulders of her dress.

BENEATH THE PALACE, beneath the crypts, lay the aquifer the priests called Apsu. From Apsu rose springs rich in minerals, and within these, Damkina birthed her son, the one child she would finally—after losing the chance with both her daughters—have the chance to raise herself.

Upon a stone in the pool, submerged below her waist in warm water, she cradled little Marduk to her breast. How was she to believe the beautiful, innocent babe in her arms could serve as a catalyst for the apocalypse? How could any mother ever suspect her flesh and blood of being capable of such unfathomable carnage? Looking into his eyes, as he clutched her finger with his whole hand, she mused upon such thoughts over and over.

Was Ananke, as the name implied, necessity?

It was one thing to discuss the concept, but to imagine it real now ... to see this adorable, squawking bundle in her arms swimming through oceans of blood and scaling mountains of death, it tore at the soul. It carved pieces of her heart away until all that remained was a raw, bloody sliver that refused to die.

Mithra came in, regal and distant, this man to whom she had given millennia of—almost—unquestioning service. He knelt beside her pool and held out his arms, and she let him hold his son. "Have you named him?" he asked, though she suspected he knew his name, for he claimed the names of all eight Destroyers were carved into the Tablet of Destiny upon the first iteration of the Earth.

"Marduk," she said.

"Marduk," he cooed, tickling the babe's cheek.

Damkina opened her mouth, choked on the words she could not say. Then forced them out anyway. "He'll die. At the end, he'll die."

Mithra frowned, shutting his eyes. "Not even Titans live forever, whatever they tell themselves. It is the lot of the Destroyer to perish in triumph." When he opened his eyes, he had this faraway look in them. "Well do you know the price, should he fail to make his stand."

The price ... *everything*. All the cosmos, swallowed in consumptive Darkness. Every soul in creation subjected to agonies that would make Tartarus seem but a stroll on a summer eve in comparison.

But Marduk must die for it.

She thought of Odysseus, whom she had loved and allowed to die because she had not tried hard enough to change fate. She thought of dear, sweet *Pandora*, her first child. Her babe, out there, lost in the sea of time. Giving her up had rent Damkina's soul asunder. She thought of Kassandra, whom she had denied and allowed to wither into shadow in the name of Ananke. In the name of Mithra's accursed Wheel of Fate ...

"No mother can stand by and watch her child die without fighting, tooth and claw, against the end, inevitable or not." Though weakened from the birthing, she fought to infuse iron into her words.

Mithra nodded slowly, looking at her. There was a sadness there, running so deep whole cities could have drowned in it. "No, I know that. And you shan't have to watch, dear Kirke." He shook his head. "Not watch." Before she realised what he was about, he had slapped a hand over her mouth and nose, clamping them shut. With his other arm, he yet cradled Marduk.

In a surge of panic, Damkina flailed, smacking his arm, desperate to pry it free. Her vision faded to black at the fringes. She poured what

Pneuma she had remaining into Potency, but still, his arm was an adamant rod pinning her place. She'd sooner have lifted the whole palace than move him.

"Much though I wish otherwise," Mithra said, staring into her eyes, "the boy cannot grow up with a mother. To be what history needs, I must hone the softness out of him. Besides, this body is but a vessel. You see, the Destroyer has not yet died. When he does, I will use the soul-stealing sorcery of the Queens of Mu to ensure his soul is brought into this body. You would not allow that, I know, for it would mean the soul of your boy would be suppressed. I don't know whether you'll believe this, but I ... I'm sorry, Kirke. I would have given you better, if Fate so allowed."

Her frantic attempts to escape had begun to wane. She knew, then, why Ningal could have betrayed her father, this god-king. For one willing to make any sacrifice to achieve his aim rendered himself inhuman in aspect. If this was god-like dedication, then the divine was a toxin, a pollutant of fanaticism.

She was so tired ...

"Trust to the Wheel of Fate ..." Faint words, whispered into the oncoming sea of darkness that rose around her.

17

PANDORA

400 Dark Age

*P*andora appeared nestled in the folded hands of the enormous statue that lay within the Anunnaki temple in the Hursag Mountains. A flood of dizziness swept over her, sending her toppling to one side, close to plummeting over the thirty-foot drop to the floor. A murmur of voices from below greeted her, unaware of her presence, though to keep it that way, she had to stifle the urge to retch. A sharp, metallic taste filled her mouth. When she brushed her lips with her hand, her palm came away stained crimson.

What was happening to her? She had become so reliant upon the Box she had never once stopped to question whether being shunted through time and space, over and over, might have some deleterious effect on her body. Even flush with Pneuma as she was, perhaps a mortal form could only stand but so much strain. She wiped away more blood. It mattered little; she was nigh done with all this.

In the temple below, Mithra and Nunamnir stood on either side of the central fire pit, the sputter of its dwindling flames limning both Titans in eerie light and squirming shadows. Her investigations had revealed that, whilst Mithra's fleet converged upon Mugedang, he had already landed a number of other vessels amid the mountains of the Dreaming Lands. It had seemed a fair assumption that, as he tried on Elládos, here he planned a two-pronged assault upon Mu, one by land, and one by sea.

Thus she had come here, to the mountain redoubt, knowing he must intend to marshal his forces alongside his ally.

"Suen's forces close in upon Shalmali," Nunamnir said. "As for ours, if we push through the desert, the queens will never see us coming. In their shallow minds, they cannot imagine anyone would dare chance the sands or endure the losses the merciless sun would inflict."

Mithra spread a hand, perhaps in acknowledgment. "But then, why ever should we seek to approach them unknown? If our troops storm their capital, we might well conquer it before the queens have the chance to turn to their Arts."

Nunamnir nodded in understanding. "They will call forth Rahab the Leviathan and, in so doing, ensure their own annihilation."

"Yes."

"And we are certain some vestige of life can endure in this Realm, even beyond apocalypse?"

Mithra stepped closer to the flame. "I have made arrangements. The Tablet of Destiny told, even in bygone Eras, of the catalyst. It fell to me but to ensure he has the will and the might to fulfil his role."

"Destroyer and preserver."

Pandora stifled a gasp. The Unseen Order counted on Prometheus's Destroyer gambit not only to ensure the Eschaton, but to ensure something of the World survived so Man could rebuild. Everything was all a cycle of creation and destruction, each blazing forth a trail for the next. And just who was the Destroyer now, that they he might stop Tiamat from unmaking the whole of Gaia?

Though she thought herself silent, Mithra tensed, cast about and, slowly, turned to gaze up into the shadowed recesses of the statue where she crouched. "You ..."

Gaze locked upon her adversary, Pandora rose to her full height, the heat in her breast blazing, turning into an inferno with her wrath, and beyond the wrath, with the passion of her final hope. She could feel the raging flames behind her eyes and, with a will, allowed the fires to ignite along her hands and forearms, to spark aflame her hair and blaze around her in a fiery halo. "You, the complicit servants of a corrupt order, have wrought unforgivable ruin upon individual lives and on Mankind as a whole. I *deny* you your facile excuses about a future that is written. That you were made at the dawn of time does not abrogate your responsibility for those choices. You are culpable for all the suffering your mistresses have unleashed across the breadth of history."

Mithra chuckled, shaking his head. "Despite your timewalking, despite your tutelage under a Watcher, still your worldview remains laughably nescient. You continue to try to impose conceptions of morality upon an indifferent cosmos that exists far beyond such binary human conceits of good and evil. Your ethics pale in the face of the infinite. They are but the egotistical creations of a species arrogant enough to see itself as the centre of the World. As for our Order, we were born from the Time Chambers of Vulgeth, and thus, in turn, from *you* and your futile attempts to alter an already perfect Tapestry. This, this flawless symmetry, it is the only good this World shall ever know." The Watcher, always so expressionless afore now, flashed a malicious grin at her. "Yet even were I to accept your faulty premises, does that not then make your beloved Prometheus equally answerable for the death that arises from his fateful choice? Who do you imagine first *carved* the Tablet of Destiny and set in stone the cycle you abhor?"

Pandora leapt from the statue, soared over the fire pit, and landed on the ground level a dozen feet from the Titan men. "Though you have known him across the bounds of eternity, you fail to understand him. I have seen his soul, and unlike yours, it is *ravaged* by guilt for those who suffer because of his choice." That, and in the end, Mithra was but a willing servant to parasitic gods. How she longed to challenge his arrogance, to reveal that, whilst the Unseen Order did as they were told in acquiescence to a pitiless cosmic system, Prometheus did all he did in opposition to that obscenity. But she could not reveal his subterfuge, nor did she owe this man answers.

"Last time you sought my death, it ended in your utter failure."

Pandora favoured him with a grim smile of her own now. "I have since benefited from some further training." She spread her arms and fires flared within the pit. Spiralling coils erupted from that blaze, surging toward her hands.

Mithra and Nunamnir each dove aside and came up in fight crouches. Pandora whirled, turning the coils of flame into lashes upon either arm, each stretching forty feet long. Her whips snapped at both her foes, holding them at bay, whilst her flames scorched and blackened the stones of the temple.

Nunamnir flipped over one of her whips, dodging one way and the next, closing in upon her. Pandora whirled the other whip in an arc to drive Mithra back. In the same motion, she swept the one on Nunamnir into a circle, end meeting end, forming into a disc. As he closed in, she flung the disc at him, and it shot for him like a hurled blade. The Titan dove beneath the disc. As he did so, Pandora clenched her fist, and the fires detonated in an explosion that sent burning cinders raining over him.

Even as she spun back to face Mithra, the Watcher leapt into the air, wings bursting from his back. His flight carried him too high over her whip, beyond the arc she could bring it to bear. He landed beside her, swinging his fist. Pandora blocked his attack on her free arm, at the same time leaping into the air and spinning in a kalaripayat move Prometheus had taught her. Her whip flashed down at Mithra, flames igniting his hair and driving him back.

Before she could press her advantage, Nunamnir charged. Though burns covered his face and torso, and his shirt lay in smouldering tatters, he'd managed to snatch up a spear from some corner of the temple. His thrust damn nigh took her in the gut, and Pandora had to topple backward to avoid getting skewered. She kicked her legs together, intent on tripping the Anunnaki. He leapt over her attack, and all she had time to do was roll to the side before his spear scraped over the spot she'd lain.

Abruptly, someone seized Nunamnir and flipped him over her shoulder, sending the Titan sprawling across the floor. Her rescuer turned, and another Pandora cast her a brief glance, a nod. Blood dribbled from her ears and nose, and she'd not bothered to wipe them. The look lasted but a single heartbeat, then the other woman bounded off after Nunamnir. Pandora reeled, scarce having time to recover from the shock, much less dwell on the implication.

With a shriek, a winged form descended upon her, Mithra diving fist-first at her. Pandora rolled over backward, gaining her feet. Mithra's fist split the worked stone floor, a spiderweb of cracks spreading out from the impact. She reached for the remaining flames in the fire pit, but Mithra surged in like a mountain wind. His blow hammered into her chest and sent her careening backward, unable to claim the fires. Already he was on her again and forcing her to block time and again, using every technique Prometheus had taught her. Mithra had a relentless intensity to his attacks, but unlike against Kala, Pandora could see them coming, could block, maybe even manage to counter—

A knee caught her in the gut and hurled her into the base of the statue. Her head cracked against the plinth, and red spots swam across her vision in a wild dance.

"One of us, reduced to mortal folly," Mithra said. He swung, and she blocked inside his elbow, slamming her opposite palm into his clavicle. The blow sent him stumbling away, and Pandora scrambled back to get her bearings. "Your utility to the timeline has run its course, timewalker."

Pandora hopped onto the plinth and dashed around the statue's legs, pulling the Box as she did so. A second Pandora. Second Pandora ... but wearing the same clothes she wore now. Same time. She spun the Box's panels to set it back mere moments, then, as Mithra rounded the statue in pursuit, popped the top. An awful, gut-wrenching scream echoed through the chamber before the light bubble enwrapt her.

The Box transported her into the shadows behind the statue. It felt like something burst inside her head, and hot wetness dribbled down her cheeks. Blood seeped from ears and nose. Pandora pushed herself up, though vertiginous waves threatened to send her spiralling into unconsciousness.

She came around the statue to see her past self scorching Mithra with a flaming whip as she landed from a whirling leap. From the side, a burnt and furious Nunamnir charged in with a spear, intent on impaling that Pandora. The woman toppled prone, avoiding the attack, even as the now-Pandora raced forward. As Nunamnir continued to attack, Pandora snared his arm, swept his leg, and flipped him over her shoulder with a Potency-fuelled throw that sent him flying aside.

She looked to the fallen Pandora, and for a heartbeat, their gazes met. She would know what to do when the time came, Pandora was certain. Pandora dashed off after Nunamnir, trusting the younger version of herself to keep Mithra busy. She ignited the flaming wings from her back to carry her toward her foe, the fires immolating her khiton. He had gained his feet and hefted his spear for her to impale herself on. Pandora turned aside—barely—in the air and slammed down beside him. Though he'd failed to run her through, the butt of his spear whipped around and clapt against her head. Only Pneuma in Steadfastness kept her skull from cracking, and even so, the impact had her reeling.

The Anunnaki whirled his spear, thrusting for her throat. Pandora twisted and caught the haft, and the two of them struggled for it, strain causing veins to pop along Nunamnir's face. The Phoenix's Pneuma made her more than a match for even a brawny Titan.

"Your utility to the timeline has run its course, timewalker," she heard Mithra saying. Not much time left to finish this, and then Mithra would be on her again.

Growling, Pandora shoved Nunamnir back, then kicked the spear. The force of her blow splintered the haft and sent the man staggering away, gawping at his damaged weapon. Another beat of her fiery wings sent Pandora careening into him, driving him down. She willed the heat to burst along her fingertips, then seized the Titan's skull as they both hit the floor. The sickly-sweet stench of burnt flesh filled her nostrils as his skin sizzled beneath her palms. He was wailing, casting about in a desperate attempt to dislodge her. Her fingers bored holes through his cheeks and melted into his sinuses. Stomach churning, she wished she could apologise for the awful death she gave the man, but time permitted no such mercy as yet. Instead, she yanked his head up and smacked it against the cold floor, twice. Thrice, until the impact sounded wet.

Something smacked into her kidney at the same time a hand snared her hair, and she was hurled aside, skittering along the floor. She tried to rise but retched up gobbets of blood that rained in spatters along the ground.

"Wretched *child*," Mithra snarled above her. "Think you the petty tricks of your Box enough to overcome one who has walked the Earth and Realms beyond since the days before Man yet took his first breath?" Utter wrath limned his visage now, and she began to think he, who seemed to care for no one save the Moirai, might have truly loved Nunamnir. "I am eternal. Had you but walked away, accepted the immutability of Fate, I would have left you be, content to allow you to weather the storm as best you may. Now, you shall die here, alone in this cold hall, and leave your benighted lover to his grief."

Pandora managed her knees, gasping. "Vinata was a Watcher, and I saw the Destroyer slay her. What makes you think yourself immune to such an end?"

"You are no Destroyer." He pointed to the dark hall behind the towering statue. "The Destroyer slumbers *there*, in fitful dreams, wrestling with incipient memories, awaiting the clarion of cataclysm that will summon him to his task. You are naught save ash compared to his ilk."

"I—"

Light warped behind them, and Mithra spun to see three more bubbles deposit three more Pandoras in the chamber, surrounding the fire pit. All were naked, all bruised and bleeding, some worse than others. All bore a gash alongside their left temple. One fell upon her hands, blood streaming from every orifice. Another collapsed entirely, though, groaning, she pushed herself up and snarled.

Open-mouthed and wide-eyed, Mithra turned back to Pandora as she gained her feet, swaying in place before managing to get a sense of equilibrium. "The Phoenix rises from ashes," she growled.

Mithra lunged for her, palm shooting toward her throat. It took all she had to knock aside his attack, and the next cracked along her jaw. His fist shot toward her temple, but one of the other Pandoras snared his shoulder and yanked him away. Pandora, though reeling, charged back in, landing a body blow against the disoriented Watcher. Mithra unfurled his wings, a beat of his powerful pinions sending the other Pandora hurtling aside, to crack her head on the ground, opening her left temple.

A third Pandora seized Mithra and tossed him away from the now-Pandora, giving her a moment's reprieve. Flames in the fire pit flared once more, and she realised the last Pandora must have reignited the spark. Pandora looked to her, the weakest of them all, her face fixed in grim determination as she reached for the flames. Each of the others did so as well, in turn, and parabolic arcs of fire lanced through the air, streaming between the three other women.

Pandora realised their intent and too reached for the flames. Around each of the four, those arcs bent, turning the last vestiges of her garments to cinders, leaving only Pandoras, each holding the Box. A lattice of parabolas burst from all four, an inferno net exploding in all directions.

Paling, Mithra began to fade from sight, as if to escape the Mortal Realm. But the outer edge of a flame washed over his arm, flash burning away flesh and leaving a skeletal arm to begin to crumble. The rest of the lattice crashed over the Watcher, immolating him, stripping away skin and muscle, blackening bone. Even his skeleton cracked from the heat and turned to dust.

"Embrace Fate," Pandora spat at him.

Slowly, the fires all winked out, leaving the chamber darkened. Two of the other women exchanged glances, then began setting the Box. The last collapsed in a heap, face-first onto the stone floor, and Pandora winced. Did all this use the last of her Pneuma? Did it cost her very life?

Yet, she had no choice. If she did not make those jumps, *all* of the timewalks, she would not have saved herself, and Mithra might have won. She began setting the Box, even as the other two women vanished.

Just as the bubble rose around her, Marduk came stumbling into the hall, half-drunk seeming and dazed, but incensed with fury at what he beheld.

The Box deposited Pandora before the fire pit, rimmed by two others. Her stomach convulsed. Her vision blurred as blood dribbled from her eyes, tinging her vision crimson. The other two crumpled, even worse off than Pandora felt.

"The Phoenix rises from ashes," growled past-Pandora. But Mithra launched at her, and she was hard-pressed. Pandora rose and dashed in to join the fray. She grabbed Mithra's shoulder and tore him away before he could pummel past-Pandora. The Watcher buffeted her with his wings, sending her flying backward. Her head smacked against the hard floor, the impact knocking all sight and sound from her. Utter darkness reigned. Then, slowly, receded, and the sounds of battle resumed.

She looked up to see another Pandora drawing fire from a reignited blaze in the pit. Pandora scrambled to her feet, though her knees tried to give out, and pulled the fires to her as well. The four Pandoras engulfed Mithra in a conflagration that spread across the whole of the chamber, giving him nowhere to flee or dodge.

"Embrace Fate," past-Pandora spat.

Bone-weary as she was, Pandora realised this was far from finished.

There were two more. After exchanging a glance with another Pandora —they knew what this would cost—she activated the Box.

She appeared beside the pit once more, and pain lanced through her whole body like a white-hot blade. Overcome, she pitched forward onto her hands. Blood streamed from every orifice on her body. Inside her core, the Phoenix quivered, struggling to keep her heart pumping. Without its power, perhaps her body would have given out long ago.

"The Phoenix rises from ashes," she heard another Pandora say, engaged with Mithra.

Gritting her teeth, Pandora stumbled to her feet. She made it two steps before crashing down on her knee, sending a jolt of lightning shooting through her leg and into her hip. All she could do was swallow the yelp of pain, spare some Pneuma to push down the agony, and rise again. Again, again once more. She charged forward, caught Mithra, and hurled him away from a prior Pandora.

Then the fires within the pit burst to life once more, and she was turning, stumbling back. Another Pandora reached to it, called forth the fires, and Pandora knew she must do likewise. Flames whirled about her, hurtling like wild flares about the chamber. All four of them were caught aflame then and weaving lattices of fire about their bodies. As one, they released a torrent of fire, and Mithra was swept away in the conflagration.

"Embrace Fate," a Pandora spat at the Watcher's ashes.

Pandora looked to another Pandora, their gazes meeting, and she knew what her prior self was thinking. She set the Box and activated it once more.

This time, appearing around the fire pit, she could not support herself. Instead, she pitched face-first into the warm bricks around the pit and lay there, unable to manage even a moan. She felt it, her blood seeping from her, stealing away her strength. The Phoenix inside grew quiet, dwindling even as the flames in the pit below had burnt down to embers. She couldn't do it. She was meant to light the fire, but she had not the strength left.

No more ...

Each breath threatened to become her last.

And if she failed here, the loop became broken. All of the others would, without her support, falter as well. All of it would be for naught, and Mithra and the Unseen Order would win this day. There had to come a reckoning for all he had done. There must be an answer made if the future Era was to have a better chance than this one. She would not see another iteration of the Earth languish beneath Mithra's heel.

Gasping, she pulled herself along the floor, closer to the fire pit. A nudge, a hair closer. With quivering fingers, she reached to those embers. But they were far, so far ...

"I know it burns," Prometheus had said, long ago. "It sears within you and wants to spread. But you can yet bring order from the chaos inherent in flame. Fire is consumption, yes, but it is also life. Burning, searing, life, Pandora."

And her life, though almost spent, was not yet over. Not while even the barest cinder of hope remained. The distant ember responded to the welling of her will, turning incandescent. Wisps of smoke rose around it as burnt tinder curled away from the heat.

"Please ..." she whispered. "Burn ..."

Burn. Burn. BURN!

The Phoenix burst to life within her breast, a flash fire ignited from a single, stubborn spark. The embers of the pit sparked, then detonated, erupting into a roaring bonfire. Pandora drank in Pneuma from the fire like its warmth was Ambrosia. Despite the pain, the blood loss, the faltering of her mortal form, she found the strength to stand one more time. She reached for the flames. Arcs of that fire surged toward her, wrapt around her arms, and hurtled in wild bursts between the other Pandoras, all of whom had followed her lead.

She wove the flames about her, crossing her parabolas, then thrust her hands forward, sending the lattice erupting outward in all directions. The conflagration blackened stone across the chamber even as it incinerated Mithra.

"Embrace Fate," a past-Pandora said, somewhere.

But bereft of the Pneuma that had kept her standing, Pandora pitched forward. Once more, she fell face-first into the stone, and there she lay, the room swirling about her in wild gyrations, as though she were caught in a maelstrom.

Perhaps the others had timewalked already. Pandora was, once more, alone, and now helpless, spent and broken. She struggled to turn her cheek to look, though the effort seemed momentous, and her vision blurred in the process.

A colossal roar, as of a thousand bellowing drakons, it sounded from beneath the mountain. Gaia protested, contracting and convulsing as if in pain. All around the temple, mortar between the bricks cracked, spilling down in a hundred curtains of dust. Another heave of the land, and a crack rived the statue's legs. Pandora managed to look up, to look to the statue for a drawn-out heartbeat. Then stone and dust burst from the crack like an arterial spray, and next she knew, another roar echoed through the hall. That of a fifty-foot-tall idol toppling.

It was happening.

She grabbed the Box. Set it for Mugedang.

18

HEL

20 Dark Age

Given the threat presented by the empousai, it came as small wonder that Milucra at last deigned to descend from the lofty heights of her tower and join the fray. Perhaps the Winter Queen thought engaging in battle beneath her station, or perhaps, as Hel had done, she waited to see what hand her foe had to play. Either way, when Milucra came amid the gathered army, she came with a sudden violence that shocked even Hel.

Before Hel could so much as cry out a warning, a twister of frigid Mist came spiralling down from the firmament. Shades were rent asunder, cast about like detritus. Poor Persephone was among those where the tornado touched down.

Hel dashed for her, hand reaching in denial of impending inevitability. But she couldn't even see as her friend was blown apart.

Wailing, Hel stumbled toward the chaos. Persephone ...

With a wave of her hand, Milucra sent the ice twister crashing through Hel's army. Enyo was battered and cast aside, leaving Hel to wonder if even a Mistwraith could survive such an onslaught. How had

Milucra called up such power? What mammoth expenditure of Pneuma did it take to reshape reality on such a scale?

But then, the answer was obvious. Achlys, the Elder Goddess of the Mist, her power flowed through Milucra. That was the reason Hel had come here. She needed to be ready. She needed everything in place for when Keuthos at last finished the final incantation.

Closing her eye, Hel focused her will a moment, not upon the empousai but rather on another wretched entity she had bound to her will.

When she opened her eye, she saw Milucra had allowed the twister to dissipate and now stared at the dark clouds rumbling overhead. Perhaps the Winter Queen had some inkling of what now impended. If so, she did not tremble, though still, she could not seem to tear her gaze from the sky.

Small wonder, for blood began to rain from those thick clouds, a drizzle at first, then a shower. A skinless leg plunged through the vapours, followed be another. Then the Old One strode before the silver towers of the Winter Court, trailing that colossal mace. In Hel's mind, Aeshma raged, livid at its enslavement. But the demon was bound to her now, its fury impotent against her will.

It hefted the mace as it approached the towers, and Milucra broke into a run, suddenly realising her throne would be cast down. Let the Winter Queen drain herself fighting such an adversary if she dared. Aeshma's massive feet stomped upon lampads too slow to evade it. Its raining blood left pink smears upon the snow fields, a macabre trail running behind the demon, cast between its enormous footprints.

It swung that mace and the tower rang like ten thousand gongs all struck at once. Mortal eardrums would have burst from the clangour, and even the gathered eidolons clutched hands to their heads in agony. Even Hel. Shards of ice exploded down over the Winter Court in a rain of hail. A spiderweb of cracks shot through the silver wall, the sigils engraved therein flaring in dying gasps.

Another hefting of that mace. Then a mountain of ice burst from the ground beneath Aeshma's feet. Crystalline lances a hundred feet long ruptured the landscape, exploding through the demon's legs and turning its flayed flesh into a grisly ruin. Naught remained of the demon below its knees. The Old One toppled, a careening, widening shadow that seemed to fall with agonised slowness, as if plummeting through water.

The impact sent a quake through the landscape, great shelves of frozen earth heaving and splitting like shattered ostraka. Hel tumbled to the ground, as did most everyone on the battlefield.

When she looked up, Milucra was on her hands and knees, trembling. Then the Winter Queen steadied herself and rose to one knee. Hel gaped. This was the power of Achlys? If such awful puissance flowed through Milucra, had Hel miscalculated? Moreover, she had not imagined Achlys would allow such violence upon her spawn. Clearly, Hel had overestimated any bond that lay betwixt a Primordial and its offspring.

Legless, Aeshma was dragging its mace along the ground, intent on bringing it around against Milucra, but the Old One had little leverage from its prone position. The Winter Queen gained her feet. With a wave of her hand, a flow of ice crystallised over the demon's body, encasing it and putting an end to its struggles.

Hel rose too and strode for Milucra. Miscalculation or not, she had invested too much into this course to turn back now. With a mental command, she summoned her Mistwraiths to her side. Melinoë, Inanna, and Hypnos appeared. She could only assume Nephthys was occupied, and Enyo had been reduced to the barest hint of a tether in her mind.

"Did you think you could overthrow an order that has persisted across Eras?" Milucra panted as she spoke, yet a fierceness still glinted in her eyes, a milky depth that bespoke hidden horrors. Mist wafted from her mouth with each wispy word she uttered. Her stark white hair and stained robes billowed in the swirling gusts. "Did you think you can intrude into the Rimefells and challenge *me*?"

With a hiss, Melinoë broke from Hel's side and flanked the Winter Queen. Hypnos edged around the opposite side, while Inanna placed herself between Milucra and Hel. As the empousai distracted the queen, Hel broke into song. Her words thrummed into the ether and the air around Milucra thickened. A miasma would cloud the lampad's mind, sapping her will and aggression, even if only for a moment.

Taking advantage of the chance, Melinoë lunged in, massive axe swinging.

"Don't slay her!" Hel shrieked, abruptly breaking off her song.

Milucra twisted, arm outstretched at the empousa. An explosion of ice burst from her hand like a rapidly expanding limb. The crystals seized around the axe haft, jerking it to a stop. At almost the same moment, the Winter Queen stepped forward, swinging her other fist at Melinoë. The impact of her blow on armour resounded, and Melinoë was sent hurtling away, disappearing into the Mist.

Hel resumed her song, but Milucra shrugged it off. Hypnos's fist collided with her head. The queen whirled upon him and plunged her hand into the void beneath his cowl. The Mistwraith shuddered and convulsed. When Milucra jerked her arm free, a coil of shadows came with it, ripped straight from Hypnos's core. Icicles burst out from the seams of his cheires. Then the empousa *melted*, his essence torn from him.

No, damn it! No! Hel could not afford to lose one of her Mistwraiths.

Inanna surged forward, tackling the queen and bearing her down. The next instant she was sent flying skyward, a kick from the queen hurling her dozens of feet into the air. Lightness allowed Inanna to twist around before falling and drift back down some distance away.

A moment of hesitation struck Hel. Her song faltered. Then, even as Milucra closed in, she began another song. The queen lunged, but Hel twisted aside, for her song bent air currents around her, allowing her to avoid harm. Twice and thrice Milucra tried to seize her, and just as oft Hel danced out of her grasp. The lampad sneered then. She placed her palms together and drew them apart, pulling a sword of ice from the air as she did so. Its razored edge glinted in the moonlight, the sword longer than any with which Hel was familiar.

"You still shan't strike me when reality conspires to impede you," Hel taunted.

Then a chill hand seized her shoulder and shoved her forward. Stumbling, she could not dodge as Milucra plunged that ice blade into her gut. Its awful cold froze even her, a glacier spreading through her core. She managed to look back and saw Khione there, sneering.

Whatever Hel's former slave might have said was lost when Milucra seized the back of her neck and forced her gaze back to the queen. "For your treachery, I shall draw your consumption out across the breadth of a thousand years."

Hel flailed, her limbs deprived of all strength by the sword twisting in her insides.

"Whilst the greater portion of your soul shall serve to sate myself and Khione, whom you so wronged, I shall enjoy carving bits of you up to hand out to those myriad enemies you have earned yourself." The lampad leered at her with an almost salacious glee, drinking Hel's pain and growing dread like heady wine. "And when I have stretched your agony long enough, even then, you shall enjoy no blessing of oblivion. You may have forced me to strike down the demon with claim upon your soul, sorceress. But its mother will stand in Aeshma's stead, wracking you with eternal torments the likes of which you have yet to imagine."

Oh, but the nightmares Aeshma had plagued her with had shown Hel more than enough.

Inanna was racing back to her side, but Khione cut of the Mistwraith. Even if Inanna could overcome the lampad, it would be too late.

Milucra's nails carved rivets into the back of Hel's neck. "Your hubris and its inevitable consequence shall serve as a warning to all the Ages to come against challenging the order of the cosmos. I shall enjoy ..." Milucra's face convulsed. The lampad blinked, her eyes pale blue instead of swirling milky white. Abruptly, the ice sword in her hand turned brittle and collapsed, and she staggered away from Hel. "Wha— What in the black walls of Tartarus have you done?"

Keuthonymos had done it. He had finished the last seal. And Hel needed but complete the final incantation to draw the power out of Milucra and into herself. Gasping, black filth dribbling down her ruined lip, Hel lurched forward. She wrapt her skeletal left hand around Milucra's jaw and the Winter Queen—too taken aback with the sluice gate slamming down upon her power to recognise the real danger—did not even fight back.

The Supernal cant burbled from Hel's lips. "*Urghst ell'r stukravmas n'ghestall ...*"

A breath escaped the queen. A breath—Pneuma—life itself.

All at once, Hel was elsewhere. Whether she had been bilocated, moved, or induced into a vision, she could not say. Around her opened a vast cavern enveloped in a cloud of Mist that swirled like the slowest of maelstroms, almost frozen in motion. At the eye of that storm knelt a woman cloaked in a pale shroud. The figure craned up her head a hair and her regard slammed into Hel with the force of a collapsing mountain, an avalanche of malice. Hatred matched only by a hunger, one vast enough to swallow stars. To consume the whole of the World and not be sated.

TEMERITY! HUBRIS, HERETOFORE KNOWN BUT ONCE IN THE AMBIT OF TIME!

The words bombarded her mind, more catastrophic than ever Aeshma's had proved. This *thing* spoke of time, and yet behind the word lurked an unspoken contempt for the concept. For this being had emerged from somewhere beyond time, beyond the World and all its boundaries of order. Here, Khaos knelt before her, chained by the invisible fetters of one of the greatest workings of sorcery in history.

The air shimmered, the weft of the cosmos pulled taut for a moment. And in that instant, before her was not the human-like guise the Archon wore, but something vast beyond imagining. A living, churning cloud of Mist within which writhed a thousand grasping skeletal arms, as if the enormity before her sought to yank itself into the World more fully. She was struck by the sense that, blessedly, some part of this abomination lay wedged inside the walls of the cosmos, unable to quite pull free one way or the other. A shuddering moan wafted out of the Mist, accompanied by the charnel stench of innumerable rotting carcasses. Mauve lightnings crackled within the clouds.

The vision broke as swiftly as it had arisen and the humanoid figure was there again, her presence all the more profane for having seen the glimpse of what lurked beneath the surface.

But this was why Hel had come. This was the endgame she had intended all along. And she opened herself up to Achlys, drawing her in with gasping breath after breath. The sluice gate of power that had slammed shut upon Milucra now creaked open within Hel.

A torrent of energies slammed into her, inundated her. Drowned her in a surging tide of Pneuma. The rush of power threatened to burst her frail form apart. Her mind flailed, pieces washed away by the undertows, until Hel could no longer even say for certain what had been lost.

A long time, Hel knelt in the cavern beneath the Hvergelmir, trembling. Almost unmade.

Almost.

When at last she rose—feeling as though perhaps years had passed her by—she was no longer what she had been. Now, now she was like unto an Elder Goddess. Now, she was fit to bend the cosmos to her will.

SOME AMONG THE damned had taken to calling the Rimefells by a new name: Niflheim, and Hel found it suited well enough. Now, the whole domain bent to her adamant will. Within Niflheim, she could reshape the world as suited her whims. So beyond the Fimbulvinter Mountains, beyond the Hvergelmir whence flowed the rivers of cold, amid the tallest peaks of Niflheim, she raised a new fortress straight from the stones.

Iron-banded double doors over a hundred feet tall greeted the procession of dead souls that flowed here out of the Roil. This place, too, the damned named for her, inspired by that first sight they beheld of her new necropolis. They called the place the Gates of Hel.

At its heart, Hel raised a throne of skulls and bone, and here she oft sat, lost in her dark musings, wondering which pieces of her mind had fallen away in her quest for power. But considering the alternative, perhaps any price had been worth paying. Thus she sat here, dead and damned. *Queen* of the damned, of Niflheim, and one day, more besides.

Mist billowed out of the entryway, announcing Keuthos before he came drifting into view. The empousa paused at the foot of her dais—she'd had it forged of the living corpses of no few who had opposed her, condemning them to forever sit beneath her heels. Among them writhed the almost empty husk of one who had once called herself queen of the lampads. Her presence here would serve as a warning that Hel could bring even the mightiest of foes to heel.

After a moment, Hel rose and descended the steps to stand before her greatest ally. Keuthos had, she suspected, misliked the changes wrought in her once she had begun feasting upon Achlys's power and soul. The bond betwixt them was strained—he could never imagine the awful glimpses of yet greater Ontos she had pulled from Achlys's mind—but she had no doubt time would ease that, as it had all strains of their past. She could not again be who once she had been, but Keuthonymos's loyalty had never once wavered, not in life nor in death. His faith in her would weather this onus as well as all the others.

"The last of the lampad nobles still in the Winter Court have sworn fealty to the new goddess of the Rimefells." The name Niflheim had not yet taken root with the empousai, much less the lampads. In truth, there were a great many names for each domain of the Spirit Realm, and Hel did not truly care what anyone called them.

"Khione?"

Keuthos shook his head. "Vanished along with the others who fled the court after the fall ..."

Hel hissed but waved it away. "Leave them be." Raising this fortress had taken much of her stolen strength, and she needed time to regain her energies. "A handful of malcontent lampads on the fringes pose little threat. If they do not come to grovel before me, they risk starving for want of souls upon which to sustain themselves. Let them destroy themselves, if they so desire."

The end of an Era drew nigh, she had grown almost certain. With it would come an Eschaton, a cataclysmic loss of life. The remaining Archons would glut themselves upon the feast of souls served up to them. Even as they did so, Hel too would gather what dead she could from the influx, restocking both her army and her larder.

"You scheme once more ..." Keuthonymos rasped. "Are you not content to rule here ...?"

Hel chuckled. "Content ... Oh, my Keuthos," she said, trailing a finger along the chill plate of his armour, "one Archon is fallen. Eight still remain before us."

And from the depths of Achlys's mind, Hel knew that, when she had broken the last of the Elder Gods, still one more lay beyond even them. The future ever called to her. There were no limits to what she would do to preserve the cosmos from damnation, even taking that damnation upon herself. She was, after all, the Queen of the Damned.

19

ARTEMIS

399 Dark Age

"The Nusantarans again manoeuvre against us," Mithra said, standing over the map table in his war room and indicating a display of ships. "Sirsir sends word they grow bolder, perhaps thinking our forces committed to the war against Elládos, and thus seek to weaken our hold upon Phoenikia and the coastal water."

Artemis sighed, staring at the little wooden ships. Neither of them had commented on the fact the board held far fewer Babilimian models than it had before Salamis. She may have succeeded in bringing down an Olympian, but they had paid a price for it, both in lives and in the strength of their navy. After a moment, she straightened. "They are not wrong, my Emperor. To counter their raids on Phoenikia, we'd have to redirect forces away from Elládosi water. That, or pull back from patrolling the waterways between Kumari Kandam and Mu." Which, of course, Mithra could not risk, given it would expose their homeland to invasion.

"The Queens of Mu know their days draw to an end. Thus, rather than accepting Fate, they thrash against it like beasts in a trap, heedless that their struggles only serve to wedge the snares tighter. They strike against us in a vain attempt to preempt our inevitable invasion of their sorcery-steeped continent."

Artemis hoped the god-king would not command her to move against Mu now. She needed to return to Elládos, to press the offensive against Zeus before he had time to recover from the battles already fought. That the king had not deigned to show himself at Salamis or Thermopylae meant he, in his cowardice, must have known he could not win in the end.

Mithra was staring hard at her now, perhaps reading her fears and ambitions off her features. Artemis made no attempt to hide her intentions. She doubted it would have mattered if she had tried. The god-king had unfathomable intuitive abilities and could guess, most oft, what any Man or Titan before him thought at any given moment. The only other person she had ever seen with such abilities was Prometheus.

"I will attend to Mu myself, with the Magi, and soon. Marduk, my son, you too must come. Mugedang must be brought into our empire or else laid waste. Artemis, you must return to Helion."

"Helion?" The abrupt change of subject had her off-balance. "You think the Muians would dare reach so far."

"Not them." Mithra tapped the Elládosi models remaining in the Strait of Korinth. "Even in the abduction of Helen, you failed to draw Zeus into open warfare. The blighted Gnostic mirrors show him foes gathering all around, driving him into craven bouts of self-doubt forever at odds with his ponderous ego. That internal battle so long paralysed the king, and so he sent his daughter to fight for him. He will grow frenzied in the paroxysms of his desperation to avert the inevitable."

"Zeus will strike at Helion? Now?" The idea seemed insane. To bypass Phrygia, Lydia, to not bother to secure Phlegra, even. And for what, an island separating Elládos from Phoenikia?

"He knows you lead his enemies. How better, in the mind of one such as he, to punish you than to inflict his fury upon your kin?"

Artemis's gaze darted back and forth between Elládos and Helion. "Father ..." Of course, Mithra was right. Of course Zeus would strive for petty vengeance, even over strategy. "I must leave."

Mithra shook his head. "Evening has already settled in. Take tomorrow to gather supplies."

§

MORE THAN HALF ASLEEP, her head upon Marduk's chest, Artemis had not heard anyone approach her door. At the urgent rapping upon it, though, she lurched upward, snatching a sheet to wrap around herself. It was well past midnight and no one would have woken her for aught save the direst of emergencies.

Marduk, too, was on his feet, though the man had naught to hide his nakedness.

Sparing him a single glance, Artemis flung open the door to find Phaethusa. Her half-sister opened her mouth, but whatever she'd intended to say died on her lips as her gaze swept over Marduk. She licked her lips.

"You best have a good reason for this intrusion," Artemis snapped.

"Hmm. Your 'dear friend'?"

It took Artemis a moment to know what Phaethusa spoke of. "Nike?"

The Heliad nodded. "She just tried to kill the god-king."

§

BETRAYAL WAS A BARBED, poisoned lance. Though one might yank out the weapon, the venom would still course through one's veins, and those wounding tines would forever seem to worm their way deeper into the flesh. A thousand recriminations—self-recriminations!—shot through Artemis's mind each time she envisaged the look she had seen upon Marduk's face. The guest of his betrothed had attempted to murder his father, and he might well consider that a betrayal of him as well. They had split up to hunt for Nike, scouring the city.

Artemis did not even like to imagine what might have happened had the woman succeeded. Mithra sought to stop the Gnostic Cabal from breaking the Wheel of Fate and consequently unmaking the cosmos. Did Nike serve the Cabal? Did she serve Zeus? Was she a fool?

Somehow, even the thought of the cosmos unravelling paled next to the thought of Marduk losing his father and, worse still, blaming Artemis for it all. How could Nike have done this?

Of course, Artemis found her tracks. Not even the cover of night could conceal prey from the huntress, least of all this prey. She followed the treacherous woman back into the Hanging Gardens, as if Nike could be fool enough to think she could hide among nature's bounty. Maybe from another hunter—not from Artemis.

"You betrayed my trust," Artemis accused when she spied Nike crouched amid ferns like some common bandit. In each hand, Artemis clutched an akinakes, her grip so tight her knuckles hurt as she imagined carving Nike's heart from her chest. No, but Mithra would want her alive to interrogate, and Artemis would deliver her that way.

More or less.

Nike rose, slowly, hands up to forestall the inevitable thrust of Artemis's daggers. "I sought not to betray, but to save. I am trying to save the *World*."

"So am I!" Artemis shrieked, closing in. "For two and a half millennia, Zeus has ruled as the greatest tyrant in history! His death will free the whole of the Thalassa from his megalomania and oppression! It is through Mithra the land has the chance to be free of him."

"You don't understand—"

"I understand well enough! You serve him still."

"No! Never! I despise Zeus with every breath. But Mithra will destroy Gaia in the process of bringing low the one you loathe. How hollow shall your vengeance ring when enjoyed upon continents piled high with corpses?"

Artemis snarled. "Lies!"

Alacrity flooded with Pneuma; Artemis lunged. Nike blocked one of her wrists on her forearm, but Artemis's other blade opened the woman's gut. Not enough to spill entrails, though blood flowed in a heavy cataract. Nike seized her wrist, but the other woman, though strong, was not fast enough. Artemis leapt onto the garden wall and ran around behind Nike. Her momentum spun Nike around. Artemis caught her, flipping her over her head, and slammed her onto the ground.

Nike tried to rise, but Artemis smacked a Potency-infused fist into her temple. She kicked the woman in her ribs, sending her flying away, off the terrace on which they had stood. Nike tumbled through a palm tree, hitting the ground of the next level down, and Artemis leapt over the side to join her. Her foe rose, and Artemis attacked. Nike dodged, but Artemis's relentless attacks left Nike covered in gashes. Enough to weaken her. More, for Artemis owed her *pain* for her perfidy.

Nike sought to escape and Artemis rammed an akinakes through her thigh, drawing a shriek from the other woman. With her now-empty hand, she grabbed Nike's arm and slammed the pommel of her other knife into the woman's jaw. Flames burnt in Nike's eyes. Uncanny strength arose in her, and, before Artemis could react, she seized Artemis's arms.

Next Artemis knew, she was hurtling through the air sideways. Her back slapped against the tree, sending lightning bolts of agony shooting up her neck and along her limbs. All control fell away. Nike had her up again, though Artemis could scarce see; another impact against the tree stole her senses. Another hit, and she didn't know what was happening.

She saw fire the moment before a heavy impact cracked her skull.

She saw no more.

ARTEMIS AWAKENED TO PAIN, guttering light from an oil lamp stinging her eyes. She lay upon her bed in the room she shared with Marduk. The windows were mercifully shuttered, so it was only the glare from the tiny flame she had to contend with. With a groan, she sat up. Lances of pain shot through her back, lightning bolts coursing into arms and legs. Nike could well have broken her spine like that, and that Artemis lived at all meant the woman had chosen to spare her.

Which did not excuse the betrayal the woman had wrought here. She had come into Artemis's home, called her friend, and tried to kill Marduk's father. Why? Why plot such a course?

Waves of vertigo threatened to send her pitching back into the bed.

"Whoa," Marduk said, slipping in through the door, though she'd not heard it open. "Morpheus gave you poppy tears, and it may not have worn off."

Oh, she hoped it had, elsewise Artemis had no idea how she would contend with the pain in her back and limbs. "Where ...?" Her tongue felt thick, heavy.

"Nike?" Marduk paced to her side and sat on the floor beside the mat of their bed. "I captured her, but Nemesis insisted I turn her over to her custody. I do not know what happened after that—I came to retrieve you and see you attended." So Marduk had succeeded into overcoming Nike where Artemis had failed. He placed his hand upon hers, his thumb stroking over her wrist. "I feared ... a moment, I feared I lost you."

She snorted without mirth. "Leave you ... free to chase some other ... woman."

Marduk shook his head. "You know, I don't recall my life before I met you. That day you came to us, it was one of my earliest memories. You might say my life began when I met you. I cannot imagine what it would be if I lost you, but I can say I would not be chasing anyone. Not ..."

She squeezed his hand to let him know she'd spoken in jest. For a time, silence held, and Artemis began to doze.

"I have begun to see things," Marduk said, drawing her from herself. "Sometimes, when I linger on that threshold betwixt waking and dreaming, I find I am plagued by a cavalcade of visions that make little sense to me, Artemis. I am not myself, and yet I know who I am, see lives not my own, face battles I cannot know. Yet for all that, these phantasms are too vivid to be mere fancy."

"Dreams are like that ... Did you ask Morpheus?"

He returned the squeeze, not looking back at her. "If I am plagued by portents? If I might be an oneiromancer myself? I have thought long on speaking with him, but I dread what the Magus might say. There is so much carnage in my mind, as though I bear witness to the birth and dying of worlds. No ... worse than witness, for in my mind I see my hands awash in oceans of blood, as though it falls upon me to usher in these cataclysms and the nascent realities that should emerge from such travails."

Artemis's mind was too cloudy for such weighty discussions, but Marduk seemed so burdened she struggled to focus. "How long has this gone on?"

"Since Thermopylae, though these apparitions have grown more frequent, more intense, of late." He looked to her now, eyes wide, face wan with dread. This man, this seemingly invincible warrior whom none could stand against—not even Nike!—and he looked to her, stricken by terror at what lurked within his breast, within his mind. "Your friend, she claimed ... said she had seen the future. Said ... 'I have beheld a world inundated by waves that rise like flowing mountains.' Such seems a claim too specific, too dire to dismiss as the wild ravings of a prisoner seeking mere distraction. Or so I have wrestled with whilst you convalesced." His eyes held hers, so desperate. "Is Nike an Oracle?"

Artemis blinked, breaking from his gaze. "No. She cannot ... I mean ..." She had never given any indication she was such. Like Apollon, she had been drenched in the blood of Python. Could it have sparked the Sight in her? But if so, Nike had never revealed such. "I don't know what she meant by that. All I know is that she betrayed us. Why then should we let her words vex us?"

Artemis was in no state for such things. In truth, she could do with another sip of the poppy tears, if not of some damn Ambrosia.

Marduk leant over her, kissed her brow. "I am bound for Mu with the tide."

"No, I'm coming with you. I cannot let you face the Queens of Mu alone."

He shook his head. "You've not the strength at present. Besides, Father says he has another task for you. Take your rest, love. When next we look upon each other, it should be in a world where our enemies are broken and we are free to wed."

But she could not shake the sense of looming dread, rising like a dark wave all around her. "What of your visions?"

"I am no Oracle, and neither, you say, is Nike." His voice held all the conviction of a man desperate to delude himself. "Let Magi attend to such things." From the table with the lamp he took up a cup, stirring the contents with one finger. "Sip the poppy, love. When we wake, the future will call for you."

Next she awakened, Artemis was summoned by the god-king and thus, after washing and dressing, came to attend him in his private chamber. The space showed no sign of the battle he'd fought against Nike here. Artemis wondered how long she'd laid abed, or how quickly the servants had cleaned the mess from here. Mithra stood on the balcony, staring east, in the direction of Mu.

"He has already sailed," she said. Not a question, for she could feel it, that Marduk was gone from the city.

Mithra turned to her. "I too am soon bound for Mu."

"And you still wish me to sail for Helion."

The god-king strolled back into his chambers, forcing her to follow. "We are past that now. As ever, we adapt and thus account for all turnings of the Wheel of Fate. In all things we serve the will of the Hidden God."

"Good thoughts, good words, good deeds," she intoned, scarce thinking of the mantra.

Mithra made no answer, instead kneeling beside a footlocker. From within his robe he produced a key and opened the chest, then folded back a silken shroud. Beneath this glittered the rose-gold of orichalcum treasures. Armbands and rings, fetters, and amulets. And a single dagger he withdrew, forged in the style not of an akinakes, but—unless she missed her guess—in Hyperborean workmanship. He unsheathed the blade and held it before her to examine. "In days long before the Time of Nyx, when the cities of Dark Faerie dominated the world, the Smith Lord wrought great works of old." Artemis knelt beside him, having no real idea what he spoke of. The god-king held the blade as if reverent, though, and she could almost feel the antiquity of it. "Many things, fair and foul, came from his hand, not least among them the spear of great Lugus. When that spear was at last broken, its point was retrieved and forged into a knife, a blade yet imbued with some of the power of its crafting."

The god-king proffered the blade and she accepted it, running a thumb along the leather-wrapt hilt and examining the intricate knotwork decorating the hilt and pommel. The blade was long, almost enough to qualify as a sword, and it seemed to radiate a faint heat.

"This blade," Mithra said, "might strike down even one whose skin is turned adamant-hard with Pneuma. It might even serve to ground against bolts of lightning, should the wielder manage to interpose it betwixt herself and the source."

Realisation struck her like a blow. "You would have me fell Zeus with this blade."

Mithra nodded, once.

So the time, at long last, was upon her to make an end of the tyrant king of Elládos. "How am I to face him alone? With you and Marduk and the Immortals striking against Mu, how can I, alone, even so armed, stand against the mightiest man on Gaia?" Oh, but she could see herself doing it, even as fear gripped her. She could see the hilt of this blade protruding from his chest, see the searing blade punching through his accursed heart.

"You shan't be alone. Nemesis, though she knows it not as yet, must needs face off against him as well, for so the Moirai have decreed. Make sail for Atlantis, and perceiving threat to his Ambrosia, the Storm King will come to face you."

Artemis balked. "If he turns his storms upon the fleet, the loss of life will be catastrophic."

Mithra nodded, face a mask of stone. "Such comes the price for this one chance to make an end to his madness. The Olympian Order is rived with cancerous corruption that, unchecked, spreads across Gaia. Is that not why you came here, centuries prior? Did not you seek any chance to destroy the blighted lord of Elládos? Will you now turn aside to learn the cost shall come dear? Think you the loss of your ships so different than if they had gone to war against the gathered Elládosi? All of your life, all of your sacrifices have led you to this moment." Now, the god-king handed her the dagger's sheath, and she slid it in. "Make an ending of this Age of Olympus ... or else abandon your pursuit of vengeance, Artemis."

The god-king played upon her pain, she knew. Mayhap he had always planned it this way, or perhaps he merely adapted, as he said, to circumstances as they revealed themselves. Either way, she would not delude herself into thinking he did this for her.

No, nor would she do it for him.

Rather, because Zeus was a blight upon Gaia, a plague that had poisoned Mankind from time long gone. This plan would lead to countless deaths among her navy. Mostlike, it would end in her death, as well. But if she succeeded, she would have left the World a hair better than it had been.

Artemis had been an Olympian. She had been part of this corrupting rot that rived across kingdoms. For that, there was no amends ... but she could try. And she would relish the look upon the tyrant's face when she rammed this blade home.

Slowly, deliberately, she rose and strapped the dagger to her hip. "The last days of Olympus have arrived."

20

ATHENE

400 Dark Age

Many claimed Atlantis the greatest polis upon the face of Gaia. Beneath the sprawling metropolis grown far beyond its earliest intent, a discerning eye might yet catch glimpses of the elegant designs at its heart. Airborne, Athene found such insights easier, gazing down at the latticework of canals that carved apart the city. Far below, little more than specks from this height, people busied about their lives, having not the least clue their World would soon come crashing down around them.

The thought tore a rent inside Athene, had her ready to deny Ananke like one of the Gnostics she hunted down, ready to strike down any path to avert the end. But therein lay the trap. To deviate from the Wheel of Fate, to deny the impending Eschaton was to damn all the cosmos. She might buy these people a year, a day, an hour, but the cost would be the World, the rise of a Khaos that, unlike what Mithra said of the Leviathan, would never subside.

The people may not have known apocalypse closed in around them, but they knew that danger came. Soldiers sworn to Hebe piled into triremes making for open water, their sweeps straining for speed. Others, already away from the shore, manoeuvred to gain advantage. Word had come that the Babilimian fleet closed on the city.

From her vantage, Athene could see them, a carpet of ants marching across the waves, dooming Atlantis. Each ant a bireme or trireme, each one laden with armies of Mithra, come to burn these people. Did Artemis lead them? Instinct bade Athene descend upon those ships, drive the foreign invaders from the shores of her people. But to what end? Whether by the spears of Immortals or the monstrous wrath of an Elder Goddess, these people were all going die, and soon. Athene had come not to save them but to ensure those who threatened the continuance of Mankind did not survive what was to come.

The Gnostic Cabal, in their incessant clinging to free will without regard to its cost, could not be allowed to persist into another Era. Kronos was gone. Athene needs must ensure his disciples could never revive the movement her grandfather had begun. So she flew past the city, keen vision hunting for her stepmother. Olympus knew Artemis closed in on Atlantis. The Huntress, Athene assumed, had decided to force a confrontation at long last; surely she realised that, on threatening the source of Ambrosia, Zeus would call every last Olympian to its defence.

From the storms gathering above Mount Evenor, there had her father built his camp, intent on surveying his foes. Thunderclouds black as stygian depths roiled overhead, crackling with fulgurations. Even as she looked that way, a streak of white lightning ripped from the clouds, blasting upon a Babilimian ship. Athene turned to look, saw the flames erupt among the vessel, imagined the agonised screams of her crew. Watching, she saw the next strike, another trireme sundered by a bolt from the heavens. Another, and another. The sea turned turbulent with typhoon-like winds.

Flashes of lightning burst around her. Blinding light, deafening thunder, they dazed her senses, forced her to land. Ungraceful, Athene slapped against a hillside beneath the mountain. But even as she fell, she espied a camp on the lower slope, one where pegasi gathered. The other Olympians would be there, preparing to command their Titan and demigod forces against the invaders. Preparing to make their final stand, though they knew it not.

She was on her knees. Pulled off her helm. Rubbed palms against her eyes as if to work out the spots those flashes had left lingering across her vision.

The Gnostic Cabal has infected *the Olympian Order, and you do not even realise you are no longer masters of your actions.* So Artemis had spat at her, before the battle of Salamis, and Athene had refused to countenance such a thing. The Phoebid had claimed Zeus but a puppet to the Cabal. Then Hera had shown up—on a battlefield! Hera!—and demanded Athene hunt for and slay Nemesis. Athene wondered if Hera knew, back then, it was Athene's destiny to become Nemesis. If she had sought, with her words, to doom Athene to some sort of circular suicide.

There was no denying Hera had become a different person sometime during Athene's exile from Olympus. Her words, actions, demeanour, all had changed by the time Athene returned to the mountain. And now she knew. The Gnostic Cabal had a spy on Olympus. The traitor, Ningal, could shift her face. How long ago had Ningal slain the real Hera and taken her place?

Such were Athene's musings as she worked her way to the camp she'd seen. It was not large. The Olympians would have sent most of their minions to battle. Still, it would not do to be seen before she found her target, so Athene glamoured herself to invisibility and stalked up the mountainside. More thunder, lightning rent the sky; the rains began, turning the slope muddy. Winds battered her but could little impede her progress.

A thought occurred: Was her father so oblivious he could not see his wife had become a different woman? A bitter revelation settled upon her then—she was not certain that, if he knew, he would have cared. Artemis had been right. Zeus cared for naught and no one save himself. And women—they were no doubt interchangeable to him.

In the end, your father will cast your life aside as a mere token and never once grieve for your death. At best, it will serve as a pretence for venting his petty rage. The Phoebid's words rang in her head, over and over, as they had on the long voyage across the sea, when Athene sat as Artemis's prisoner. How oft had she denied those words. How she had sought to deny them.

She shook her head, unwilling to let grief claim her, though part of her wanted to weep in frustration at it all. For millennia, she had served

Zeus, so desperate to win his approbation. But Mithra claimed all Olympus had become corrupted, for beneath the mountain lay the Tartarian Gate. Zeus, in his arrogance or ignorance, had chosen to build his fastness above a blight, thinking himself immune to its toxins. Or maybe it was not just the Olympians ... maybe all Titans were a blight. From Elládos to Babilim and beyond, Titans reigned over Men, called themselves living gods, and dominated. With hubris, with cruelty, they thought themselves above other sentient beings of Gaia. Some Titans claimed they shepherded Men, as befit gods. Others made no pretence, claiming rulership in virtue of strength. But Men needed neither shepherds nor tyrants, and they would have done better in a world free of gods.

A stray flash of lightning struck a nearby tree and the thing exploded. One more victim of beings given too much power.

Oh ... such musings did not behove her, least of all in present circumstances. Athene replaced her helm on her head. Nemesis, the assassin of Fate, had come here to ensure Mankind could survive. That end was achievable only through the destruction of the Gnostic Cabal. If whatever remnant of Man survived this was to flourish, their means of doing so was not her present concern.

She closed in upon the camp and was not surprised to see it consisted only of Hebe, Hera, and Hestia, and their respective pegasi. Given the choice, Athene would not hurt Hebe or Hestia. Though they too would bear the corrupting influence of Olympus, she did not want to strike against either her sister or her grandfather's pyromancer apprentice. Instead, she circled the camp, trying to get close to Hera. At least, when Hera moved to one side to fortify her nerves with some wine, Athene was able to follow. Was there the least chance she was wrong? What if the woman before her was her stepmother after all? It would mean Hera had become a better person, had begun to care for others ... Athene wanted to believe that, couldn't. Mithra said Ningal was here. She had to be one of these three women. It wouldn't be Hebe; Athene's sister had lived on Atlantis, too far to influence their father.

Of a sudden, Hestia whirled, looked dead at Athene. She followed the pyromancer's gaze, saw the impressions her sandals left in the mud —empty footprints had appeared around the camp. Not even the glamour would hide such a thing. "Hera!" Hestia shrieked.

Athene's stepmother flung herself to the side, a dagger appearing in her hand from within the folds of her peplos.

Well, then.

Athene allowed the glamour to fall from her like rainwater streaking over a facade.

Hera balked, fell back. "Nemesis! Bah! I told that wretched daughter of Zeus to slay you, but it seems she failed in that as in everything else that day."

Athene stiffened, then pushed the indignation aside. She had come here to kill this woman. What should she care what Hera—Ningal—thought of her? She stripped off her helm and tossed it aside, savoured the widening of Hera's eyes. So she had not known. A point in her favour, Athene supposed. She eased free her xiphos.

"What treachery is this?" Hera demanded.

"Athene?" Hestia asked. Already, Hebe was by the pyromancer's side, hand on the hilt of her own xiphos. It was the pyromancer Athene looked to, then. The woman's expression was that of someone at last putting together the pieces of a puzzle that finally made sense. What visions had forewarned her of this, Athene wondered? Visions, all fragments, given, she assumed, only to ensure the turning of the Wheel of Fate, never to allow an Oracle to alter it. She supposed she would never know the extent of Hestia's burdens, even as Hestia might never know all Athene had borne.

Ignoring Hestia, Athene pointed her sword at Hera. "For too long the Cabal has whispered poison into the ears of my father. Small wonder, I suppose, given you cherish those vipers like children." Though Ningal had not brought her pet snakes here, at least.

"What is this?" Hestia demanded. "What Cabal do you speak of, Athene? I saw you fall to the traitor, Artemis. Did she infect your mind?"

"When did you kill my stepmother?" Athene spat at Hera.

"Ugh," Hebe moaned. "It had to be *my* sister who turned her brains to mush, huh? I mean, as if I've not tedium enough in dealing with"—she waved her hands as if to indicate all Gaia—"the war and shit. Psh, and now I've got to cope with a crazy person in the family."

No one bothered so much as looking at Hebe now.

"'Tis funny you should mention poison," Hera said, "and claim 'twas I who introduced it to your father. Oh, but that petty, hubristic buffoon has venom in his veins, child." Even as Athene's glamour had melted, so too did the illusion masking Hera fall away, revealing beneath her a Kandamian woman Athene had never seen before.

"Well ..." Hebe said. "Shit. Me, I did not see that coming. So, ugh ... you've got two faces, Mother? Like, literally two of them? Are there more?"

"You name serpents my children," Ningal spat back at Athene. "Yet, children I did have, and two of them sacrificed upon the altar of your master's vanity, of his cruel idolisation of merciless Ananke. When did I slay your contemptible mother? When she was fool enough to think to rid herself of a burdensome husband and thus seek allies in so doing! Oh, but Zeus is more useful to us alive, putting a stop to the villain whom you serve, Nemesis. Surely, even a despotic megalomaniac is better than the one who strives to end the world."

"Do you serve Mithra?" Hestia demanded. Even as she spoke, she reached toward the campfire, and its flames flared up, called to her hand in a churning spiral. Like a fiery serpent, it coiled about her arm, sizzling in the rain. "I do not know what obscenity had this woman slaying the queen to take her place ... but I find myself in agreement that, if she sides with Zeus rather than Mithra, her side is the one I must cleave to."

"Whoa," Hebe interrupted. "You mean, you slew my mother? And I'm supposed to, what? Say, 'oh, all for a good cause, anyway'? Psh." Hebe drew her xiphos and pointed it at Ningal. "That's an ill blow, it is. You know I have to avenge matricide, damn it all."

Finally, Ningal deigned to acknowledge the woman. "Your precious mother sought to assassinate your father."

"Well ..." Hebe moaned. "Aww, shit." The woman wavered, looked to Athene, the point of her xiphos drooping. "I don't ... Can't we just decide who's in the right? Ugh. Ethics and figuring stuff out is not my forte. I mean, better to bribe a philosopher to fuck or drink with or something, am I right?"

Athene wondered what it said about her that the closest she had to an ally in this moment was a moronic half-sister. "Hebe. Help me avenge your mother. The rest will bide until that's done."

With her right hand, Hestia drew a knife. The flames around her left hand surged higher, brighter. "Hebe, stand down. Athene, drop the sword while that option yet remains before you." That fiery serpent broke into two, each rearing back as it meant to dart in, immolate Athene. "I shan't ask again—"

An arrow abruptly sprouted betwixt the Olympian's eyes and she pitched over dead, flames extinguished in an instant. Everyone turned to see Artemis tossing aside her bow and pulling a pair of daggers. "Not a single Olympian shall survive this night."

"Oh, fuck," Hebe moaned.

Athene lunged at Ningal, who twisted aside with uncanny speed. The woman's blade clattered against Athene's xiphos, beat it aside. Athene kicked out, smacking her greave into Ningal's shin, drawing a shriek from the Titan, who pitched over. She must have reinforced her bones with Pneuma, for they did not snap, but still, she rolled aside, clutching her leg. Athene leapt across the few feet between them, stabbing downward.

Ningal whipped her dagger up, deflecting. Barely. Athene's xiphos gouged her face and sent her spilling over backwards.

A sudden rage blossomed in Athene's chest, born of her vision of Typhon and all the empty horror that lurked forever just beyond sight. Of the profane knowledge of what awaited the World, should the Gnostics succeed—eternal damnation for every soul in the cosmos. "You would dare thwart Ananke!" She kicked, her foot taking Ningal in the ribs and sending her hurtling aside. The fallen Titan's flight was halted by the trunk of an ancient, twisted juniper, one that cracked on impact. Ningal pitched to the ground, moaning.

Athene closed in, blade rising as she stalked the Gnostic. "I can no longer separate right from wrong. Neither praise nor condemn what you did to Hera, what you've done to my father. Only this ..." She pointed the blade at the woman, the Anunnak who should have been allied to the Unseen Order. "I am Nemesis, sworn to serve the Moirai and thus preserve the hope of life, even if that hope comes through the burning crucible of Eschatons. For threatening that hope, your life is forfeit, daughter of Enki."

"Enki ... is Mithra," Ningal spat. Athene faltered, cocked her head. So weary was she of these endless machinations, of the game the Gnostic Cabal and Unseen Order played across the ambit of history. She had to believe she had at last chosen the right side. She could not ... could not stand to think, once more, she had picked allies no better than those she had left behind. "Aye, let the weight sink in," Ningal taunted. "Let the unvarnished hypocrisy bloom before those azure eyes of yours. Let—"

She was cut off as Athene rammed her xiphos into her throat. Whatever lies Mithra had told mattered little compared to the stakes. Athene had seen Typhon, had spoken to the Moirai. She knew the threat the Cabal posed in trying to break the Wheel of Fate. She was Nemesis.

When she looked back, Hebe was dead at Artemis's feet. Of course she was. There were so few left on Gaia who could stand against either Artemis or Athene now. Among the last of the great Titans who had so long ruled this Earth, trampling Men beneath their sandalled feet.

"You killed my sister," Athene said, shocked by the lack of emotion in her voice.

"You killed my brother." Artemis's voice was *not* unemotional, but the wrath that started to limn her face melted away after a moment. "Zeus must die."

The words struck like a blow to Athene's kidney. Worse, because she knew they would come. Worse, because she knew them for truth. She slipped to one knee, driving the point of her sword into the ground. Leaning upon it, shaking her head, wanting to deny truth. She'd spent so much of her immortal life striving for her father's love. Why, why must it be *her* to betray him?

"His madness grows beyond all bounds," Artemis said, pointing at the raging storm above them. "He scorches the very heavens with his petulant fury. Do you believe, were he to be shown the Truth, he would surrender the least semblance of his power even for the sake of preserving the cosmos? That man, up there, he would see everything burnt to cinders if it meant holding his glory for a single heartbeat more. There is naught in his heart, nor his head, save for *himself*. There never has been. And on that poisoned, corrupted mountain, his madness festered for Ages. And we allowed it! You and I, the other Olympians, all of us!

"Because it stroked our egos to be told we were better than Men, told we were gods! We became the hand choking this world, Athene!" Artemis paused, looked hard at her, but not without sympathy. After all that had passed between them ... could still there be some fragment of love, as yet unbroken?

Artemis's words, in haunting echo of Athene's own dark musings, stung Athene to the pith. They were truth, she knew in bitter realisation. Too much truth. Titans were a blight, Athene had known. An Elder Race who had abused their power, as power, in the hands of the few, would always be abused.

"Not a single Olympian shall survive this night." When Artemis repeated her earlier statement, Athene looked to her, apprehended the depth of her meaning. Her erstwhile mentor included the both of them in her decree of an ending. "I go now to slay Zeus," Artemis said. "Will you seek to hinder me?"

Athene swallowed. Rose, plucking her xiphos from the ground with the sound of squelching mud. "I shall not." Because Artemis was right. "His madness ..." The words threatened to choke her. "It must end."

Artemis nodded. "Then ... let us make an end of it, side by side, as in days gone."

And end ... for Athene was weary, indeed.

BESIDE ARTEMIS, Athene climbed the slopes of Mount Evenor as a cataclysmic thunderstorm raged overhead. Lightning, seeming fierce enough to set the heavens ablaze and immolate the clouds, darted about the land and sea in annihilating fingers. Everywhere they touched, Gaia and the life upon her withered, cracked, or exploded. Dancing bolts touched down by the hundreds, now indiscriminate in the carnage they unleashed; fury, feeding upon itself, existing only for its own sake.

The galvanic apocalypse must have slain as many Elládosi as it did Babilimians, mayhap more. But what care had Zeus for such causalities, so long as his foes perished in the carnage? Athene had so long deluded herself about her father; so long, and not one moment more. His hubris was writ now with blinding flashes, heralded by the deafening trumpets of his thunder.

Cyclonic winds buffeted them as they ascended, threatening to tear them from the mountainside. Neither spoke. What more had they to say to one another now as they bore witness to the ending of the World? No, not merely bore witness to it. Titans, all Titans who had dared reign as living gods, they had wrought this ending, Athene and Artemis not least amongst them. Perhaps, even were the Eschaton not needful to perpetuate the Wheel of Fate, there came a time when the edifices of the World grew so corrupt that only total destruction could suffice to sweep them clean. Hope could endure only if given a fresh start.

A small megaron sat upon the upper slopes of Mount Evenor. The palace had belonged to Hebe, though Athene had never deigned to visit her sister there. Now, the marble columns of the portico seemed to wilt before the awesome fury of the storm Zeus had unleashed. Athene's father stood there, on the open porch past the entablature, arms raised as if in ecstasy at the carnage he commanded. A fierce, almost demoniac expression limned his face, his eyes too wide, his beard and hair swirling in the winds. A moment, Athene watched him, feeling her heart clench at the sight. Well did she know what was needful, what she ought to have done centuries back, yes. But the knowing of it only served to shatter her further. Her father, the man for whom she had done so much, the one for whom she had shaped her being in the hopes of pleasing him—and he stood here, an aberration against order. And she, a fiend, come for patricide, was no better.

She looked over her shoulder, sought for Artemis in the hopes the woman's presence might strengthen her resolve, but Artemis had disappeared. Perhaps she skirted the periphery to catch Zeus unawares; Athene did not think Artemis would back down. Either way, the time had come and Athene could not turn from this, even knowing her felling blow would strike down herself as well as Zeus. She blinked away the tears, strode up the steps of the megaron, rainwater sloshing beneath her sandals as they struck the slickened marble floor.

At last, Zeus noticed her, lowered his arms, and let the winds abate, enough to be heard. Though she'd have not thought it possible, his eyes grew wider still as he took in her armour. She knew that look though. Such came upon a person who at last understood the merciless weavings of Ananke and knew all their striving against those threads had only served to tighten them into the noose settling upon their neck. Well did Athene know that feeling.

"It is not possible," Zeus protested. "*You*. The child who would dare betray me ...? A girl!" It settled upon her then, a leaden weight, that he was more aghast to think a woman might overcome him than at the thought of his own blood bringing him low. They had tried to tell her, Athene knew. Artemis, Kirke, others, they had demanded she look upon the depths of the disdain with which Zeus viewed her gender. She'd known, of course. Had known, hadn't wanted to parse it, nonetheless.

There were no more illusions left, least of all those needful ones which allowed one to endure an otherwise intolerable existence. Athene eased free her xiphos. "I have come to stop your madness, Father. At the end, you have left me no choice but to become the spectre you so long dreaded."

Her father sneered at her, hefting a hand as if he might summon his lightning and strike her down. He did not act, though. "Ingrate child! I made you a living goddess! I made us all gods, gave us the World, to bend over and use as we willed!" Athene glowered at his wretched metaphor but saw no reason now to bother castigating him. Not now, blade in hand, ready for his throat. She advanced upon him. Abruptly, Zeus stiffened. "Do you not know what the Elder Gods are, you petulant cunt? They are the abominations lurking ever upon the fringes, hungering for the souls of all with the ambit of this World! Who, if not I, would shelter us from their wrath? By my hand alone does Gaia endure!"

"I know what they are ..." she said, still making one painful advancing stride after another. "Incarnations of Khaos, of evil. Only now am I forced to cast aside the scales upon my eyes and acknowledge that you, Father, are as twisted as the dark forces against which you claim to strive."

Again, that loathsome sneer came upon his face. It hurt less this time. His eyes crackled with lightning as Athene charged forward, wind racing behind her with the speed of her movement, throwing up a curtain of water. Her blade raced for his throat, a darting serpent. He caught it in his bare hand. Her sword crunched beneath his strength. Metal squealed, bent. No ichor seeped between his fingers, and Athene gawped at his apparent invincibility.

"You cannot imagine the depth of Pneuma so much Ambrosia has given me." He advanced, closed in upon her, leered at her in a way that had her skin crawling. His foot came up before she could recover her composure. The impact—forceful as an avalanche—crunched her insides despite her Pneuma and sent her hurtling away like a missile. Her back crashed into a marble column. The surface split, sending a rain of dust and pebbles hailing upon her head.

Gasping, arm to her gut, Athene struggled to pull herself into a sitting position. He had knocked her beneath the entablature, but the wild gales still sent rain splattering her from the side. She blinked, tried to clear her vision. Even surging her Pneuma only served to blunt the pain, not completely remove it. She cast about for her xiphos, but the bent, useless thing lay tossed at her father's feet. The luminance in his eyes deepened. Galvanic arcs jumped between his fingers.

He spoke; she could not hear him over the ringing in her ears. Even as he thrust that hand forward, even as lightning leapt from him, coursing toward her, Artemis dropped down from the roof betwixt Athene and her father, blades in hand. Zeus's lightning crashed into one of her knives as if drawn to it, an electric stream of searing radiance, roaring so loud it drowned all other sound. That knife turned incandescent, absorbing the cataclysmic energies.

Then, gaping, Zeus broke off the torrent of his attack. Power still coruscated along the blade and Artemis whirled, whipping her knife in an arc. A parabola of lightning leapt from it, hit the pooled rainwaters upon the portico, and rolled along the ground in a wave. That voltaic blast surged back into Zeus and sent Athene's father hurtling backward, thrown off the porch.

Athene blinked, rubbed her ears to try to force down the ringing. Artemis was looking at her, she knew, demanding she rise. Yes, because this would not be ended so easily. The other woman did not offer her a hand, instead turning back to race after Zeus, so fast her form blurred, visible only in momentary fulgurations. Athene gained her feet, though fresh agonies tore through her insides in the process. Zeus had ruptured internal organs, she suspected. With enough Pneuma, perhaps a dose of Ambrosia, she might heal such injuries. She doubted she would have any such chance.

The sound of fighting rang out, over the thunder, metallic clangs. Blades meeting—or Potency-infused Titan blows striking against Pneuma-hardened Titan flesh. Athene flooded more Pneuma not into healing her wounds but suppressing the pain of them and charged forward until she beheld Zeus and Artemis in melee. Lightning had flash burnt away much of Zeus's shirt, singed his beard and brows, and turned his flesh ruddy. He did not seem pained, though, so much as seized by a paroxysm of rage. He had caught Artemis's wrist that held that frightful dagger, whilst her other blade clattered uselessly against his reinforced skin.

Athene's father twisted his arm, and Artemis shrieked. Athene could not hear the bones break, not above the clamour of the storm and the fight. No, but she saw when Zeus dropped Artemis, her wrist was bent at an unnatural angle, the edge of her ulna punching out of her flesh. The Phoebid was clutching her ruined right hand, wailing in agony Athene did not want to contemplate.

Athene surged forward, focusing Pneuma to make herself as fast and strong as she had ever managed. She crashed into Zeus as though flung from a catapult, hurling the both of them toward the mountain's precipice. They burst into open air and Athene kicked away from him, summoning her wings to forestall her plummet. The winds were too strong and tossed her about like a doll. Then a bolt of lightning streamed out of the clouds, smacked into her like the fist of the cosmos.

Next she knew, she was at the bottom of a slope, covered in scree and ichor, smoke rising from her ruined cuirass and smouldering wings. Zeus was standing over her. With a kick to her abdomen, he spun her over, then seized one of her already ruined wings. Too late, she realised his intent, tried to dismiss them. But already he had a hand on it, and she could not retract her wings. Zeus planted a sandal upon her back and bellowed as he yanked. Flesh and sinew shredded. Red agony blinded Athene as she was certain her entire body was being torn apart.

With the sickening sound of rending flesh, her right wing tore free. Zeus tossed it aside with a wet *plop*. He grabbed her by the hair and heaved her aloft, forced her to look into his stormy eyes. The fury that simmered there was beyond the ken of Man or Titan, something altogether Otherworldly.

"After I cut off her hands and feet," Zeus drawled, "I'm going to fuck every orifice of that cunt friend of yours—"

A shadow dropped down from above, crashed into the pair of them. Zeus wailed like a toddler as he and Artemis toppled to the ground. Artemis sprang up, flipped around in midair, and landed to face him, her ruined arm cradled against her abdomen. Only belatedly did Athene realise Artemis's strange dagger now jutted from Zeus's back, just above his right shoulder blade.

"How's that for a new orifice?" Artemis spat.

Shrieking, Zeus jerked a hand toward the Phoebid, lightning dancing about his fingers. The energies surged, burst forth, and shot not at Artemis but back into the king's body. Lightning coruscated over Zeus and back into the dagger, sending him tumbling end over end like some mummer doing cartwheels, limbs flying akimbo. Athene's father crashed down on the slope, pitched over the side, and fell off into a gulley.

"What ...?" Athene gasped, trying not to weep at the waves of agony breaking over her. She bent back, looked to the ichorous stump where a moment prior a wing had been. Seeing such a thing only redoubled the pain. She withdrew her wings inside herself. That failed to mute the torment and Athene grieved to think a missing limb might hurt worse than an injured extant one.

"Remnants of the days of Dark Faerie," came Artemis's answer as the Phoebid advanced to the precipice over which Zeus had fallen. Athene saw her brace, no doubt directing the flow of her Pneuma, then she leapt over the side, disappearing into the gap.

Once more, Athene staggered to her feet. This must be ended. This must ... A rumble shout through the island, became a colossal roar as of an army of enraged drakons all wakened at once. The ground shook with such force, a crack rived the mountainside. With a convulsive heave, one half of the slope jutted upward whilst the other fell away. A wave passed beneath the ground, and geysers of sulphur and magma shot up in sporadic intervals. Clouds of dust and ash mingled with the cyclone already raging about the mountain until everything grew dark as a moonless night.

Athene staggered to the precipice and peered below, unable to spare any Pneuma to enhance her senses. There, on what had become an island of rock sundered from the rest of the slope, stood Artemis and Zeus, both of which could only use one arm. Artemis gave him no pause to withdraw the dagger in his shoulder, and he could not use the lightning whilst it remained. The Phoebid danced around the Kroniad, so fast he could not land a hand on her. Which was fortunate for her, given Zeus had the strength to tear her limb from limb should he catch her. Artemis was a whirlwind, though, darting around him, landing blows with fist and foot. Each rang as though struck against solid iron. A Titan could not keep their skin reinforced like that forever, but Athene suspected, given how Zeus had glutted himself on Ambrosia, Artemis would tire first.

Panting, Athene backed up. It was a long way, and she had no wings, nor Artemis's ability at Lightness. But Athene needed to be there. It had to be her. So she flooded all the Pneuma she could to her legs, broke into a run, and leapt. She soared some forty feet afore the cyclonic winds seized her in midair and sent her careening off course. The gale flung her against the upraised side of a chasm that had torn open, and, having directed all her Pneuma to the leap, she had none to fortify her flesh. The impact knocked her breath away, and Athene pitched toward the heaving, tumultuous ground. It rose up to meet her, smacked her senseless.

Next she looked, pushing up on her elbows, Zeus had managed to get a hand around Artemis's ankle. The king roared, spun, whirling the Phoebid around before releasing her. Artemis hit the island's surface, skidded along it, tumbling end over end. Athene hoped the woman had Pneuma left to reinforce her skin. Either way, each jarring impact must have been torture upon Artemis's ruined wrist.

Rising once more—swaying despite her Pneuma—Athene leapt over the gulf separating her from the island where her father stood. A geyser of magma burst as she passed, incandescent and foul smelling. Athene landed in a crouch, then, as Zeus reached awkwardly around for the dagger in his shoulder, she sprang catlike at him. She collided with his midriff and bore her father down, smacking him into the dirt.

"Traitor!" he spat, shoving her off him, stumbling to his feet. Tiring at last. Even he had limits to his Pneuma.

Instinct bade her dispute his accusation, defend herself, justify her actions. But something forestalled her, made her hold her tongue. Maybe it was that she owed this man naught more than she had already given to him, Age upon Age, in thankless service.

Her lack of answer served to enrage him further, and he lunged at her, swiping with his good hand. Athene blocked on her vambrace and jerked her elbow up into his jaw. He staggered away, ichor dribbled from his split lips, her father seeming even more shocked than she was. It had been like striking solid rock, but he could no longer ward against Pneuma-enhanced Titan strength. Would he run out before her energies dwindled? He swung again, reliant on brute force rather than technique.

Athene caught him in one of the earliest pankration holds Artemis had ever taught her, flipped him over her shoulder, and slammed him to the ground. She followed up with a fist to his nose. Cartilage exploded beneath her blow, and ichor seeped down, into his beard.

"Fucking cunt," he spat—or tried, for his words were garbled by his broken nose.

She hit him again. She wanted to weep. She wanted to scream, to rail against the Moirai at the inequities of life, at the sheer obscenity of saddling her with such a parent. But as Nemesis, she knew better than any the futility of raging against Fate. The Wheel must turn, or the cosmos would crumble. For good or ill, the Moirai had woven this perverse tale, brought her here, to the moment when she must strike down her father. When she must become a patricide, the most loathsome of creatures on Gaia.

Zeus tried to spit some vulgarity at her again. Unintelligible, though she imagined he relied on his usual term for women. She hit him again. Again, twice more. He tried to spew some other incoherence at her. Another blow landed across his temple, cracking the stone around them.

Again, the land heaved. Through the ash and raging storm, she could see a mountainous wave arising, come to swallow the whole island of Atlantis. From the feel of the tremors, perhaps the land would break apart afore the wave even reached here. She heaved Zeus to his feet. Saw Artemis behind her, watching, arm against her gut, other hand upon her knee, struggling to stand.

Part of her longed to apologise to her father for the need for this. She wanted to beg his forgiveness—though it would never come, of course—for what she must do. She could not voice those words, though. She owed it to his myriad victims to do this without sentiment. He had treated so many people, women most of all, as less than persons. So how could familial bonds now join them in connection? How could Athene allow herself such an indulgence?

"Imma ... fuck ... yer ..." he mumbled.

Athene kneed Zeus in his stones. The blow doubled him over, allowed her to grasp the blade embedded in his shoulder. Even touching it, she could feel the Pneuma coursing through this ancient object, this remnant, as Artemis said, of Dark Faerie. She wondered, a moment, what dire days had seen such a thing made, and what Eschaton had ended those days, as well. Then she jerked the blade free, drawing a hiss from her ... from the broken king. Grabbing his hair with one hand, Athene jerked his head back.

"The assassin of Fate condemns you for your crimes," she spat at him. And she rammed the blade under his chin until the point burst from the base of his skull. Then she let him drop like a stone.

A cacophony of roars erupted around them as waves lapping upon the shore deposited tremendous saurian bulks before the city. Sea drakons, perhaps wakened by the churning deep? Blue and aquamarine scaled, they came, like giant lizards swarming over the crumbling polis of Atlantis.

"The Muians call those taniwha," Artemis said, having limped over to her. "Supposed to be legend more than ..."

"What do you see?" Athene asked, for the Phoebid had sharper eyes.

"Atlantean ships try to flee. They shan't make it, I think. The drakons ..."

Athene shut her eyes a moment. "You said no Olympian should survive the night. You had the right of it—this island is finished. But let us make an end slaying drakons and see if we cannot spare what Men we might."

When she looked to Artemis, the other woman nodded. "The least we can do, given all we've done." There were tears in the Phoebid's eyes. Perhaps she thought of her betrothed, thought how she would never again look upon his visage.

"Artemis," Athene said. "The Wheel of Life spins out souls again and again. Maybe ... we'll have another chance ..."

The woman bent to retrieve the dagger from Zeus's corpse. "Maybe we'd make the same mistakes," she said, not looking up.

"Maybe," Athene admitted.

But then, to try to do it better perhaps was the most that could be asked of any person.

21

PANDORA

400 Dark Age

*T*he collapsing bubble of the Box deposited Pandora outside the city of Mugedang. Her timewalk had caught up pieces of the falling debris from the Hursag sanctum, and they showered about her. She scarce noticed, given the colossal roar of a city imploding. Even as she had witnessed the fall of Atlantis, she saw the beautiful streets and wondrous architecture of Mugedang tumble inward, swallowed by rents torn across the land. The earth shook with such violence she could not gain her feet, though she managed her knees, gawping at the cataclysmic destruction.

As she looked, she realised it was not the city tearing itself apart but, so far as she could tell, the entire continent of Mu. Explosions burst from distant mountains. Incandescent blooms of lava lit the night sky with reddish gleams. Volcanic lightning streaked through curtains of ash and dust obscuring the sky.

And all around, the sea rose, liquid mountains crashing in toward the land. The Deluge was come. She saw it, then, a shadow within the monstrous waves, a darkness looming in the deep. She saw it, and though she'd known it would come, still Pandora could not fight down her shriek of atavistic dread on beholding an entity of such horror.

Though she had thought the waves mountainous, when she saw the eyes, each larger than a city, she realised the scope of her error. A chain of lidless wells of incandescence gleamed beneath a shroud of water, faintly illuminating a draconic head ... or some profane amalgamation of drakon and cephalopod. Numerous tentacles writhed in the deep, blessedly concealed—for the most part—by the darkness, such that she could, at least momentarily, deny the vast breadth of them. Each of those tendrils might encompass and crush a polis. Each might tear worlds apart.

When its behemothic bulk shifted, a swell of the tides came crashing onto Mugedang, inundating the city, ravaging what little of it might have survived the quakes.

So came Tiamat, the Leviathan. So came the ending of the World.

She had to do something. She had to stop this demon god, no matter what it took. She must save what lives might be saved, must ensure life could endure—though she knew Prometheus had given that role to another. Still, she could not stand aside. Pandora rose, legs wobbling. She had so drained her Pneuma, so battered herself with timewalking.

She advanced. Toppled back to one knee. She needed fire to call upon ... Pandora looked, saw the distant rivers of lava cutting troughs through Mu now. Lava flows swept away rainforest, everything aflame. She crawled in that direction. Would never make it.

The Box ... The Box could take her there. Using it again might render her unconscious, mayhap drain the last of her life away. But without the source of flame to absorb and refill her Pneuma, how was she to stand against the Leviathan? She took up the Box, began to set it.

The surging tides swept in. Fast, too fast. Water hit her. Something washed over her, shielded her from the impact, at least partially. Still the waves struck with colossal force, stole the Box from her weak fingers, obscured all vision. She was pressed down, against the new-formed seabed, held secure against the rushing currents. A fishy tail abraded her naked flesh. Had a siren ... saved her? Her lungs were going to explode, she couldn't see, couldn't breathe, couldn't think ...

Then she was seized in iron-strong arms, surging upward. A leap carried the both of them above the churning water, and Pandora sucked down a ragged breath. They landed upon a rock outcropping just above the breaking waves—might have been a hill afore now. Soon, it would be underwater.

Her rescuer had formed legs now, held her in his arms. His eyes nictitated. She knew this siren. "Sirsir ..." The former servant of Themis had lost half his face in some recent battle, seemed scarce clinging to life now.

"Pandora." Sirsir cast a glance over his shoulder, winced as he saw the Leviathan. So, even this god of the sea feared—dreaded—the apocalyptic horror that had wakened unto the world. "Marduk commanded I save lives as I might." He looked pointedly skyward, back toward the eldritch abomination that had closed with Mugedang.

No, he was not looking at the Leviathan. He was looking at something else, a figure so tiny as to seem insectile against the backdrop of the Elder Goddess. Yet that figure leapt in, soaring a hundred feet in the air, streaming arcs of lightning as he surged toward the Leviathan.

And she knew. That was Marduk. The man ... who had, afore now, been held in fitful slumber as vestiges of past lives began to surface for him, that he might face a threat to the very existence of the World. The Destroyer was Mithra's son, primed and groomed for the role by his father. He would fight, but not even he could stand against a threat such as this. Not alone.

Still, he struggled, leapt among thrashing tendrils pulverising a city, striking with that mace. Each falling blow brought crashing thunder and cataclysms of lightning. It would not be enough.

"I need flame," Pandora rasped, pointing toward the erupting volcanos. "I must be closer."

Sirsir looked solemn a moment. "He knew, now I think upon it. Enki knew this frightful end he brought upon the Earth and named it all Fate, said it was carved upon the Tablet of Destiny." Where Marduk's name would be carved as the Destroyer that might stop this, might ensure something survived. But could Pandora trust him to do so alone? No, she would not bide and allow such. "We believed in him. Yet still, I ... could not have imagined this."

"Enki is dead!" Pandora shrieked. "I slew him for callous disregard for life." She was shaking, half afraid he would kill her for the admission, breathless, maybe dying from draining so much of her Pneuma. "He was wrong! Now, I need flame!"

"Aye," Sirsir said, grim faced. "Then grab my shoulders. As the water rises, those peaks become islands. I can swim you there."

Pandora wrapt her arms around the siren's shoulders, and he dove back into the surging water, resuming his tailed form. It was awkward, holding on whilst he beat his tail to hurl them through the water. Focusing on that task helped to keep her from dwelling upon the unspeakable carnage unfolding all around them.

She knew, of course, Atlantis was ripping itself apart, even now. She did not understand what had caused the quakes, but she knew the continents were shifting, tearing themselves to pieces. She knew, all that would remain, soon, was scattered islands and endless sea. She had failed to stop the ending of the Era, yes, but she would not fail to see the Leviathan driven from the Mortal Realm once more. She must ... must win this.

She looked back, saw Marduk—a gleaming speck of light encased in coruscating energies—leaping from tendril to tendril, striking blows that could never fell the Leviathan. He could not do this alone. For all his fearful thunder, he was a mosquito trying to down an elephant. He had not enough power.

Sirsir bore her close until she could feel the heat as lava poured into the newly risen sea, throwing up curtains of steam and obscuring all view. The water grew scalding, and the siren gasped, no doubt agonised. Pandora reached a hand toward the searing flames of the earth, let their Pneuma flow into her and replenish her own. She heard, within those flames, the heartbeat of Gaia. It became Pandora's heartbeat. Faster, stronger, hotter.

Burn, burn, burn.

"Help me breach the water," she commanded. "Then get gone from this place, save whomever you can."

Sirsir flung her skyward, enough for Pandora to manifest her flaming wings and hurl herself above the waves. Her shrieking flight carried her through choking fumes, amid flashes of volcanic lightning that passed too close, ever too close. Once more, she could not breathe.

Through the haze, through the fear, she saw it as a tentacle seized Marduk. As it broke him upon the mountainside. As the Elder Goddess crushed the last of their hopes, of Prometheus's *great* hope for the continuance of Mankind. A wail escaped Pandora.

Her fiery leap carried her there, and she too crashed upon the slope, beside Marduk's broken body. Her flames, afore she managed to extinguish them, ignited the forest around her. She paid it no heed, for there, beside her, lay the shattered corpse of the Destroyer, his useless mace still clutched in a death grip.

How could this happen? How could the Destroyer fail? Her hand went to her mouth, stifling a scream, stifling weeping. Holding back all emotion, for she felt empty, bereft of everything to which she might now cling. Was she ... to fight the Leviathan alone? She knew she would fail. She was not the Destroyer, besides which, she knew Marduk, in past lives, had defeated every foe before him. Time and time, the cycle ... the cycle ...

It was broken now. The World would end, the cosmos winking out as though they had never been. Whatever dregs were left when the Leviathan finished, the rest of the Elder Gods would consume, damning all souls to eternal torment. Prometheus's great gambit had, in the end, played itself out and he had lost.

Pandora kindled a flame in the palm of her hand, saw how paltry it looked before the boundless scope of the abomination closing in. She could never defeat this Elder Goddess. Only Marduk had ... only ...

She had risen from her death, when Kanaloa had slain her. She had been reborn from ashes. She had brought Kadmus back from death. She ... Pandora gasped.

She pressed her palms against Marduk's chest. Trembles wracked her whole body. She could do this. She must do this. She pushed her Pneuma into his still, broken form. She believed in him ... because she believed in Prometheus. Because Prometheus had wagered all on this gambit, and Pandora would not allow it to fail. Not at any cost.

She screamed, pouring more and more of herself into Marduk's body. She felt the Phoenix within her, sparking, flaring, seeping into the Destroyer alongside her Pneuma. Mentally, she wrapt herself around its smouldering core, unwilling to let too much go. Just enough to restore him ... But would that be enough to stop the Leviathan?

A memory, a flash. Prometheus made this for her.

"There was ... a legend, Pandora, a thought I chased after for ages until, at

last, I realised I must create what I sought myself, even as I created the Box. All for you."

"What are you saying?"

"As best I reckon it, I spent some three decades bound in Tartarus. And in that time, I kindled a flame … an ember broken off the First Flame."

A broken piece of the First Flame, itself a fragment of another Elder God, a god of scorching flame and destruction.

"It will burn in you. Through you. With more Pneuma than you can ever imagine—if you can but harness it. For I stole this Flame from Agni, when the world was young and I was another man. It is brighter, scorching hot, Pandora."

In her mind's eye, Pandora stood before the Phoenix now, in a darkened cave, the only illumination coming from the bird's smouldering pinions, from the embers gathered round its feet. The bird, at least ten times the size of the greatest of eagles, stared at her, its black pupil boring into her, the incandescence of its iris burning her soul.

Burn, burn, burn.

It was in her, a part of her. Because Prometheus had torn a piece of the Flame inside himself and given it to her. Because he had trusted her to push through the endless tribulations he'd known would lie ahead of her. He had known she would need to be armed against the coils of the ouroboros, to strive again and again against Fate. And to do so now, this was the way, the last way.

Attuned to her thoughts, the Phoenix rose, spread its wings, and bared its breast. She raised a trembling hand toward it. Prometheus had created the Tablet of Destiny, had chosen the Destroyer for this, even as he had made the Phoenix for her. Here, at the end, all that was left was trust. He had trusted her to use well this power, and now, she needs must trust his choices might one day lead them to a better future.

Reaching inside the Phoenix was reaching inside an inferno. Heat overwhelmed all other senses, though Pandora did not burn or her hair catch flame. From within the breast of the Phoenix, she withdrew a glowing ember the size of her fist. It pulsed, heart-like; she wondered if it was from the bird or a piece of her heart.

Grasping it with both hands, Pandora ripped it in twain, deliberately breaking off but a tiny chunk. A last, glowing ember that might sustain her heart. For it would be too easy to surrender now, to pour everything into Marduk and let go the future she had so long sought. But doing so would be sacrificing the hope she held for herself, and this, Pandora would not do. Hope, she swore, would never flicker out.

The smaller fragment, she pushed against her breast, over her heart. The greater piece became as magma in her hands, flaring bright as the sun.

PANDORA WAS BACK in her body, kneeling over Marduk, still pushing her Pneuma into him. Pushing the Phoenix—the greater piece of it—into him. It rushed out of her in a surge of heat that, in its passing, left her chilled, especially sodden and naked as she was. Pandora pitched over sideways, gasping, feeling as though every breath had fled from her. The taste of ash filled her mouth, seemed to clog her airways.

And still, still, a piece of that ember wakened inside her.

A radiant flame burst into life beside her, a bonfire scorching skyward. A dozen feet, two dozen, three dozen, the fire raged, a miniature volcano. Its heat raced over Pandora, flooded into her, restoring her strength, though that Pneuma remained at the barest fraction of what once it had been. The better part of her power, it was gone from her.

Gone from her, not from the World. As the flames dwindled, from the pyre rose a man, eyes lambent with the fires now burning in his core. He was naked, all he'd carried burnt to ash, save for that mace, now turned incandescent by the heat that had consumed his body. That fearsome weapon dripped and ran, its shape ruined, though the growing coruscation of lightning along its head told Pandora its power remained. And he, now, with more Pneuma than he could have ever imagined coursing through his body, primed to pour into that weapon.

All around her, the continent continued to rip in half. Tendrils of the Leviathan had sundered all Mugedang, were now crushing mountains, reaching out to destroy any cities surviving the Deluge. Other tentacles seized those ships which sought to flee the carnage, pulverised the vessels, and tossed the wreckage into that cavernous saurian maw, where she knew souls would be feasted upon and brought to unspeakable torment.

Marduk looked to her, then his mace. His lucent gaze raked over her once more. Trembling, on the edge of weeping, Pandora mouthed, "go." For he alone might face this, and into Prometheus's champion, she too had now poured the last of her hopes. Of all Gaia's hopes.

With a nod—an acquiescence that he, too, would not survive this—Marduk leapt. Flames burst from his heels and hurled him skyward as fiery wings sprang from his back. He was hundreds of feet in the air, shooting into the heavens like a falling star in reverse, streaking toward the eldritch abomination ending the World.

Through the haze of storm cloud and ash, through glimpses granted by flashes of volcanic lightning, she saw their battle. Through the brilliant, blinding light of the galvanic cyclone Marduk unleashed, she saw the monster blasted and scorched as the Destroyer streaked across the sky on wings of fire. She watched, saw mere flickers as gods destroyed one another. One, a demon of the Khaos beyond the World, an Elder Goddess from outside of time and space, hungry. The other, a living god come to bring destruction, if through it time might persist. She and Prometheus, they had helped forge this dark, violent god, who stood against the encroachment of forces darker still.

The thought brought a grim smile to her face, and she rose.

Waves still fell around her, drinking the land, the Deluge claiming its due. Pandora raced up the mountain slope, seeking higher ground. She could no longer manifest flaming wings, but she would not surrender her life. She leapt to a rock ledge above her, still blessed with enough Pneuma to make superhuman bounds. Further she pushed on. Because so long as breath remained in her body, Pandora would not stop, would never accept the inevitable.

So long as life remained, so too, would hope. Always.

EPILOGUE

1 Worldsea Era

Having dispatched Nemesis's minions, Prometheus turned, saw the so-called Oracle of Tides—the octopus god Kanaloa—seize Pandora in an arm and drive her to the bottom of the pool. Panic raced through him like the foreshocks of the quakes he knew must come in mere moments. She could not die; he could not lose her. Flooding Pneuma for speed, he surged toward the pool, charging across the cavern of the Soul Hollow. With a single bound he covered the last thirty feet and dove in water that had—blessedly, she yet had a chance! —already begun to boil.

The curtain of bubbles made it almost impossible to see, so Prometheus swam toward the greatest concentration of heat. The Phoenix was wakening in her, bringing her back, it had to be. He flailed through the searing hot water until his fingers brushed over flesh, caught her, kicked off the bottom, and launched them out of the water to come crashing down alongside the pool. He spared a single glance over his shoulder, but Kanaloa had fled the flames burgeoning within Pandora's … corpse.

She was not breathing. The thought flensed his soul, filled him with a profound desire to shout denials at the heavens, to curse the Moirai, as he had done time and again across the passage of eons. Mentally, he shrieked, *"Not again, not again!"*

Effulgent red streaks seeped through her flesh, like veins of fire coursing just beneath her skin. The whole of her body turned lambent, then immolated, raging flames bursting from her. Prometheus had dared hope for this, but still his breath caught. Still, he feared to believe ... He seized her. "Pandora! Wake, Pandora!"

The radiance grew so intense he could no longer see through the fire. Her body turned to ash. And from those ashes, it was reborn. Pandora convulsed, retched seawater from her lungs as the quakes began. The Queens of Mu had broken the Veil, called forth the Leviathan, the Archon of the Deep, the one the Elládosi named Echidna and the Babilimians called Tiamat. All around, the Earth convulsed from the breach, continents tearing themselves apart, unable to bear the strain of the connection to the Eternal Depths within the Spirit Realm. He had known the Deluge was coming, had foreseen it. Still, he'd dreaded this moment.

All around them, men and women were screaming. Vinata was gone, perhaps fled through the Time Chamber. Which was, he supposed, where he must send Pandora, much though it pained him.

"Pandora!" Prometheus yanked her to her feet. "We have to go now!"

"I died!" she shrieked, eyes wild as realisation struck her. "I died! I died!"

He wished he could give her the time to parse all that had passed, but this place would mostlike be buried under a mountain of debris in moments. If not, then the rising sea would claim it. Either way, Mugedang was lost and they must flee. He grabbed the sides of her face. "The Phoenix is a manifestation of pure Pneuma, enough to rekindle the spark of your life when it had been reduced to ashes. I ... I saw you rise from your pyre, Pandora. I begin to hope, perhaps, like myself, you might have moved beyond the constraints of death."

She shook, scarce herself, and little could he blame her. "I ... we failed. They summoned the Elder Deep."

All he could offer to that was a nod. For, of course, he had known she would fail here. The future existed and could not be gainsaid merely for the asking. History was merciless.

She was so weak now he draped her arm around his shoulders to usher her from the Soul Hollow. Only a few steps, and it was clear she could not move at speed, as yet, so he swept her up in his arms. Even as he did so, a massive stalactite pitched down in the space before them. Prometheus shielded Pandora from the cloud of debris with his body, then broke into a wild dash. Part of him wanted to keep *this* Pandora with him, to see her to safety. But in flame, he had seen another, and that one would need him. In order for that Pandora to exist, this Pandora must flee another way.

Pandora still in his arms, Prometheus escaped the palace and, surging Pneuma, broke into great bounds, each carrying them dozens of feet. All around them, Mugedang was rent and sundered, the wondrous city meeting the same grinding end as Murias before it. The land convulsed, bucked in pained waves. Schisms ripped open, half of streets sent skyward whilst the other side pitched into gulleys and were swallowed by the sea. Entire city blocks vanished into sudden crevices.

The Eschaton reaped its rich harvest, adding to the incalculable tally of Prometheus's guilt.

He saw the mountainous wave rising in the distance, soon to break over the city, over the crumbling continent. Saw it, felt the colossal intellect within the wave stretching out, seeking souls; Prometheus chose not to look. Pandora felt it too, screamed.

Prometheus raced through the ruins of Mugedang, back to the ruins of Murias, where lay the Time Chamber that might see Pandora to safety. The central plaza split apart before them, the columns in the colonnade crashing in succession, bringing down the stoa's roof. People died by the thousands and he, much though he wished to save more of them, he could do naught now. Instead, he jumped down to a lower level, and again, splashing shoulder-high into the water, racing into the canal that had, moments earlier, been a dry bed. The flood was blocking the way to the ruined city beneath Mugedang, but he must reach it, nevertheless. Pandora depended on it.

"Can you find your way back to the Chamber?" he shouted.

"Come with me!" she pleaded.

"I cannot! I am needed elsewhere!" That, too, he had seen, and the pieces were beginning to fit together now, the fragments slotting into place. "You must go, Pandora!" The hesitation was writ plain upon her face. She no more wanted to be separated from him than he from her.

He cupped her cheek with his palm. Would that he could linger here ... But doing so might damn Pandora, and anyone he might manage to save in the next moments. So he allowed himself no more time, not with this Pandora. He raced away, charging back through the surging water that threatened to cast him aside and hurl him out to sea. He caught a block of masonry, scrambled atop it, and from there leapt to the canal's edge. Mortar crumbled beneath his fingers, but still he managed to reach what remained of street level.

He made his way toward the harbour and, on spying it below, found it completely flooded. Ships had broken free of their moorings and were flung wildly by waves. Dhows smacked into one another or crashed over the saddle roofs of nearby buildings, scraping off chains of tiles in the process. People were screaming, he knew, but he could hear no words over the world-ending cacophony erupting in all directions. With a great bound, he leapt onto a roof. His bare feet skidded along the steep incline of soaked tiles, then he caught himself and raced forward, leaping from building to building toward the ships.

He could, if he joined a vessel, help guide it to safety. Perhaps, some few of the children of Mu might yet survive this cataclysm. Then he looked out to sea and saw the onrushing wave containing the Leviathan *stalled*. There, before it, stood Pokoharau, the Sea Queen, feeding all of her Mana into holding back the inevitable, into buying time for her people to escape. A handful of ships fled the harbour in the time she bought, sailing in two different directions, and Prometheus might choose but one of them.

He leapt to another roof, and another, then espied an enormous double-hulled canoe. Surging all the Pneuma he could, Prometheus broke into a run and leapt for it, cleared almost fifty feet. But the waves dropped out from beneath the canoe, pitching the boat wildly, and he fell short, crashing into the churning sea. Currents strong as a maelstrom seized him, hurling him hither and thither. Momentary dread rose—he could not permanently die from drowning, but he could find himself locked in an endless cycle of so doing, reviving only to drown instantly once more, never again to stand upon dry land.

A hand seized his, hurled him above the waves, and he landed upon the canoe's connecting planks with a breath-stealing *thud*.

"Maui?" someone shouted, peering over him, and Prometheus belatedly recognised Nu'u. His wife, Lilinoe, was there too, and many others. The Snow Queen had taken charge and was issuing orders. "Praise the ancestors, Maui!" Nu'u cried. "Malah found you?"

"Malah ... Sirsir?" Prometheus asked with a groan, rising to grasp a line and steady himself on the bucking, wild outrigger. He had heard the Nusantarans name Sirsir thus.

"Aye, the Adaro has a line beneath the ship, is trying to help pull us where sails and sweeps fail." Nu'u pointed over to the man at the helm. "Captain Atrahasis and the spirit have an accord."

Prometheus knew Atrahasis, a noble of Mugedang. He and Pandora had once dined with him, almost two decades prior. Clutching a succession of lines, Prometheus made his way to the captain. "The mountain!" he shouted, pointing to what had now become an island. "Hina is there, we must save her!"

Wild-eyed, Atrahasis looked back and forth between the place Prometheus indicated and the surging wave about to seize them all. "Maui, I ..."

Prometheus grabbed his shoulder. "I have foreseen where islands will survive this and can guide us there! Pass around that mountain and we will be on our way. I beseech you, old friend! My wife is there!" He could not lose her again, not like this. The fragments of his visions, they clarified in his mind, and he was certain now, as he so oft became certain of the future only when it was far too late to change it.

"We can get there," Lilinoe cut in. "We must save as many Muians as we can." Prometheus did not miss that, as Maui and Hina, the queen counted them still among her people.

With a grunt, Atrahasis yanked on the tiller until, a moment later, Sirsir surfaced to demand what he was about. Whether the Deep One approved, he made no comment, instead diving below once more, helping the ship come about and sail over what had once been the continent of Mu.

Prometheus looked back, saw cataclysmic flashes of lightning cast the Leviathan in stark relief. For a moment, he wondered if the Destroyer might, in fact, manage to annihilate an Elder God. More likely,

Marduk would drive her into torpor and force her back into the Spirit Realm, buying the Earth a few more millennia of existence. It would cost Marduk his life, Prometheus knew. It always did. Such was the bargain the Destroyer had made, such the price of Prometheus's gambit.

The outrigger drew nigh upon the shore of the mountain until Prometheus could spy Pandora climbing higher and higher, fleeing the rising water. She was naked, must have burnt off her clothes with the Phoenix again. She saw the ship and he thought she would leap for it, manifest her wings. Her gaze met his and she shook her head. Did she lack the remaining Pneuma to make such a leap? Prometheus's gut fell at the thought.

"We can come no closer!" Atrahasis bellowed. "We risk foundering upon the rocks!"

She was right there, not two hundred paces from him. There, still out of reach. And he was going to lose her. For it was this moment he'd seen in flames, him reaching for her, her stretching a hand toward him in the distance. He could not leap so far, nor hope to make the swim in the raging currents. In bitterness he cursed himself for destroying his Watcher ring—and the wings that came with it. Even knowing the self-recriminations pointless, that had he done otherwise, the World would already have ended, still he could not suppress the guilt, the grief.

She was right there! And he could not reach her. She was going to die alone, and Prometheus could not reach her. He wanted to rip out his heart, to have done with this accursed life. To cast away the immortality the Moirai had thrust upon him with their bargain, ensuring he must shepherd Era after Era through their bitter endings, a tool of Fate. Was this too the price of his gambit? Was losing her, over and over, the cost of him giving Mankind a glimmer of hope within the sea of the Dark surrounding the World?

At the canoe's edge, Lilinoe had a hand in the water, was screaming. The Snow Queen poured so much Mana into the sea, Prometheus could feel it thrumming over the waves. Mayhap, had Pokoharau survived, the Sea Queen could have stilled the water enough they could draw close to the island. Lilinoe had no such power and was trying something more desperate still. The surface froze before her touch. Sheets of ice crashed together, broke apart, unable to hold into more than small floes against the turbulent waves. The ice slapped back against the hull, jarred the outrigger. People were screaming, clutching each other. This choice of the queen's, it risked sending other survivors pitching into the deep.

And Prometheus could not waste the chance she gave him, mad though it seemed. Ragged, desperate breaths tore through him. It was so hard to aim at the ice floes as they churned, twisted, rose and fell and smacked together in almost total chaos. His mind whirred, struggling to calculate geometries and gauge probable trajectories. In the palace of his mind, time slowed. He spent so much time in probability trances, predicting possible futures based on fragmentary pyromantic visions. But never had he sought to achieve such precision on a moment-to-moment scale. If he erred now, Pandora would die and Prometheus would be swept under with little chance of re-joining the ship. And for her, he would risk it a thousand times over.

He braced, surging Pneuma to his legs. He leapt, his bound wild, lifting him airborne. A rush of wind, an arcing fall. He struck down upon a floe, his feet skidding along its sea-slickened surface. The ice pitched over, beginning to capsize from the impact. Prometheus leapt once more, trusting only to hope—was that not Pandora's greatest gift!—that his initial calculations meant a floe would be passing beneath the arc of his next bound. Soaring high above the water, flailing, he saw it and was uncertain he'd make it. But he landed upon the ice. Too close to the edge! He had no time before he leapt again, this time clearing the space between sea and shore and landing upon the mountainside.

Pandora was thirty feet above him, skidding down over scree. She crashed into his arms and wrapt herself around him, weeping. "How in Ares's arsehole did you do that?" she shrieked, though he doubted she expected any answer. In silence, he held her until she spoke once more. "I ... I gave up most of the Phoenix ..." she half-shouted, half mumbled into his shoulder.

He stiffened with the shock of that, but he had no time to parse the revelation. Lilinoe could not long continue to generate those ice floes. Prometheus swept Pandora up in his arms as he had held her past self not long before—from his point of view, leastwise—and allowed all sensory inputs to fade as he made calculations to bound back to the outrigger. Now, even his final destination was moving, tossed about on the waves. But he would not fail her.

Then he leapt, was soaring through the air once more. Because he was going to save her. This time, he would not be parted from Pandora. This time, Maui and Hina would have the future they had fought for.

IN THE DAYS THAT FOLLOWED, they called it the Worldsea, for all that remained above the surface were scattered islands forced up by seismic shifting. Maui had seen the Earth made and remade before, but even so, still it came as a shock. He knew some of the refugees of Mugedang had made it to other archipelagos. But the survivors were too few to mount any voyage across trackless sea in search for kin they might never find. The heirs of Mu were parted and unlikely to meet again for centuries.

Instead, those few who landed on what they named the island of Kahiki began to build. Maui helped them, for they were few in number and fewer in learned craftsmen. They had lost the skills of agriculture, of trades, of most of the disciplines Men must spend centuries reclaiming at the dawn of any Era. But those centuries tended to be more peaceful, so perhaps these simple times were the greatest of blessings.

With Hina, Maui built a modest home, not unlike the one they'd once shared outside Mugedang, set upon the mountainside, on the eastern slope, where they could watch the sunrise together, spot birds, or gaze upon the sea and muse on what had been. When he returned from the village, he found her roasting mahi mahi over the cook fire.

Weary but pleased, he settled down beside her, careful to look not in the flames but at his wife. Oh, sometimes he saw things there, still. He knew many taniwha—sea drakons—had come across from the Spirit Realm whilst the breach lasted, and many more Deep Ones, enough they were building their benthic empires and would one day seek to rule over Mankind. He knew even the Worldsea would not last forever, and that, in passing, it would give way to an ice age, and a savage world held in the grip of perilous Mist. Many things he knew, and many more he predicted based on his visions. But if he was to have peace, sometimes, it was better not to know what lay in distant days. Sometimes, the only day that mattered was the one here, now.

"I saw a pod of whales swim by, just offshore," Hina said. "I wonder what they make of this changed world."

Maui laughed. "Yes, they are intelligent animals, and that must leave them wondering and perhaps somewhat aghast at so sudden changes. But they'll adapt, as all things do ..."

His mirth faltered. Enough of the Phoenix remained inside Hina to slow her aging to a crawl. She might live far longer than a Titan unfortified by Ambrosia—a draught now blessedly lost to history—but time would have her, sooner or later. Whilst Maui endured forever, Hina would wither and one day ... No. He forced the thought down. This time, here and now, this was what they had so long sought for each other. Did it lack value for not being eternal?

No, all experiences were transitory, and the more precious for it. So together they would cherish each moment, each quiet day and blissful night. Insightful, she saw it upon his face and nodded in silent understanding.

"I love you," she said.

"And I, you," he agreed, reaching over to take her hand.

The Cycle would continue, the Ages come and go, time marching on toward its merciless end. But for now, Pandora had taught him to hope once more. And that hope was a fire he would never allow to burn out.

Join the Skalds' Tribe newsletter and get access to exclusive insider information and a *FREE* ebook and audiobook for your collection.

(Already have this book? Let me know and I can hook you up with something else.)

https://www.mattlarkinbooks.com/skalds/

ALSO BY MATT LARKIN

The Eschaton Cycle

Arc 1: Gods of the Ragnarok Era

The Apples of Idunn

The Mists of Niflheim

The Shores of Vanaheim

The High Seat of Asgard

The Well of Mimir

The Radiance of Alfheim

The Shadows of Svartalfheim

The Gates of Hel

The Fires of Muspelheim

Arc 2: Tapestry of Fate

The Gifts of Pandora

The Valor of Perseus

The Inferno of Prometheus

The Madness of Herakles

The Threads of Theseus

The Face of Hekate

The Wrath of Artemis

The Circle of Kirke

The Eyes of Athene

Arc 3: Heirs of Mana

Tides of Mana

Flames of Mana

Arc 4: Tales of Dark Faerie

Waves Breaking Over Ys

ABOUT THE AUTHOR

Along with his wife and daughter, Matt lives as a digital nomad, traveling the world while researching for his novels. He enjoys reading, loves video games, and relaxes by binge watching Netflix with his wife.

Matt writes retellings of mythology as dark, gritty fantasy. His passions of myths, philosophy, and history inform his series. He strives to combine gut-wrenching action with thought-provoking ideas and culturally resonant stories.

In exploration of these ideas, the *Eschaton Cycle* was born—a universe of dark fantasy where all myths and legends play out. Each series in the Eschaton Cycle represents a single arc within a greater narrative.

Learn more and get a free book at:
https://www.mattlarkinbooks.com/skalds/

For Juhi. For Kiran. Forever.